Feuds and Interludes

Rock 'n' Romance Legends Book One

Road to Rocktoberfest 2024

R.L. Merrill

 Created with Vellum

ABOUT FEUDS AND INTERLUDES

Boone Collins and Shane Butler are two of rock music's brightest stars today. Their grandfathers founded a powerhouse rock supergroup that ruled the airwaves in the late 1970s, and the grandsons grew up in their shadows to become front men of their own successful bands. The epic rivalry between Boone and Shane is notorious, and it's about to blow up.

When Shane's grandfather Bruce inducts his deceased bandmate into the Rock Hall of Fame, he admits to the world that he wrote the band's biggest hit about his best friend's widow—Boone's grandmother Vera Jean. His admission kicks off a courtship that leaves the feuding grandsons scrambling to keep their beloved grandparents safe from harm...and heartache.

Only, the men soon find that working together for a common goal reveals surprising similarities between them, as well as a chemistry they cannot ignore. Shane sees behind Boone's glittery facade to the secrets he hides from his bandmates, and Boone is there to pick up the pieces when Shane's professional world implodes. Together, they plot a musical collaboration to celebrate their grandfathers' accomplishments —a star-studded tribute at the storied Rocktoberfest event in the Nevada desert—but will being in the spotlight prove to be too much for their fledgling romance to handle?

Feuds and Interludes is part of the multi-author Road to Rocktoberfest 2024 series. Each book can be read as a stand-alone, but why not read them all and see what antics our bands get into next? Hot rock stars and the men who love them, what more could you ask for. Kick back, load up your kindle, and enjoy the men of Rocktoberfest!

To those struggling with chronic illnesses:
You're perfect in your messiness.
You deserve all the happy.

ONE

F*eedback Magazine*
March 2024

Love and Fame
  Boone Collins Talks Hall of Fame, His Famous Grandpar-
ents, and That Feud.
  By Sammara Gunderson

Boone Collins of Stellar carries himself with confidence and poise
as he greets me in the foyer of his grandparents' estate in Laurel
Canyon. The confidence, no doubt, comes from his many accom-
plishments, and the poise he comes by genetically. As the only
grandson of John Boone, British-born singer/guitarist for the
'70s supergroup California and Academy Award-Winning
British actress Vera Jean Collins, Boone's success is a combination
of right place, right time, relentless determination, and pure
talent. No one on the rock scene today can keep up with his vocal

pyrotechnics, and Stellar continues to wow audiences and critics alike with their combination of classic rock roots and alternative edge.

Boone is days away from his performance at this year's Hall of Fame Induction Ceremony, where instead of playing Stellar tunes, he'll be sharing the stage with his grandfather's former collaborator, Bruce Duncan, and playing some of his grandfather's biggest hits. I asked Boone to tell us about the plans for the show.

"Our goal is to showcase not only my grandfather's brilliant guitar compositions, but also to recreate the one-of-a-kind sound produced by putting him and Bruce together on a microphone. I'm not my grandfather, but I learned his songs down to the note as a young person, and I want to do my best to celebrate his career. We've got a lot of great material to choose from."

He says "young person" as if that was long ago, but at 30, Collins has an old soul that comes from the trauma and grief he's experienced. While he may have been raised with everything he needed in a material sense, Boone's early life was tumultuous to say the least.

His mother, Jean, met his father, actor Michael Cannon, on the set of her first film when she was still a teenager, and the two had a whirlwind romance documented in the tabloids. She became pregnant at age eighteen and, when Boone was five, Michael was arrested for domestic abuse against Jean, and charged with gun possession. While out on bail awaiting trial, he violated the protective order the court placed against him and assaulted Jean again. Michael was sentenced to ten years in San Quentin. He was murdered six months later.

Jean died of an overdose a week after his death. Boone was six years old. John and Vera Jean took custody of him and attempted to give him a sense of normalcy, but as he's shared in the past, those losses took their toll.

Boone is open about his history, but rather than ask him to recount tales he's shared a thousand times before to people like me, I'd rather focus on his plans for world domination. It's obvious he's most comfortable talking about Stellar, who recently returned to Los Angeles after two years of heavy touring, so let's dig in and discover what's currently the buzz for the band.

"This was our first time playing larger venues in Europe. We'd mostly played festivals and clubs before, and this change was a blast. We played Japan, Australia, and Brazil as well. It was our most extensive tour to date, and we were overwhelmed by the fans' support. They were so good to us. It has us contemplating how to build on this momentum with our upcoming album."

I ask him how much preparation has gone into his impending performance with Bruce.

He laughs.

"Our managers talked to each other. Isn't that how everything gets done these days?" He takes a sip of herbal tea, which he cryptically points out is part of his new normal. "Touring is hard on the body," he adds as his only explanation. "I've met Bruce many times, but he and my grandfather hadn't been social for a long while. Rehearsal will be the first time I've seen him in probably two years? Maybe since my grandfather's funeral."

Boone shows me around the main floor of the mansion, which contains the massive collection of memorabilia from California and John's solo career that Vera Jean has curated over the years. Their family bond is strong.

"I miss him every day. I wish he were here to play these songs himself, but I'll do my best to honor him. My grandmother celebrates him with her annual gala that benefits the Collins Foundation. We do our best to keep his life and music fresh in people's minds."

Boone is such a together guy for a rock star who's experienced so much trauma as a child. Although he definitely looks the part, speaking with him feels more like having a conversation with an historian or music academic, which is surprising, until you recall that he's a classically trained musician, educated at the prestigious Berklee College of Music.

It's when you read stories of his epic feud with Shane Butler—lead guitarist for Wicked Soul, and grandson of the afore-mentioned Bruce Duncan of California fame—that you question his façade. For two men with impeccable rock 'n' roll credentials, they've chosen completely different paths and each found success in their own right. So why the feud?

"You'd have to ask him, honestly. Shane is insanely talented as both a musician and songwriter, and while I think he sells himself short sometimes, he's created some great music."

"Just not 'Faker'?" I ask him about Wicked Soul's smash hit from three years ago, which was reportedly written about Boone after the two bands made memorable appearances at the iHeart Radio festival in Las Vegas.

Boone chuckles and rolls his eyes. "If that song is even about me. I try not to listen to the rumors."

"Is it true you requested not to play the same day as Wicked Soul and threatened to pull out of the lineup if they performed after you?" I have to ask.

"Our manager handles those things, so it's not even realistic that I would make a threat like that. Look, if Shane has issues with me, it's completely one-sided. I have a lot of respect for him as an artist."

From there, Boone makes it clear he's done discussing his rival, which leaves a lot of questions unanswered. He concludes the tour of his family's museum and we walk out front to Vera Jean's rose garden. I ask him what he's got lined up next, and he grins slyly.

"No rest for Stellar, that's for sure. We're headed into the studio as soon as the Rock Hall gig is done. I spent the last six months writing new material for our next album, which will be our fifth, and we're all anxious to get moving on a new project.

I'll also be helping my grandmother with next year's benefit for the Collins Foundation. Gotta stay busy."

And he is. He doesn't mention the collaborations he's got scheduled and the score he's working on for an upcoming Dreamworks film, which his manager filled me in on. Feedback Magazine will share the details as they are available. The next few years are going to be busy for Boone Collins. His star continues to rise out of the shadow of his grandfather's music legacy to shine brightly on its own.

Two

Boone

"Boone, honey, will you zip me up?"

Vera Jean Collins possessed the kind of beauty that turned heads, the grace of a royal, and the unshakeable poise to shrug off even the most rabid paparazzi. And tonight, all those characteristics would be put to the test.

"Gladly. How are you feeling?"

She turned with a huff. "Is it over yet?"

I chuckled. I'd never get over how stunning my grandmother was. The only constant in my life, she was my home, my role model, and my best friend. Wearing a form-fitting, sleeveless black dress adorned with iridescent rainbow sparkles, she had a youthful glow about her at nearly seventy years old and still commanded attention. A statuesque former actress, beleaguered rockstar wife, and now passionate philanthropist, Vera Jean Collins carried herself with an elegance that belied her years spent married to my lovable scoundrel of a grandfather.

"That tuxedo is very flattering," she said as I stepped behind her and carefully zipped her dress to the nape of her neck. She'd pulled her long silver hair into a twist that looked professionally done, and with her heels on, she stood nearly eye-to-eye with my five-eleven frame. "I love the vest, too."

I looked down at the navy velvet suit and gold brocade vest and smiled. "The tailor did a nice job taking it in. I think Papa would get a kick out of me wearing this. He loved this one."

I held up the matching bow tie and she took it from me, gesturing for me to let her tie it. She looped it over my head and went to work, a wistful smile on her face.

"He certainly did. He bought it to irritate me, and then was frustrated when I told him that I loved how it brought out the blue in his eyes. He was always trying to pull a fast one on me."

"And you'd always call his bluff."

She handed me her diamond choker to fasten, and I winced when I noticed her hands were shaking. She was so brave, no matter the challenge before her, but I'd learned to notice the subtle traces of her struggles. Tonight her task would be smiling and waving at her deceased husband's adoring fans and colleagues as he was posthumously inducted into the Rock Hall. I knew she missed him terribly. We both did.

"Kept things fun," she said with a little shrug. She ran her fingers over her choker and relaxed her shoulders. "Always kept him guessing."

I had my own reason for being nervous. My band, Stellar, was chosen to lead the tribute performance. In a few hours, I would be performing for an arena full of my musical heroes. With Bruce Duncan. I usually did my best when under pressure, but this was ridiculous.

"It was weird seeing Bruce at rehearsal."

I'd grown up hearing the stories of when he and my grandfather ruled the world, but I had no idea what to make of him as a person.

"Oh? How so?"

Gran stopped what she was doing and turned to face me.

"He talked to everyone else in the room but me. Well, he scolded me about the timing on one of the songs."

"Relax, darling," she said as she fastened her bracelet. "He's probably just as nervous as you."

"I'm not nervous. I know these songs like the back of my hand."

"Right," she said as she looked me up and down. "And that's why your shirt is misbuttoned."

I ran my hand down my shirt, and sure enough, I'd missed a button and the thing had a big bump in the middle sticking out from my vest. I went about undoing and redoing my shirt and vest. You'd think by the age of thirty, I'd be able to dress myself. You'd be wrong, apparently.

"Yeah, well, his infuriating grandson has probably told him terrible things about me."

"Oh, nonsense. Shane is a good boy."

"Boy? He's two years older than me."

"You two have more in common than you'd think."

"He's determined to be rude to me, so I guess I'll never know."

She was right in the sense that we came from similar backgrounds, but that's where the similarities ended. I put together a band of unique artists interested in playing smart rock music with a point and a backbone. Shane was a hotheaded, brilliant musician who, instead of following in his grandfather's footsteps, had chosen to while away his time in a mediocre albeit popular metal band. He could do so much better.

"Maybe if you two walked a mile in each other's shoes, you'd get along. Speaking of which, do you *have* to wear those shoes?"

I looked at my feet and back at her. "My Chucks? Of course, I'm wearing my Chucks. They're custom-made. Most comfortable shoes I own." I'd managed to get a sponsorship from Converse a few years back and they made some amazing inserts for people like me, who are on our feet a lot and need more support than your average skater or ball player. Now more than ever I had to take care of my feet, so I lived in these damned shoes. I'd chosen my gold sparkly ones tonight to match the tuxedo, so they really stood out.

She exhaled through her nose and raised an eyebrow at me. "You're lucky you're so handsome," she said as she fastened her dangly diamond earrings. "You get away with a lot more that way."

"And you wouldn't let just anyone escort you tonight. Right. You said that already." She could tease me all she wanted. I knew how much she loved me.

"Are you almost ready? Or do you have more metal to put in your head?"

She smiled sweetly at me and I rolled my eyes. I adjusted my septum piercing and ran my fingers over the thick silver rings in both ears. I had a stud through my tongue as well.

"I think I'm good." I crossed my eyes at her and she wrinkled her nose. Then her smile morphed into that grandmotherly look of concern she'd had frequently as of late.

"How about *you*? How are you feeling?"

"I'm okay. All good."

A trip to the doctor when I returned home after our tour landed me a brand-spankin'-new Type 2 diabetes diagnosis and a whole host of pamphlets, apps on my phone, and gadgets. I was young for an illness like this, but thanks to years of regular drinking and smoking, very little sleep, and a pervasive family history that I knew nothing about—thanks to my bio dad—it was time I started making some changes, and Grandma was all too ready to see me change.

I'm not changing the shoes, though. I mentally stuck my tongue out at her.

"You had enough to eat today?"

"Yes, Gran, I'm fine. I'll be all right." *I hope.*

"Good. Because we can't both be falling apart tonight." She winked at me.

"Right. Like you'd ever fall apart in public." Oh, sure, she was prone to the occasional dramatic histrionics at home from time to time. But never in the public eye.

"There's a first time for everything, my darling."

She threw a lipstick and some breath mints in her tiny purse, showed me that she had my inhaler and a package of crackers in there in case I needed them.

"Thank you," I said, feeling six years old again, which was when I came to live with her and Papa.

My phone buzzed, letting me know our car had arrived. I helped her into her coat and we made our way downstairs and to the lobby of the hotel, where a dude in the black suit was waiting to whisk us away to the ceremony. Gran slipped her hand through my offered arm and I leaned over to kiss her on the cheek.

"Chin up, tits out," she muttered.

"I'll try to remember that."

She subtly hip-bumped me and put on her most dazzling smile, no doubt practicing for the evening ahead.

I loved this woman, owed her my life, and I would stand by her side no matter what. I wanted her to be happy. She deserved happy.

As for me? I just needed to survive without making a fool of myself. I knew I was good enough to keep up with the likes of Bruce Duncan, but he'd rattled me more than I let on at that rehearsal. The idea that I wouldn't do my grandfather's music justice terrified me.

My career may not have happened if it weren't for my connection to one of rock's greatest artists of all time, despite the fact that I was talented enough in my own right. I'd never intentionally ridden his coattails, but I never turned down a connection or networking opportunity, either. My family got me in the door, my playing and singing got me and my band a record deal, and our collective hard work won us two Grammys, sold-out shows around the world, and a platinum-selling album.

Papa taught me everything I needed to know to launch my career. I would do him proud tonight.

And if that meant dealing with the likes of Bruce Duncan or his aggravating grandson, Shane Butler, so be it.

THREE

S hane

Teeth-chattering is not very metal.

I pulled my suit coat a little tighter and tried not to shiver.

It was bad enough having to fly out to New York in the wintertime, but then to have to get dressed up in a damn monkey suit and play nice? The worst. I was surly about the whole thing and doing a terrible job of hiding it from my beloved grandfather.

"You could have stayed home," he teased. "I know you had a whole weekend of...what are you playing now?"

"Fuck off," I said with a laugh, knowing full well he was going to give me shit about my obsession with Warhammer, a humble pastime that kept me sane in between tours.

"As long as we can both agree I'm the hippest one in this car."

"Yeah," I snorted. "You're the hippest, hep cat."

It was fun joking around with Pops, but I knew he was trying to distract me from my beef with this whole Rock Hall of Fame bullshit.

"I can't believe the committee asked *his* band to play the tribute and not yours. So wrong."

"Now, Shane," Pops answered in his lilting Irish accent. "I have no problem playing with Stellar and letting Boone Collins take the lead. It gives the show buy-in with the younger fans and might get us some movement. It's been a while since the band has had a moment in the sun."

We rode in a stretch limo from our hotel to the venue, and I wished I was anywhere else. I loved being my grandfather's escort, don't get me wrong, but I hated New York. Nothing good ever happened in this city, and even though my band spent a lot of time here, I never felt comfortable. Always felt like a small fish in a big sea when I *should* feel on top of the world.

"I just think since you co-wrote most of the songs from California, you should be the one singing."

Pops shook his head. He knew he wasn't going to convince me that Boone was a great guy. That ship sailed a long time ago.

"He's got that voice, though. Even better than John's."

I grunted my reluctant agreement. Boone Collins had the most sultry and sensual tenor in all of rock music. He had more range than Elvis, more sex appeal than Jim Morrison, and more balls than Mick Jagger and Steven Tyler combined when he was onstage.

And yet he was a total prick in person.

"Anyhow, it'll be great to play the songs. I'm glad Vera Jean will be there."

Pops got a thoughtful smile on his face whenever he mentioned John's widow. She was a nice enough lady, did a helluva lot to support the LGBTQ+ community and folks in the music industry who were in need.

But how my grandfather could be so charitable after everything that had happened to him as a result of his friendship with John Boone was beyond me. John had been painted as the hero after California split up over "personal differences"—yeah, John insisted they keep their drama to themselves so he would continue looking like the good guy. But I knew the truth. I seethed whenever I heard people gushing over John Boone and his schoolboy grandson.

Meanwhile, Pops spent twenty years nearly killing himself while touring with hired guns until he finally mended fences and reunited with the other former members of California. They formed the band Brothers, and their collaboration was a massive success, a comeback that lasted over a decade. Now mostly retired, Brothers played the occasional casino tour or Vegas residency, but Pops spent most of his time alone these days.

"I heard you talking to Mack the other day. You guys still planning the anniversary tour?"

"We're talking about it. Mack said there's a lot of interest, but I'm not sure how many of the guys are physically up to it."

I knew he was happiest on the road, even though it was terrible on him physically, as well. I hated to think he'd miss out.

"Maybe a few festival dates? A livestream or Pay-Per-View show would be cool—"

"Let's just get through tonight. I know yer always onto the next set of plans."

"Yeah, you know. Headed up to Oregon to Bolder Breed Studios for a stretch, then rehearsals for Rocktoberfest. Then a tour in November and December before the album comes out. Gotta stay busy to stay relevant."

He gave me a sad smile. "Probably drives yer bandmates nuts, huh?"

I cracked my knuckles and stretched my neck out. "Probably. But it's why they've all got sports cars and big fancy houses."

Pops slapped his hand down on top of my thigh and squeezed. "I'm so damned proud of ye, ye know that don't ye?"

I patted his hand. "Thanks."

I did know, and I was grateful. Grateful for *him*. If my parents would have had a say, I'd be working some boring nine-to-five out in the valley with a husband and two-point-whatever kids. My mother hadn't spoken to me—well, not civilly—since I'd left home fifteen years ago to make it as a musician. She wouldn't admit she was wrong when she said I'd never amount to anything if I pursued music, and so I had nothing to say to her. Or my father, who let her run the show without ever standing up for me.

The limousine pulled up in front of the Barclays Center and we stepped out to the familiar sounds of screaming fans and the flashing lights of cameras. Many voices shouted out my grandfather's name, but even more shouted mine, which was always weird. I wished they all appreciated him as much as I did.

I put my hand on his back and waved to the crowd, loving the smile on his face. People didn't recognize his genius as much as I'd like, but there were definitely adoring fans here.

Once we were inside the lobby, we were whisked away to our table and there were lots of well-wishers who stopped by and said their hellos. Grandpa and I gave plenty of hugs and backslaps. There were so many faces, I started to lose track.

Until I saw the one that made my blood boil.

Damn that Boone Collins, looking like the devil he was in his navy-blue velvet tuxedo. He'd lost weight since the last time

I'd seen him, and his long auburn hair curled handsomely around pronounced cheekbones under deep-set innocent-looking blue eyes. He wore his long hair parted in the middle from a widow's peak and it was always so damn healthy looking, it was as if he'd stepped off a modeling shoot. Premature balding hadn't affected *him*, no. I was the lucky one in that department. I finally started buzzing mine to the scalp about five years ago, which I got complimented on, but still. What did they say about plumage and the male of the species? It was our glory or some shit? It felt like I'd had my damned peacock feathers plucked out.

Oh well. Some people thought bald was beautiful. I'd have to go with that.

Vera Jean walked in on Boone's arm looking like she was at the Oscars rather than the Rock Hall Induction Ceremony. She was a stunner, to say the least. But she'd always seemed like she was too good for the plebes in the music business. The sea of people parted to let them through to the table next to ours. I hated that I couldn't take my eyes off of them and tried to force myself to remain sitting when my grandfather practically launched himself in her direction.

Here we go.

I hurried after Pops, though why, I don't know. Did I think I'd keep him from embarrassing himself? That I'd save him from getting his feelings hurt? I've no clue what I hoped to accomplish, but I followed nonetheless and planted myself at his side with my hands clasped in front of me like some burly bodyguard. I even had my stupid sunglasses on still, why? To protect myself? To hide the eye rolling?

Whatever my reason, I was acting like the quintessential douchey rockstar, and I hated it. Boone Collins always seemed to bring it out in me.

"Vera Jean, you look lovely."

Pops took her hand and kissed it as though he was a knight

or some shit. But I saw what maybe no one else did. First, his sheer happiness at being near her...and her grand dame façade slip to a genuine smile. Her eyes watered. I'd never seen the glamorous woman let her guard down at all, and yet here she was, having a moment. With my grandfather.

And Boone saw it too. He moved to support her, placing an arm behind her back. He whispered something in her ear and she gave him a nod.

"It's wonderful to see you, Bruce. It's been too long." She pulled him closer by the hand and leaned in to kiss him on the cheek.

And he blushed.

"How are you, Shane?"

I almost didn't see Boone's extended hand; I was so caught up in my grandfather's reunion, I'd missed Boone's attempt at a greeting. By the time I noticed, he'd pulled his hand back.

"Or not," he said with an eye roll.

Shit. There was no recovering from that.

"Collins." I kicked my chin out in his direction. "Hope you've been practicing. Sounded like there was some trouble in rehearsal," I said. I couldn't help myself. He needed to be taken down a peg.

"Shane." I didn't miss the warning in Pops's tone.

Boone's returning smile was so condescending, I wanted to slap it away.

"I can certainly handle my own. I was practically born playing this music."

"Yeah, but you didn't write it."

Why did I have such animosity toward a guy who shouldn't matter to me? Maybe because my whole life I'd heard how great he was, how successful he was, and damn if I wasn't a little jealous.

"Shane, that was very thoughtful of you to donate your piano to the auction." Vera Jean was irresistible, and she had impeccable timing. It was hard to accept her compliments, and yet she always had them. "You've always been so generous to the foundation."

She held out her hand, and I shook it.

"It's the least I could do."

She gave my hand an extra squeeze before she turned her attention back to Pops.

"He's so much like you," she said, squeezing Pops's biceps.

"He's smarter, more handsome, and more talented...but similar, yes," Pops said, and he winked at me.

"Whatever." I hated this shit. The compliments, the kissing up, the fake humility. My pops meant it, but I hated the one-up bullshit.

The house lights flickered and it was time to take our seats. Pops and Vera Jean shared one last smile and turned to go—but this interlude wasn't over.

"He's right, you know."

I felt Boone at my back, and it raised my hackles. I turned to face him and was surprised at his proximity, but not enough to step back.

"He's what?"

Boone did that big blue-eyed demure thing he does that's sold Stellar a million albums. It didn't work on me. No. His "thing" didn't work on me. At all.

"Your grandfather's right. You *are* smarter, more handsome, more talented."

Fire shot straight down my spine. Was I pissed? Furious? Or something else?

"The fuck you talking about, College Boy? You don't know anything."

His goddamned blue eyes flared, and he flinched at my words. I think? Or did I imagine it?

"Right," he said with a smirk. "I don't know anything.

Keep telling yourself that."

I saw red and acted before I could even consider where I was or who was around. I pushed him. Not hard, but still. He stumbled back with a laugh, and crashed into fucking Roger Taylor from Queen, who patted him on the shoulder and moved on to his seat. And then he was right back in my face. Still laughing. Was he laughing at me? Was he covering up his embarrassment? Or did he really want a piece of me?

"Boys," Pops snapped. "This is not the time or the place."

Vera Jean caught Boone's eye and somehow managed to smile at him *and* give him a "how dare you" look at the same time. The woman had a gift.

My heart was still pounding in my ears as Pops led me to our table. Boone stared me down the whole way to his seat, and even as he lowered himself into the chair, he kept glaring his challenge my way. What was his game? What the hell was he trying to prove? Why the hell did he have to say anything? Why the *hell* did I always let him get a rise out of me?

"Why do you let him get a rise out of you?" Pops asked close to my ear. The bastard and I were still staring at each other, and I knew for certain if you took my blood pressure right then it would've been through the roof. I downed my water and reached for the pitcher to pour another one.

"He's the one...he just...he's always...*grrrr*." I felt my nostrils flare as I looked at him across the aisle, smiling and laughing with Vera Jean.

Prick.

Someone was speaking over the PA but my heart still thundered in my ears, quieter now but still. Then I heard the opening *chug-a-chug-a-chug-a* of "Edge of Midnight," and I realized the show had begun. The ever-magical Stevie Nicks had taken the stage, and all eyes were on her.

Except Boone's.

And mine.

Why the hell was he still staring at me? Why did he always *do* this?

Why did staring back make my heart beat faster?

I told myself over and over to stop giving him the power to set me off, but there was just something about him that made me...weak. Which was probably why I reacted. Definitely why I reacted. But what the weakness was about, I hadn't figured out. Shit like this had happened every time we ran into each other over the past few years.

Well, someday we were going to have it out, because I was sick of him acting like he was better than me when we both put our fucking pants on one leg at a time.

Why the hell am I thinking about his pants?

Four

B oone

God, he's hot when he's mad.

I half listened to Stevie Nicks and The Cure perform because I couldn't stop thinking about the drama that had just played out.

In all the times that Shane Butler and I had faced off, he'd never gone speechless like that, and all I could think about was how to make him do it again. Because never in all of our years inhabiting the same planet had I *ever* walked away from one of our arguments feeling like the victor, and tonight I did. Maybe it was my ego flexing because it knew I needed to be in rare form in order to perform for these people tonight. But it had to be more than that.

I *liked* knowing that Shane reacted to me. I'd touched a nerve.

All I'd wanted to do was let him know that I saw him. I

saw how hard he worked, toiling away with his band, and I knew that with them, he'd peaked. He could be so much greater. He had a brilliance that could reach across genres and touch so many people if only he'd get out of his own way. He was a renaissance man like Trent Reznor, Dave Grohl and Jack White, living in an Emo world he should have outgrown by now. Those teenagers who grew up with his posters on their walls had moved on. Well, most of them, and he could be so much *more*.

I wanted to write with him. Create with him. But he hated me. *Haaated* me. With a passion that started wars. He hated me the way Helen of Troy's face launched a thousand ships. And I couldn't figure out why. I'd spoken highly of him in the press, I sang his praise every time I was asked about him. Our families hadn't socialized often despite the fact that our grandfathers had been best friends at one point, but he was a constant presence in my life from the minute I picked up a guitar and the comparisons began.

Movement grabbed my attention, and I looked over to see Bruce stand up, shake hands with fellow musicians and move to the stage. I'd be playing with him in a few minutes, and I was ready. After my little sparring match with Shane, I was *so* ready.

"You're going to be great, Boone."

I turned to smile at my grandmother and kissed her cheek. "I know." If I said it, I'd *have* to be great.

I wished I could get up and pace. It felt weird to just stand up and walk onstage, sling on a guitar and start playing.

The Cure finished their set, there was a lighting change, and then my grandfather's face lit up the screen. His long sideburns and flowing locks identified the picture as from the late '70s, which was just after California had broken up. A round of applause filled the place and the spotlight shone on Bruce

Duncan as he ascended the steps to the stage. He waved as he took his place behind the microphone.

"John Boone was a lot of things to a lot of people. At different times of my life, he played different roles. My musical collaborator, my sparring partner, my nemesis, my best friend, my rival. He was the creative force behind a legendary rock band, and then had a solo career that was the envy of all of his peers."

"Time to go," my drummer Brandon said, and we all stood from the table to make our way down to the front. I shook out my hands on the walk and tried to center myself. I took a moment to say a silent prayer.

"Papa, if you're listening, I could use a little of your magic right about now. I want to celebrate you in the manner you deserve, and I want to make this entire auditorium weep. I know that's ambitious, but it's what you taught me to do. Help me make you and Gran proud. I love you, old man."

Bruce was still talking as we got to the foot of the stage, and I realized that actually, the committee had done a great job in choosing him to do the induction. Bruce knew my grandfather in ways I never would, the ways that counted to the people in this room. He was a witness to my grandfather's greatest rock 'n' roll moments, where I'd merely read the history books and heard second- and third-hand tales. Everything happens for a reason, and I had a warm feeling in my chest for the old man tonight. It was obvious how much Bruce cared for Grandpa Boone.

"Competing with John meant becoming a better songwriter. I never would have written a song like 'Paisley,' which remains my greatest accomplishment as a musician. He pushed me to be better in all aspects of my life, even when it meant losing the woman I loved. John, you may have gotten the girl, but the song is mine."

Laughter filled the arena, along with applause, but my

hearing had hollowed out. I turned to my band and they all gawked at me.

"Bruce and Vera Jean?" Brandon asked in awe.

"'Paisley' is about your *grandmother*?" my bass player, Brandon's twin sister Annie, chimed in.

"Dude, this is epic! You could have been related to Shane Butler." Brandon usually got a pass for being a dumbass, and thankfully Annie stepped in to handle her brother's smartassery, because I was dumbfounded.

He wrote "Paisley" for Gran?

And then it was time to take the stage. I walked to my spot, took the guitar from the tech, nodded to Annie and Brandon to make sure they were set, and then I turned and looked at Bruce.

And he smiled at me like the damn cat who ate the canary.

Who the hell was this man to—

He played the opening riff to "Too Late," one of California's biggest hits, and I nearly missed my cue to join in. When I did, I let everything fall away, looked out over the crowd and sang as though my grandfather was sitting in the front row. Forget the fact that it was actually the members of Def Leppard sitting in my line of sight. If I turned the other way, I'd see Janet Jackson…I did my best to channel her attitude and sang my fucking heart out.

Bruce was there to my right, watching me, keeping a furious rhythm. He played his Gibson hard. I imagined he broke a lot of strings on tour. Papa had always had a gentler touch when he played, and his notes flowed effortlessly. Bruce's playing had a percussive quality to it that gave California that signature sound.

When it came time for his solo, he moved to the center of the stage and I stepped back, watching him in awe. For an old guy, he sure had that spark inside him. I was honored to be onstage with him, and I momentarily forgot that I was furious about his little revelation.

When it was time for me to pick back up with the vocals, I approached and he remained at the mic. We sang together, so close our guitars knocked, and I saw the sheer joy in his face to be singing the songs that he'd poured his heart and soul into. He could still hit the notes, too, with volume. The smile on my face was just as genuine. I wished once more I could have been alive to see them play together back in the day.

The song ended, the applause was thunderous, and we launched into another California hit. Bruce and I traded riffs, and we fell into a rhythm I hadn't been sure we could achieve together after he'd ignored me at rehearsal.

And then it was time for "Paisley."

I handed my guitar over to the tech and returned to the mic. I brushed my hair back from my face and took a deep breath.

"Go up to the canyon, they said
She'll greet you with a smile
And when you're feelin' low, they said
She'll tell you stay awhile

And the stars always shine upon her
Ain't no one make you feel finer
Lemon sun drops all around her
Ain't no way you'll ever forget her

My love dressed in paisley
Come away with me maybe
What is it about he

Why won't you choose me?

Go up to the canyon, I did
    She greeted me with a smile
    She knew someday I'd go
    She begged me to stay awhile

But his star shines bright for her
    Ain't no one makes her feel finer
    I could orbit all around her
    But then I would regret her

My love dressed in paisley
    Come away with me maybe
    What is it about he
    Why don't you choose me?"

As the song finished, as the applause and shouts from the audience filled the arena, I stared at Bruce, dumbfounded.

He smiled back at me as though to say, "I'm sorry you found out like this, but I'm not sorry."

This was one of my favorite songs to play. Ever. And when it was over, I could barely breathe. It wasn't my asthma, though. More like all of the oxygen had been eaten up by the sheer emotional weight of the evening.

John Boone had touched so many people with his music and had forever changed the lives of those around him, both in good ways and ways that broke hearts. I never imagined that one of those hearts might have been his best friend's.

Whether I wanted to or not, I had to know.

Bruce put his arm around me and pulled me into a hug, squeezing me tight. "Thank you for sharing that with me," he said in my ear. "I'm sure you'll have questions, but not here, not now."

And then he was gone, shaking hands and back slapping with everyone offstage.

And we had two more songs to play.

We coasted through two of Papa's biggest solo hits to riotous cheers from the audience. I'd lost my focus, however. I was in a daze until we took a big bow and walked offstage.

"What did he say to you?"

"You look like you've seen a ghost."

I was stunned. The weight of what I'd just heard, and the performance that followed, was crushing me. I needed to sit down. The adrenaline was leaving my body and I had the shakes. I probably needed to put my head between my knees.

Sounds were muddied and spots appeared in my vision. I knew my band was right behind me, and I felt Annie's hand on my back. She guided me to a spot in an empty hallway and pushed me down on a bench.

"Fucking incredible," Brandon said as he did a victory dance, bouncing his knees out and in while walking around on his tiptoes. "That old guy is rad!"

My hands tingled like pins and needles and the room started to spin. I leaned back against the wall and closed my eyes.

"Shut up, dumbass! Get him some water," Annie yelled to her brother.

Brandon grabbed a roadie with a headset and asked him for some water.

"You sounded brilliant," Annie said, giving my hand a squeeze. "Truly. I've never cried over that damn song, and you had me bawling like a baby."

I opened one eye and sure enough, her black mascara was smudged.

All I could do was grin.

"Great job, kid."

Bruce walked by with his guitar tech as he used a towel to wipe his face.

I couldn't speak. Which was good. I didn't know whether I wanted to hug him and weep or punch him in the mouth, which would be wrong. The guy was in his 70s.

I lifted a hand and waved at him, which was probably the smartest bet.

"You okay to go back to the table?"

Brandon handed me a bottle of water. I gulped half of it down, and then coughed as some of it took the wrong pipe to my lung.

"Just a minute," I said. I hated being fucked up after a performance. I'd been feeling shitty the last several months on tour, and when my bloodwork came back with an 8.2 A1C and a fasting blood sugar reading of over 180, it was enough to be diagnosed with diabetes. I did everything I could to change my diet, but some things were tougher to deal with, like a regular sleep schedule, exercise in between bus rides...I started medication and that was helping some.

The only thing that was going to help me right now was to get back to the hotel and crash.

"What was that little shoving match with Butler about earlier?" Annie asked me. Apparently, they'd had an excellent view for that interlude.

I couldn't help the shit-eating grin that spread across my face. "Saw that, did you?"

Annie shook her head. "What did you say?"

"Told him I wanted him to bend me over a couch."

"You did not!"

I burst out laughing and coughed again, my body letting

me know I needed my inhaler. Too much stress for one night. But laughing helped. Remembering the look on Shane's face? *Priceless.*

"I didn't. But it doesn't matter what I say to him, he hates me."

"Yeah, well, hatred, and wanting to tear your clothes off and lick you like a popsicle must be the same emotion to him, because that's the vibe I got."

My eyes bugged out. "No way."

"Way," Brandon said. "He wants your ass *baaad.*"

I threw my empty bottle at him, but I was still smiling.

Could it be that Shane Butler had something other than hatred on his mind? Could a round of angry sex with the gorgeous man make him hate me less? *Tempting.*

But then I thought about our grandparents making eyes at each other, and I shuddered.

Uh-uh.

No way.

Bruce Duncan better take care with my beloved gran. Old man or not, I'd take him out.

And if his grandson didn't like it...well...

Shane Butler could kiss my...something.

FIVE

S hane

"Boone Collins can kiss my ass."

Honestly, if I had to hear his name one more time...

"Calm down, Shane. Such a hothead."

Pops was the only one I allowed to talk to me like that. My fiery temper apparently came from him, though I'd never seen it. My mom inherited it from somewhere. Her mother—Bruce's second wife, Eddie Mae, a sought after Black hairstylist from Alabama—who died before I was old enough to really know her, apparently was a tough one too. Her and Pops supposedly had some epic rows.

"I wish you would have given me a heads up that you were going to use this opportunity to declare your love for your ex-best friend's widow."

The cheeky bastard just chuckled. "Yeah, well, I'm just

getting warmed up. As soon as we're back in LA, I'm going to call her and ask her on a date."

"*A date*? With Vera Jean Collins? Are you out of your mind?"

Pops's teasing smile faded and in its place was a haunted expression, one from a man who had lived a hard life, a lot of it his own doing, and who dared to want more for himself.

"No, Shane. I'm finally in my *right* mind. Vera Jean made the best decision for herself back then. I was a mess. John was a better choice for her. But now? I'm sober, I'm healthier than I've been in my adult life...I've still got a few years to kick around. I'd like to spend them with her."

My heart broke hearing him make this confession. He did deserve to be happy...but really? "Why her? Why not meet someone new?"

Pops shook his head and sighed. "Because it's time. And it would *only* be her." He locked eyes with me. "She's the love of my life, Shane. And I want to spend what life I have left with her."

I opened my mouth to retort, and I saw him brace himself. It took a lot for him to admit that to me.

"Do you think she feels the same?" I asked. Maybe he knew something I didn't.

Pops grinned wickedly. "We're about to find out."

I drove Pops across town a week later to his regular AA meeting and we argued the whole way. The plan was that I'd drop him off, and then he'd walk over to The Dresden afterward to meet Vera Jean for dinner. He'd call me when he was done. When did I become the parent in this relationship?

"Just maybe don't lead with, 'you're the love of my life,' that's all. Spend some time, get to know her again. Maybe she's not the same person she was all those years ago."

"Of course, she's not. You'd understand if you ever got out of your own way and let yourself fall in love."

I scoffed. "What do you mean? I've been in love."

He scoffed. This conversation was quickly devolving.

"Right. That bloke Remi? He was a glorified groupie and you were glad to see him gone."

I grunted. Why did he have to be right? "I was in love with Daron."

"Daron was an overgrown Boy Scout and he wanted you to quit music."

That's what I got for dating someone my parents wanted me to date.

Daron Mirigian was an investment banker my stepfather knew through his Armenian relatives. I'd fallen hard for him, so much so that I'd missed the signs. I asked him to take the next step with me, whatever he thought that should be, whether it was moving in or getting married and then cohabitating. He'd agreed it was time... Time that I quit the band. That was the end of our relationship. I pulled everything in tighter to myself and became the control freak I was today.

"I was attempting to smooth things over with Mom, you know that." I'd lived with Pops since getting my GED. My father had left when I was in middle school, tired of Mom's controlling ways. I tried to please her, but when Pops bought me my first guitar at age thirteen, I was hooked.

Mom was furious that I wanted to pursue music after I'd seen how it wrecked Pops's life. Not only had his addiction played a part in the demise of California, but it also led to friction in his relationships, and it kept him from having a close relationship with my mom, not to mention the financial strain it caused his family. I saw it differently. Pops's struggles with alcohol put me firmly in the sober camp, and I learned from his trials and tribulations, but Mom didn't believe that would be enough to keep me out of trouble. I proved her wrong, though the part of me that craved her approval kept me bitter. For years, I'd try to connect, try to show her how successful I was, then she'd belittle me, I'd get pissed, I'd go get another tattoo, another piercing, she'd bitch...

Now? We spoke when necessary, but we'd never been close.

How pathetic to let my mommy issues interfere with my life?

I'd have been a mess if it hadn't been for Pops. Bruce Duncan was the most important person in my life, and in the back of my mind, I knew my issues with him dating Vera Jean had more to do with my fear of abandonment than worrying about him. Yeah, I'd done the therapy thing. I considered myself a pretty self-actualized dude. Most of the time. Didn't mean my shit didn't crop up occasionally.

I pulled up in front of the building in Los Feliz where Pops had been going to AA for years. I did my time in Al-Anon, at his suggestion, and was glad he had the support of the program.

"You'll call me when you're done at The Dresden?"

Pops chuckled. "Don't wait up. I can grab a Lyft, or maybe a ride with a lovely lady."

The thought of my 70-year-old grandfather going home with someone?

I should have been more worried about my own lack of plans for the evening. I waved goodbye to him, drove over to Sunset to pick up my Gibson from my buddy Ty at the repair shop in Guitar Center, perused the comics at Meltdown, and then scrolled through my phone to see if there was a movie playing nearby. I could have called one of the guys in my band, but we didn't socialize when we were off tour. We had a working relationship, that was it. Sure, we cared about each other. You couldn't *not* when you'd been together for ten years, but I needed to leave work at work. I thought about going by my mom's...

"You're a fucking case, Butler." I pulled away from the curb and drove over to The Dresden. At least I'd be close if he needed a ride. If I saw him leave, well, then I'd know he was okay.

Maybe I should have looked for an Al-Anon meeting with my codependent ass hanging out.

Instead, I pulled up YouTube and, like the disaster I was, I rewatched the performance from the induction ceremony.

Fucking Boone Collins.

Six

B oone

"I don't get it. Why him? Why now? If you're lonely—"

"Boone, don't be absurd. I have all I need. I have lived a very full and fulfilling life. Bruce is part of that life, and I'd like to see him."

I rolled my eyes like a child. "What's so special about this guy?"

Gran made me sit down on the bench at the end of her bed. She sat at her vanity, looking like the glamorous starlet she still was.

"I was nineteen when I met John and Bruce at a party in Laurel Canyon. They'd just hit it big with California and they were in Los Angeles recording their second album. Photos were taken and my publicist scolded me for being seen with such ruffians. An Oscar-winning actress shouldn't put herself in such a position, he said. But I loved hanging out with them.

They had parties at the home they'd rented most nights, and I loved to go. No one there treated me like I was a snob, I could smoke grass and no one cared."

"You rebel, you," I said, loving it when she told stories. I'd heard about her party days before, but they had always led to "and then John asked me to marry him."

"Did you know they both loved you?"

She sighed. "I'm sorry you had to find out like this, but yes. I was seeing both of them. I liked the attention. They were so different. John and I eventually started meeting during the day, going to museums and galleries. The press loved us, and my publicist thought it might help my career if the news of our romance kept selling papers. But I was also spending time with Bruce. He was such a romantic," she said with a dreamy smile. "We'd go for long walks in Griffith Park or we'd just find a grassy patch somewhere and stare at the sky. And get high." She giggled! My gran! "He'd make up poems on the spot. He'd make daisy chains and weave them into my hair. He was a bit of a leftover flower child.

"But then he told me he loved me... I panicked. John hadn't said it, but he talked about our future more and more. At night, at their house, I never spent time alone with either of them. Bruce started drinking more heavily, John would make snide remarks. I didn't like the growing animosity between them. I actually stayed away from them for a while. I was filming in France for about six weeks. John called when he could. Bruce sent me letters every day. The man was such a poet.

"But when I got back, I found out the two had come to blows. I felt terrible! *I* was the cause of their friendship falling apart. It was awful, Boone. After their fight, Bruce left and no one heard from him for days. John came to my apartment, and he asked me to marry him. It felt terribly unfair to say yes when I still had feelings for Bruce, but I knew that if I married

Bruce, I'd lose myself, my career. John was the driven one. He was very career oriented, and he supported mine as well. I suppose I felt like choosing John was the responsible thing to do...if you can call marrying a rock star responsible."

I chuckled. "I think that's a stretch, Gran. I think even Papa would laugh."

She reached over and placed her hand on my cheek. "He would. We both loved Bruce and we felt awful, but when he didn't return for months, I finally agreed to marry John. I tried sending word to Bruce, wrote him letters. He responded with, 'I wish you both happiness and a long life together.' It broke my heart, but we went ahead with the wedding."

Her eyes drifted over to their wedding photos still hanging on the wall. I'd never seen a more beautiful couple.

"So what happened then? That wasn't when they broke up, was it?"

She shook her head. "California stuck together for a couple of years after that. Bruce was kind to me, stiff with John, but we were all civil with each other. Then John decided to go solo, and then we had Jean...Bruce didn't even put up a fight when the band called it quits. John attempted to keep up their friendship, but he was always so sad when he came back from seeing him. I think he regretted losing his best friend, and as close as we were, I could never be to him what Bruce was."

"I've always dreamed about finding someone I could connect with on a musical as well as a romantic level. I know it's cliche, and rock and roll marriages rarely last, but look at Paul and Linda McCartney, or Pat Benatar and Neil Giraldo. And you and Papa. I want a love like that, for the ages."

She smiled, her eyes teary. "And I wish that for you, dear boy. Don't settle for less." She looked at the clock on the mantle behind me. "Oh, my. I've got to hurry. I told Bruce I would meet him at eight."

I slumped on the bench. "Are you *sure* this is a good idea?"

She turned to face me with her mascara wand in hand and immediately donned the Gran posture, the one that let me know I was about to hear it.

"Boone Randolph Collins. It is a perfectly acceptable idea. I am having dinner with an old friend—"

"Who just told the whole world he's still in love with you."

She threw a makeup sponge at me. "He did no such thing. Now, quit your sulking. You need to find something to do with yourself tonight. I don't want to come back and find you on a bender." She raised her eyebrows and turned back to the mirror.

I fell back on her bed with a huff. "I already threw out all the ice cream and cookies. Maybe I'll do some online shopping. All of my pants are falling off."

"What a terrible problem to have," she said and winked at me in the mirror. "You're doing so well, dear boy. I know it's hard, and I'm so sorry you're having to deal with this."

I shrugged. "Guess it's time for me to develop some responsible habits."

She burst out laughing and she sounded so like a girl, I sat up. She stood in front of her full-length mirror, smoothing down the flowy dress she wore. It was a navy layered chiffon number with spaghetti straps that gave her an air of whimsy. I could imagine it reminded her of the time when she was in a love triangle with two brilliant musicians and the world held in thrall.

I didn't want to be the weight tying her to the pain in her past. I wanted her to keep smiling like she was right now.

"I'll get my keys and drop you off." Gran never drove at night because she hated wearing her glasses. She'd gotten over a lot of her vanity since stepping back from Hollywood, but every once in a while it showed through.

"My dearest dear boy."

I didn't even care that she still called me a boy.

The drive was fraught with traffic hazards, but I kept my cool while listening to her sing along to Dionne Warwick and Carole King. She had such a lovely, soft, breathy voice, but anytime I'd compliment her, she'd laugh it away.

"No, you boys were always my singers."

I pulled up to the back entrance and put the car in park. I started to climb out and Gran placed her hand over mine.

"Don't be silly. I'll call you when I'm finished."

"I'll be nearby. Be safe."

She smiled at me like a teenager headed out on a first date, and then leaned over and kissed my cheek. "Thanks, Boone."

Oh, now I'm Boone? Not dear boy?

The valet opened the door for her and she smiled regally, giving him a nod and a thank you. Her dress hung low in the back and she walked steadily on three-inch heels.

Man, I hope I've got it that good when I'm sixty-six.

I'd told her I'd be going to the twins' place, which was a few blocks away, but I wanted to be close in case she needed me. I pulled around the lot and backed into a parking spot against the fence. I had a clear view of the door. I turned on some tunes and sighed. Maybe I could read. Maybe I could write. I had my notebook with me and my tablet...

I flicked open YouTube and searched my favorite obsession instead.

Shane Butler interviews.

I'd probably seen them all, but I loved hearing him speak, hearing the cadence of his deep, smooth baritone.

The first one to pop up was from three months ago as a wrap-up to Wicked Soul's most recent world tour. I'd never seen them perform live. I'd stalked—I mean, *watched* recorded performances, and then there was that iHeart Radio festival where I'd supposedly refused to go on if we were playing the same day. Whatever. I might be a diva, but I was dead serious when it came to performing, and the only issue I had with iHeart was that they didn't appear to have a contingency plan in case of bad weather, which had been forecasted, and I wasn't about to play in an electrical storm. We nearly pulled out until the organizers provided us a plan. The other bands gave me shit for being the squeaky wheel, but I got them all protection, now didn't I? No thanks necessary.

"All right, Shane, clear up the rumors for us. Is 'Faker' about Boone Collins?"

Ugh, I hated this question. For Shane and for myself. I watched his jaw muscle twitch, which I'd learned was a clear indicator that he was fighting his urge to bite the head off the person who was talking to him. He hadn't held back when it was me though. *Hmm.*

"That song is not about any one person. It's about every person, the ones who think they're better than others, the ones who step on others to get where they want to be in life. People are going to think what they want. It was never meant to be about one person."

"So you and Boone Collins are cool?"

Shane's nostrils flared and his throat bobbed as he swallowed. "Next question." When the interviewer insisted, Shane shook his head. "Our grandfathers were in a band together. He's immensely talented. I've got nothing against Boone. Next question."

My face flushed. "Aw. He doesn't admit to hating me."

The interviewer asked him about his obsession with Warhammer. Shane spoke about the game and its impact on his songwriting, and though I got lost a bit, my ears perked up at the last question.

"Tomorrow's Mother's Day. How will you be celebrating?"

Shane's face paled noticeably. "I'll, uh, bring her flowers."

The interviewer was at least professional enough to know

that his question had led to a topic Shane was not at all comfortable discussing. They moved on to songwriting and the host talked over a clip of the one Wicked Soul song that I particularly loved, "Fall Into Pain," and I found myself wondering, what if? Shane and I were so different, his lyrics went in a direction that I never dared to go. His music was powerful, angry, passionate in a different way than mine. Would we mesh? Could we make something incredible together?

Too bad he hated me.

"All right! You heard it, folks. Catch Wicked Soul tonight at the Palladium."

"Damn, that would have been a good show," I muttered to myself, thinking it was about time I went to see them play. Incognito, of course. I wouldn't want my appearance at one of his shows feeding the rumor mill or causing any problems for him. I didn't give a fuck what people thought about me, as long as people listened to the music. Shane seemed to care. He wanted to make music that people respected, and though I didn't agree that his band was the best platform for him, I wanted to see him thrive. Truly.

The next video loaded as my phone started buzzing in my hand. I squealed and tossed the phone in the air, honking the horn in my attempt to catch it. I sighed when I saw Rose's name on the screen.

"I'm so glad it's you," I said after answering. "I nearly concussed myself with my own phone."

Rose barked out a laugh. "Please don't do that! I would hate to concuss a person. I'd *cuss* at them, or *dis*cuss them, but *con*cussing seems really harsh. I'm against it."

We giggled together for several moments before getting to the point of the call.

"I can't wait to see you next week," I said.

"I concur, not to be *con*fused with *con*cussing. I was calling to *con*firm your studio time with Morrison."

"Yes, please! Tell Morrison we are *con*pletely—wait that doesn't work. We're, uh, *con*fident in his *con*trol—oh, forget it. We'll be there."

"Awesome," she said. "Can't wait to see you. Please bring your nail stuff. You give the best manicures ever."

"And I love to do them. If you have requests for colors, let me know. I can stop by the beauty supply and pick up some fresh bottles."

Rose squealed with delight and clapped her hands. "We're going to have such a great week. You guys are going to be there, both More and Lydia are home, and Wicked Soul will be here—"

"Wait, *what*? Really?"

My whole body flushed at that news. I hadn't heard they were going back in the studio. I wondered if I'd manifested his appearance. I also wondered if Shane knew we were going to be there.

"Yeah. Their manager said the overlap was okay. Morrison wants to see you both, so we're working on a schedule to get you both time with him and Leland."

"Right on." I was certainly willing to be flexible, especially with my current Butler Fascination...I'd bend any which way to get close to him, just for a little while. Was I crazy? Was it possible for him *not* to hate me? Or was this just another self-destructive habit I'd developed? My ice cream addiction would probably be better for my heart than this.

Rose and I disconnected and I got back to worrying about the task at hand. My gran and her new grandpa boyfriend. Bruce had certainly gotten my hackles up at the induction ceremony, but I knew he wasn't a bad guy. That didn't mean I thought he was the right person for her to get back out there with. They may have had a history together, but Bruce's *personal* history was rife with tragedy. Alcoholism, loss, financial troubles, divorces…his own daughter, Shane's mom Christina, didn't speak to him. I knew that much from gossip.

He had Shane, and Shane was his biggest fan. And he could still play circles around me.

I looked at my watch. An hour had gone by. Should I check in with her? A quick text wouldn't hurt anything. Right?

I wondered what Shane thought about our grandparents reconnecting. I had the sudden urge to ask him, but I didn't have his number, nor did I know anyone who—

I redialed Rose.

"Hey, it's me again. I don't suppose you could share Shane's number with me, could you? I wanted to talk to him about the studio time." Bullshit, but easier than explaining to her the whole thing. He might not want the world to know.

"Uh, let me see… Nope, I don't have his number. Let me text Jeff Garza, their manager."

"Great. You can give him my number if that's easiest."

"Got it."

We hung up and I waited. Fidgeted. A wave of wooziness overcame me, and I looked at my blood sugar app. I wore a monitor on my stomach or the back of my arm, and I got notifications if I was too low or too high. At the moment I was okay, but that could change quickly. I was fine with my new exercise regimen, but cutting out my sweets and drinking? Hated it!

My phone buzzed a moment later.

This is Jeff Garza. How can I help you?

"How can you help me," I wondered out loud as my thumb hovered over the phone's keyboard.

It's Boone Collins. I need to speak with Shane. Can you give me his number?

This was becoming quite an arduous undertaking.

I'm not at liberty to give out Shane's personal information.

I groaned. *Can you please give my number to him and ask him to get in touch?*

Now I looked like a whiny bitch. *Great.* Maybe I should have just let it go.

May I ask what this is in regards to?

"Grrr! Jesus, this guy is nosy. Uhhh, 'it's a personal matter.' There." I clicked send and waited for a few minutes before I got a response.

I'm sorry, I'll need more information before I contact Mr. Butler at this hour.

"Fuck!" I didn't want to spill it all, but I figured this would let me know whether or not his grandfather had told him about the date.

It's about Bruce Duncan.

Again with the long wait time.

Thank you. I will pass along your inquiry to Mr. Butler, and if he's able, he will respond within 24-48 hours. Thank you for contacting Slade Artist Management.

"Yeah, thanks for nothing." I slammed my head back against the headrest of my Mach-E and groaned. Maybe this was a bad idea, reaching out to Shane. What would I even say? I didn't want to end up being rude or making him angry.

My phone buzzed from an unfamiliar number.

What about my grandfather?

I started to type a response three times, but I worried that context and tone would get lost via text. So I hit the call button.

"Why are you calling me?"

"Hi, Shane. Sorry, I didn't want to be misunderstood via text."

He didn't know me very well, and, well, I didn't want to accidentally offend him.

"Oh." He was quiet for several beats. I was trying to think

of what to say when he said, "This is weird. I never talk on the phone."

I laughed. "Me either. I just wanted to know if you knew, you know, about our grandparents."

Shane sighed heavily into the phone, making that muffled sound as though his breath traveled over the microphone. I got goose bumps just thinking about it.

"Yeah."

I smiled. I could hear the frustration in his voice too.

"It's weird, right? I didn't know, uh, about before. She and Grandpa conveniently left out the part about their little love triangle."

"Convenient."

"Yeah."

Silence.

Man, he was always ready with the snide remark. Where was the comeback now?

"Did you know? The whole story?"

I heard rustling on his end. I wondered where he was. He lived in LA, I knew that, but I wondered where.

"I knew. I knew about the song. I knew he still carried a torch for her. Had no clue he was going to tell the world at the ceremony, though. I would have cautioned against it."

"I had no clue," I said, my voice just above a whisper.

"Yeah, well, why would you?"

"I don't know. I thought I knew the whole story. That they were all friends, Gran and Grandpa got married, Bruce left the band—"

"John decided to go solo. Pops didn't leave."

"Ah. Guess we got different versions of the story."

Shane scoffed. "Yeah, you could say that."

A siren blared to life and startled me so bad, I dropped the phone again. Why I was so jumpy, I had no clue. I picked it up and...heard the siren on the other end of the call?

"Where are you?" I asked him.

"Why?"

I looked around the parking lot but of course, I had no idea what kind of car he drove. "That siren. Are you here?"

He paused. "I dropped him off. Don't want him to have to call a Lyft, so I stuck around."

I laughed. "Guess we're in the same boat. I'm parked in the lot."

My heart jumped at the thought of seeing him. Would he be pissed? Could we have an actual conversation away from everyone else and maybe not fight? I could think of nothing I'd rather do than see him in person right that very minute.

I climbed out of my car, feeling brave, and looked around. I found him quickly, in a classic car no less, a restored van from what looked like the '60s. He had sunglasses on even though the sun was mostly down, but that was his brand. He probably didn't want a bunch of lookie-loos seeing him.

So I waved like a damn wacky wavy inflatable thing and trotted over to his van.

He may have shaken his head, but I ignored that response.

He had one tanned, muscular arm resting on the window ledge. Though it was chilly out, he wore a short-sleeved black bowling-type shirt with a white tank undershirt beneath. I'd been delighted when he'd shaved his head, thinking the look suited him. Made him look more dangerous, which fit with his music. His dark brows and his thin mustache and beard added to his severe look, and when he performed, his sneers and growls showed off perfect white teeth.

"Hey," I said on approach.

I got a chin lift. "Nice shirt."

I looked down to try to remember what shirt I had on. "Oh! Scooby gang. Yeah. I love the show. And you've got the perfect van for a stakeout."

He stared at me for a couple of long moments before he

leaned over and unlocked the passenger-side door. Every move he made was hesitant, like he thought at any minute I was going to attack. Or embarrass him.

I walked around to the passenger side and climbed in.

The entire van had been reupholstered and carpeted in dark gray colors, which paired nicely with the metallic teal paint job. In the back was a cabinet with a cooktop, a small fridge and...a bed.

That discovery made my vision go a little spotty.

Wow, did I have a crush.

Seven

Shane

"This is great. How long have you been living the van life, Shane?"

I smirked. "I had it done like this so Grandpa and I could maybe travel. The bed flips up to make more storage space for hauling gear." I fidgeted in my seat, why did it matter that Boone liked my van?

"It's fantastic! Spotless, picture-perfect, and cozy. Not the kind of vehicle one would picture Shane Butler riding around in. Then again, I don't know much about the real Shane, so how would I know?"

His compliments further caught me off guard, so I looked out the window toward the direction he'd come from to gather my wits. I didn't want to make a total fool of myself. I lifted my chin when I spotted a sleek-looking electric car. "That your car?"

"The Mach-E? Yeah. Love it. Ridiculously fun to drive. I wanted something reliable and better for the environment, you know? Gas guzzlers are going to destroy us."

We both looked at the dash of my van.

"Uh, yeah, I have a Honda too," I said lamely. What did I care what he thought? Except I cared about the environment, too.

He sniffed and turned to face the restaurant. "I guess we should talk about it."

"About...it?" I asked, then I realized I was being dumb. "Oh. Them."

"Yeah. Them." He shrugged. "I think it's cute they're meeting up. I'm sure they're just talking over old times."

I ran my hand up under my sunglasses, unsure I was ready to have this discussion with Boone. I rubbed my eyes and then my stubble-covered jaw. "It ain't just old times for Pops."

He turned sideways in the seat, flicked his long hair back over his shoulder and waited for me to continue. His aqua t-shirt with the cartoon Scooby Gang was...cute, but the way it hugged his chest, and those tight, flared corduroy pants he wore with Birkenstocks...he looked damn fine sitting in my van. He'd fit in well with the SoCal set if it were 1968, when our grandparents met.

That thought gave me pause in my gawking. I pulled the sunglasses off with a huff and leaned my arm on the steering wheel. "He's still got feelings for her, you know. This ain't just about old friends catching up, Collins."

He sat a little taller in my seat. "Oh. Well."

"Yeah," I said. "You see my concern?"

He frowned. "What?"

I cursed under my breath. "My concern, Boone, is that nothing good can come of this. They may have been friends once, but they run in different circles now, and her circle wouldn't include someone like him. You know, Pops is a good man, and—"

"Whoa," he said, holding out his hands. "I know he is. And what do you mean by 'her circle'? Her circle is me, her staff from the foundation, and a few close friends. She keeps to herself mostly."

"Yeah, and nowhere in there is an old man still playing in a rock band." I crossed my arms on the steering wheel, unable to keep gazing into his bottomless blue eyes. They were so deep, so perfect, I could so easily get lost in them. So maybe my next words were more about me than Pops. "I don't want to see him upset."

"And you think Gran will upset him? She is the most caring and generous person I know, Shane."

"I know she is," I said, holding up a hand. "I've got nothing against your grandmother."

We were quiet for several long moments. I watched cars pull in, take the valet parking option, and nicely dressed couples went in and came out the back doors. A couple of teenage-looking tourists snapped pics of each other outside the old-fashioned restaurant. It wasn't really a young-person kind of place. It was a classy, old-school restaurant that was probably a little old for Vera Jean and Bruce back in the day. Pops and John had spent a lot of time at It's Boss and the Whisky on the Strip, along with other rockers from the late '60s, early '70s.

"You ever think about what it would have been like here back then?" I mused out loud.

"All the time. Can you imagine seeing all those bands?"

I didn't answer right away. I'd often wished I could have experienced first-hand that wild time.

"Who were some of your favorites?" he asked.

Could we actually be doing this? Having a civil conversation? This was the most I'd ever spoken to him. It was surprisingly kind of nice.

I blew out a breath and started drumming my thumbs on the steering wheel. "Man. I would have loved to see Crosby, Stills, Nash and Young. To hear those harmonies in person?"

"Really? That seems...tame for you."

I shrugged and frowned when he started smiling at me. God, it was that big smile that always lit up a room, that graced the covers of magazines. So beautiful. "Just because I play loud music doesn't mean that's all I like." I kicked up my chin. "How 'bout you?"

"The Doors...oh *man*. To see Jim Morrison, just once?" His eyes rolled back and he let his head fall against the seat with a sigh. God, his sex appeal was too much this close. I wondered if he knew the affect he had on people.

"I can see that," I said, my voice cracking. "You definitely channel that energy onstage."

He whipped his head around and stared at me wide-eyed. "That's a huge compliment."

I looked back out the windshield, afraid I'd give away just how much he affected me if we kept this up. "You don't need me to tell you you're good, Collins. You hear it enough, I'm sure."

"Yeah, but not from you. So thank you."

I chanced a look at Boone and, dammit, I could barely focus on the topic at hand. I wished things were different, that we didn't have this weirdness between us, because right then, just the two of us, he seemed like someone who could be that something I didn't have.

A friend. A real companion.

"So what are we going to do about those two?" he asked, and I realized I'd been staring at him. He laughed. "I feel like I skipped raising a toddler and went straight to parenting a teenager."

"It's not up to us," I said, sounding like the responsible one, a role I was used to. I often had to be the adult when Pops was in a mood. "I don't like it though. I'll be the one picking up the pieces if it goes south."

"What do you mean?"

I frowned at him. How could he not know? "Look, Vera Jean is a grand dame, a lady. She's got her life together. Pops has had...a different life. I don't know how well he'll take rejection at his age. He's had a lot of loss in his life."

"She has her moments. She's impenetrable in public, but at home? Let's just say...your grandfather isn't the only one who could be hurt by this."

We gazed at each other for a long time, the weight of our situation descending upon us like the curtain dropping on stage. *Showtime.* Whatever moment we were having was gone.

Our phones buzzed at the same time.

"Guess they're done," Boone said. "Thanks for letting me enjoy the van life for a bit." His smile fell. It seemed as though he wanted to say something else. He turned to get out, and when he shut the door, he leaned back in the window.

"It was nice talking to you. I'm not sure why we can't be civil like this all the time."

I shrugged, feeling a little guilty for all the times I'd gotten frustrated with him. He wasn't a bad guy. Honestly, his company had helped me stay chill while I waited to see what shape Pops would be in after his date.

"Yeah." I had no clue what else to say. I was honestly shocked that we'd gotten along. Maybe it was when there were folks around that he had to be extra, or maybe it was—

"Yeah," he said, rolling his eyes. "Well, thanks."

He walked away while I was still thinking of something intelligent to say. I fisted my hand and banged the steering wheel. I really needed to learn how to talk to people without being a jerk. Especially him. I got the sense that under that attitude he seemed to have, there might just be a sensitive guy.

I started the van and let it warm for a minute before pulling around to the back entrance. The last thing I needed was for the temperamental beauty to backfire and scare half of Los Feliz.

Boone had just reached our grandparents and was shaking hands with Pops as I pulled up. Then Pops took Vera Jean's hands and leaned in to kiss her cheek. I was too far away to hear but he said something to her, and her skin flushed as she chuckled.

"I'll see you soon," she said to him, squeezing his hands. She took Boone's offered arm and a deep frown marred his face as they stepped off the curb.

"Thanks, son," Pops said as he climbed in. He rubbed his hands together and smiled as he watched them walk across the lot to Boone's car.

"No problem. Everything okay?"

"More than okay." He didn't bother to further explain his cryptic statement, so I put the van in gear and tried to exit the parking lot. *Tried.* There were two cars facing opposite directions at the driveaway and the drivers were having a conversation with each other, not caring at all that they were blocking the exit. I groaned and put the van in reverse, figuring I'd use the other exit, which meant driving past Boone's car. Which he was currently abusing by slapping his hand on the roof.

I stopped in front of them, and Pops rolled down his window.

"Everything okay?"

Boone cursed then took a deep breath. "Battery's dead."

"It's all right, you two," Vera Jean said. "Boone is going to call for a service truck."

"It's late, why don't we give you a ride home?" Pops offered.

I covered my protest with a cough. I'm not sure what I would have said. "I'm not a taxi," or something rude like that. While I coughed, Pops got out and held the door open for Vera.

"Are you sure you don't mind?"

I shook my head and smiled tightly, not wanting to take a chance my inner asshole would answer.

Pops opened the back door and gestured for Boone to climb in, but I could see him warring with himself. I could only imagine he didn't want to leave his grandmother.

Feeling charitable, I said, "I'm sure your car will be fine here. I could bring you back tomorrow to pick it up," I said.

Boone blinked those giant blue eyes at me, and I wanted to tell him to forget it.

No, I wanted him to climb in and for us to keep talking, obviously without our grandparents.

"That's very kind of you, Shane." Vera Jean fastened her seat belt and smiled at me. "Boone sometimes forgets to charge that thing."

It was my turn to do the surprised blinking thing. Boone? Not be perfect? I started to razz him about it but the innocent look was gone and in its place was...anger?

He climbed in and sat on the bed next to Pops.

"Sorry, I don't have extra seat belts back there."

"Just don't take the corners too tight," Pops said with a laugh. He said something to Boone, and when I looked in the rearview, Boone looked as if he'd rather eat glass than be riding in my van.

Why so on edge, I wondered?

Vera Jean gave me the address, and I plastered a smile on my face rather than bitch about heading in the opposite direction from home and into the hilly, windy canyon road. The van was in great shape, but the hills were a challenge. I watched as Boone attempted to find something to hold on to in the back, while Bruce and Vera Jean continued talking.

"Oh! And there was the place you lot rented back then."

Bruce chuckled. "We definitely trashed that place back in nineteen-seventy."

The two of them told hilarious tales of debauchery while I tried to focus on the road.

"I'm glad you kept the house here," Pops said as we pulled into the driveway of a massive mansion. "John loved this place."

"He did. We both did. It's too big for me, really, but with Boone here, it's nice. We both have our space."

I had to bite my cheek. *He lives with his grandma?* I was close with Pops, but we both had our own condos a few blocks away from each other.

Boone stood and tried the door handle, getting a little frustrated when it didn't work.

"Oh, hang on. It only opens from the outside."

I put the van in park and got out, trotted around the backside, and opened the door, coming face-to-face with a flustered Boone. He hopped down and I got a whiff of his...body wash? He smelled like gummy bears, or taffy. I wanted to grab him and bring him back in close, he smelled that good. Instead, I reached for Vera Jean's door and held out a hand to help her down.

"It's kind of a high step."

"I've got her," Boone said, taking her other hand.

Vera stood between us, laughing at our overenthusiastic chivalry. I would have been flustered, but I was caught in Boone's gravitational pull and I couldn't stop staring at him.

"Boys, this was nice. Bruce? Walk me up?" She looked between us with a curious expression, and then accepted Pops's hand.

Boone and I were left standing. Staring. Though what he was thinking, I had no idea. He kind of looked at me like I was an alien, when he was the one who'd shocked me.

"Thank you. I know it's a pain to come all the way out here. I can't believe it. I left the damn car on when I went over to your van. I wasn't even thinking."

"I think I'd always be nervous about running out of battery with an electric car."

He shrugged and looked toward our grandparents getting cozy on the porch.

"They seem happy," he said, sounding anything but.

"For now," I scoffed.

He pinned me with his gaze once more. "I hope you'll give Gran the benefit of the doubt. She's not going to trounce all over your pops, no matter what you think of us."

"I don't think—"

"See you around, I guess," he muttered, shaking his head as he stormed off toward the house. Instead of going in the front door, he punched in a code on the garage and the door opened, revealing John Boone's classic '70s Corvette—the one he was photographed with for his solo album cover—and a late-model Cadillac, which was probably Vera Jean's.

I didn't know what to say. Boone was so different when it was just us. He seemed almost...insecure. Like he worried what I thought about him. Since when? He had everything. I *fought* for everything. But for now, we were united in our roles as doting grandsons.

We'd have to support our grandparents through this reunion, whatever we felt about each other. Whatever the outcome.

EIGHT

B oone

"Just one more time, you guys." It was our last band practice before we left for Portland to record, and I just wanted to work out this one last song. It was our practice to have solid songs together before going into the studio, and Brandon, Annie and I were a tight songwriting team.

"Boone, you need to rest your voice, man."

Brandon and Annie had been treating me with kid gloves lately and though I knew they were right to be concerned, it drove me nuts.

"I'm fine," I said, though I knew I wasn't. This fucking physical limitation crap I'd been dealing with since my diagnosis was bullshit. It had only been a few months, and I was already sick and tired of my body getting in the way of my work. The doctors had told me it might take some time to get things under control, but despite diet and exercise changes, I was still struggling with insomnia and prone to super low dips in my blood sugar. I was on the verge of throwing a massive tantrum when Annie stepped closer.

"You say that," Annie said, resting a hand on the neck of my guitar, "but you've been pushing yourself so hard. I'm worried about you."

The twins knew that I was dealing with some medical stuff, but I hadn't told them the truth. I didn't want anyone other than Gran watching what I was eating—or not eating— reminding me to drink more water, joining me in our home gym to make sure I got my cardio in.

I sighed and took my guitar off, placing it on a holder. We practiced on the lower floor of Gran's place. My rooms were down here and she lived upstairs. After Grandpa died, I came to stay and I never left. She didn't have to tell me she didn't want to be alone.

Annie and Brandon worried we'd disturb her, but I reassured them it was fine. She said she loved to have the energy in the house again. The twins totally fangirled over her whenever she came downstairs, which she did right then.

"Sounds good upstairs," she said, her eyes trained on me with worry.

Damn, I must have looked like shit.

"Thanks," I muttered, but Annie and Brandon chatted excitedly with her. I wandered over to the sink in my kitchenette, drained my water bottle, and refilled it. I stared out the bank of windows that looked over Laurel Canyon. It really was beautiful here. I often opened the windows in the middle of the night and just listened to the sounds, absorbing any of the leftover vibes from the days when great music could be heard from every nook and cranny of the canyon.

"You're coming up to the compound? Boone, you didn't tell us!"

"Oh, right. Yeah. Gran, you talked to Lydia?"

She grinned and pressed her hands together. "Yes, and she said she and Morrison would love to host the foundation's benefit show this year. They've each agreed to play as well! Rose will coordinate all of the incidentals with me."

I beamed. "That's great news. It sucks that the Bowl isn't available—"

She waved a hand. "It will be nice to hold it in a different place this year. Who knows? Maybe we'll get some new donors, even take it on the road in the future. I'm just so glad you put me in touch with them."

Gran and Papa had set up the Collins Foundation ten years ago to raise money for artists in need. Too many of our peers had struggled with health issues, and after one of Papa's good friends fell ill with cancer, he watched the man lose everything and vowed he'd build an organization that would ensure musicians wouldn't have to jeopardize their health and suffer while trying to make ends meet.

Papa's death didn't just devastate Gran and I. It was a devastating loss to the music industry as well. Vera Jean loved the foundation and had gained strength and purpose from continuing the work after she'd lost her partner.

"Bruce is going to meet me up there. He wants to help."

My shocked expression did little to eliminate her enthusiastic smile, and I had to turn away. I couldn't let my pouting ruin a chance for her to have happiness again. I drank more water and took a moment to chill the fuck out. We'd already exchanged heated words after her date, when she'd let me know that she planned on seeing him again...often... seriously.

"But Gran," I'd argued like an insolent teen.

"Boone, this is not up to you. I know I've leaned on you quite a bit, and I appreciate you being there for me, but I'm a grown woman with my own mind. And I want this. Bruce is just as wonderful as he was then, even more so now with age and experience. He makes me happy. I should think you'd want that for me."

How could I argue with that?

"I guess we can call it quits for the night. I need to pack anyway."

"You haven't packed yet?" Annie said, rolling her eyes. "Of course you haven't. Want some help?"

"No, thanks." Annie knew she'd be taking her life into her hands if she came into my bedroom. I'd lived with her and Brandon for a long time when we first started the band. My pigsty of a room was legend back then. I'd like to say that age has made me a neater, more organized person. I'd be a liar though.

"We'll pick you up in the morning, then," Brandon said. He and Annie hugged Gran and collected their gear.

I shut off all the equipment and made sure all of the recordings were downloaded into the cloud so I could access them for Morrison. Gran moved to my side and twirled my hair with her finger.

"How are you feeling, dear boy?"

I sighed and plopped down in the desk chair next to the control panel. "I'm fucking tired, and I'm fucking tired of being tired." I shrugged. "I'm not doing well with my 'new normal.'"

She tilted her head. "And you haven't told the twins, have you?"

I shook my head. "We're doing the sober thing together and they know I quit smoking. That's all they need to know for now."

Gran sighed in that way that let me know she disagreed but was going to let me fall on my face on my own. She liked it that way, then she could swoop in and say she told me so. I let her. I knew she was right. That much I knew at my age.

"Bruce said Shane was getting ready to go to Portland, too."

I nodded. "Yeah, we're splitting time with them. I'm sure he's not happy about it."

"And that makes you sad, doesn't it?"

I let my head fall back and spun the chair around and around. "It does, which is dumb. I don't know why I care."

"You care because you hate it whenever you can't win someone over."

The spinning in the chair used to help me think but right now it was making me nauseous. I stopped and closed my eyes. "Am I that much of a narcissist?"

"Boone, you aren't a narcissist! But you love to be loved, and Shane is the one person you haven't won over."

"Yet," I said with a wink. "I remember being like seven or eight years old the first time I met him. You and Grandpa had one of your wild parties, do you remember that?" She nodded and laced her fingers together. "I remember thinking he was so cool. I followed him around the whole afternoon."

"Yes, and at the end of the day, you cried to me that you'd never be a big kid like Shane. I remember that vividly. That was before his parents split up, I think. When his mum still came to functions with Bruce."

"And now I'm thirty years old and I still want him to like me." In my stupid obsession of watching interviews with Shane, I came across one in which he didn't hold back when the reporter asked him about Stellar. He'd said something to the effect that we were like candy that tasted good at first bite, but left you with a stomachache and a cavity. Not just us; he'd lumped us into the same category with several other bands currently sitting on the top of the Hard Rock and Alternative Rock charts.

"Then you go up there to Portland and you do what you do best, and you act like the consummate professional. That's all you *can* do. But I will ask that you also be respectful when it comes to Bruce. I know your experience with him at the induction ceremony rubbed you the wrong way—"

"It's not that," I said. "I was just worried for you. As long as he treats you with respect, he'll have mine. I promise. No more tantrums."

She grabbed my chin and wrinkled her nose. "You are so good to me, Boone. I want you to know how much I love you, and how blessed I am to have you in my life."

"Stop it, Gran." We both teared up, and I gave her a tight hug, which she tried to worm away from when she felt how sweaty I was.

"Now, you go shower and pack. I'm having Catherine clean up your disaster zone while you're gone, and I won't hear a word from you."

I felt the urge to stomp my foot and protest, but that would undo all of the progress I'd just made with her.

She knew threatening me with Catherine's cleaning meant I would clean up my own shit to avoid anything getting lost, broken, or tossed out, so that's what I did. I spent the entire night cleaning my room, spending an inordinate amount of time putting loose photos in an album, organizing my paperwork, alphabetizing my vinyl collection.

So when Annie and Brandon arrived, I was still dripping wet from the shower and throwing clothes into a duffel bag. I made sure I had enough protein bars, all of my test strips and extra lancets, my monitor, my Metformin, my vitamins... Oh, and my manicure kit and polish collection.

I'd sleep at some point. In between playing with my band, working with Morrison, giving Rose a manicure, and trying to simultaneously avoid Shane and make him like me.

NINE

Shane

"I'm sorry, Shane, but Stellar is booked to overlap with you for the week. Morrison plans to work with you during the evenings, but days he'll be with them. Lydia is free for the first couple of days to work with you as well."

So many ugly things wanted to come out of my mouth, but that would feed into my reputation as a total dick, and none of this was Rose's fault. As the manager of Bolder Breed Studios, it was her job to keep Lydia Pride and Morrison Jones on schedule, and to be their buffer in situations like this. The issue was on our end.

"You're right, I'm sorry. Jeff should have let me know we'd be splitting time." Our manager, of all people, should have known I wouldn't want to be in the same studio, much less the same area code, with Boone. "Tell Lydia we'd love to see her tomorrow then."

"I'm really sorry for the miscommunication," Rose said. "But the rehearsal space is open in Cabin Six for you guys. You've got your usual rooms in the east wing, on the second floor."

I didn't want to ask where Stellar was staying. I didn't even want to be breathing the same air, be in the same time zone as Boone...

Because I didn't trust myself.

He'd been all I could think about, especially after seeing him lose some of that golden-boy gloss the night our grandparents reconnected. But if I was being honest, it really hit me while watching him sing with my grandfather. Oh, man, the two of them sounded good together.

Since that night, I'd spent my time vacillating between wanting to support my grandfather in his determination to win back the love of his life and wanting to forget about the entire Collins family. Pops was hurt time and time again by his best friend and the woman they both loved, and it seemed I was the only one who remembered that.

Dude was completely gone. He was so in love with Vera Jean. He'd loved my grandmother, Eddie Mae. They married shortly after John and Vera Jean were married, and had my mom around the same time Jean Collins was born. Grandma and Pops had a tumultuous marriage that wasn't helped by their drinking. Sadly, she passed when I was little.

My mother blamed him for everything that went wrong in their lives. I overheard some teary conversations he'd had with Mom after yet another setback in his life. She thought music had ruined his life and made him an addict. She finally told him to stop coming around when I was in middle school, which was the beginning of the end of any sort of positive relationship between us. Shortly after that my father left, and though he tried to stay a part of my life, he got tired of fighting my mother as well. Obviously I hadn't had a whole lot of experience observing healthy relationships, so what did I know?

I just wanted to see him happy, and he was over the damn moon.

The guys and I carried our stuff up the grand staircase and as I turned the corner, I heard laughter behind me.

Guess who.

"Shane."

Boone stared at me with the type of grin on his face that had me thinking he was ready to dig at me again, but he said nothing.

"I'll meet you down there," Annie, his bass player, said before trotting down the steps and over to Rose's office.

"Didn't know you guys were going to be here," I said. It wasn't the douchiest thing I could have said, but it probably sounded that way to him.

Boone cocked his head and walked toward me, stopping farther away than usual. He was kind of a personal-space invader, but this time he remained out of arm's reach.

I'd been a total dick in New York.

"I thought you knew. I'm sorry if that cuts into your plans," he said with a wince, and I actually believed he meant it. "We would postpone and give you guys the time, but Gran is coming in a few days to work on the plans for the benefit show, and I need to wrap Stellar stuff before she arrives. Morrison and Lydia invited her to have it at the venue here."

I raised my eyebrows. "Instead of LA?"

Boone lifted a shoulder. "The Bowl is under renovations, and since they're donating the venue fee, it means more of the funds will go to the foundation."

"Vera Jean does good work. I'm glad it worked out."

Boone stepped closer. "Hey, Shane—"

"Butler, we're going down to the mess hall. I'm starving." Dean, Tucker, and Drew stood there staring between us like they were itching to grab some popcorn and ringside seats.

I waved them off, though they all hesitated at the top of the stairs, probably waiting for the predictable drama. Fucking Dean pulled out his phone, and I swear he hit record.

"I'll see you down there," I said, inviting them to fuck right off with the flick of my middle finger.

Boone chuckled, and my eyes shot to him, expecting him to make a smartass comment and walk away. What was he waiting for?

Dean, Drew, and Tucker left us alone, finally. When they reached the bottom of the stairs, I turned back to Boone.

We both spoke at once.

And there was nervous laughter.

For the first time, I didn't feel animosity toward him. I wanted to hear what he had to say. Maybe he, too, had been feeling some kinda way about all that happened between us recently. But then I spoke first.

"I'm sorry I pushed you." *What are you doing, Shane?* "In New York. I was out of line."

Boone's beguiling eyes as blue as the deepest sea went even rounder. "Oh, no, it was my fault. I egged you on."

I opened my mouth to speak, but then his words registered. He was actually admitting he might not be perfect? When I didn't say anything, he stepped even closer, now in his usual too-close proximity.

"I always seem to say the wrong thing—"

"It's not you," I said. "It's been bugging me. I shouldn't have put my hands on you."

Boone tucked his chin and smiled up at me. "I mean, maybe not in anger."

"I—" *Pardon?*

"Maybe I wanted you to. *Want* you to. Maybe that's why I poke you." His gaze dropped to my lips, back up to my eyes, and then he sighed. "See you around, Butler."

And he fucking winked as he walked away, his hippie pants riding low on his hips, leaving a gap of pale skin where his black stretchy top didn't quite reach.

I was left sputtering on the top of the steps.

What the…? How the…? Why would he…?

"Shane! You coming, man?"

Dean stood at the bottom of the steps with his hands out.

I was so close to making this internal dialogue external that I took a minute to breathe deeply, shake off this…whatever it was. Irritation? Annoyance?

No. If I was honest with myself, I recognized it.

Lust. Attraction. Intrigue.

I couldn't deny any longer that I absolutely did *not* hate this confounding man. There was a reason why he kept getting to me, and perhaps he saw it clearer than I did. I tended to stay in my feisty and furious mindset most of the time, which didn't allow for tight relationships with anyone other than my band, who *had* to deal with me. I was prickly. Abrasive, even.

Why the hell would the golden boy want to engage with me? And why did I want him to?

I held up a finger, trotted to my room, opened it with the key Rose had given me, and dropped my guitar and bags inside before locking it again, first taking a moment to smile at the place I'd lay my head for the next several nights. I loved the decor of these rooms. Morrison and Lydia had acquired an enormous collection of rock memorabilia over the years and they decorated the rooms thematically to make each one special. They usually gave me the one with the giant Led Zeppelin "Stairway to Heaven" mural. Dark-stained wood walls, thick drapes in case you wanted to sleep in, and a king-sized bed with a padded headboard and enough pillows to hide a body underneath looked so inviting right now, but it was work time.

I took the stairs quickly and brushed past Dean without giving his smart mouth an opportunity to talk shit.

"Everything okay?"

"Peachy."

Dean laughed and jogged to catch up with my long strides.

We headed out the front doors and down the gravel path toward the mess hall. We ate better at the compound than I did anywhere else, so we made it a point never to miss meals while we were here.

"You know, I think you and the cherub should just fuck and get it over with. No one is going to care. I don't know why you just—"

"Stop."

Dean was the only one in my band I would even allow to talk shit about my personal life. Yeah, I did run the show a bit like a dictator from time to time, but the guys were with me because they liked me being in charge.

During a period of weakness—I don't know if I should call it that or not, but a period when I was going through some shit, I tried to get the guys to make some of the decisions, take more ownership of writing songs. I was sick and fucking tired of everything being on me. They didn't go for it, and we went right back to the way things were. Some bands do change it up, some are a democracy. But not Wicked Soul. I wrote the songs, Dean, Drew, and Tucker assisted with arrangements, and I liaised with our manager Jeff and the label.

I wanted my fingers in the business. I didn't want what happened to Pops to happen to me. I wanted to make enough money that I didn't have to worry about it, and so I could take care of the old man. So far, I'd met my goals.

"Come on, Butler. You going to tell me there's not something there? Everyone sees it."

"Stop. Seriously. We're here to record. We've got a tight schedule, made tighter by this little hitch in our plans—"

"Is that what we're calling him?"

"Fuck off." But it didn't have any venom in it. Part of me was secretly thrilled to potentially get to see Stellar behind the scenes, maybe even get to watch Boone sing.

"All right, but if you want to scratch that itch, nobody's

gonna blame you. And frankly, I'd be happy to cover for you if you don't want the other guys to know."

"Gee, thanks. I'm touched."

Dean cursed under his breath. "You need to be touched," he muttered.

I let it go as we were nearing the mess hall and I knew that if I protested any harder, I'd make a total ass out of myself, and that wouldn't be a great way to start our week here.

We were well cared for by the whole staff at Bolder Breed. Felix, Morrison's chef, took extra care to meet everyone's likes and dietary needs. Dinner that night was grilled mahi mahi, vegetables, and mashed potatoes, just enough to satisfy but not too much that we'd leave feeling like we'd had a heavy meal. Then the guys really wanted to go into Portland and see a burlesque show, and even though I wanted to get some rehearsal time in, I didn't want to be a curmudgeon.

As we were walking back to the lodge together, Leland Elliot, Morrison's partner, was jogging down the steps. We'd met years ago, and I always loved catching up with him.

"You guys go ahead," I said to Dean and the others after they shook hands with Leland, and they were gone. Didn't even hesitate to leave without me. Not that we went out together in cases like this, but for some reason it niggled at me. Dean checked to see if he had the keys to the rental SUV we'd picked up and waved as he ran off.

"Good to see you, man," I said, as Leland wrapped me in a big hug.

"Been too long, Butler. I hear there was a little mix-up with the schedule, man, I'm sorry."

"Not at all. It'll be good to have some time with Lydia *and* with Morrison. They both bring something different to the music, you know."

Leland kept his arm around my shoulders. "You heading up?"

"Nah. Too restless. I was going to grab a guitar and go to Cabin 6, mess around for a while."

Leland pulled me away from the lodge. "Let me show you what More brought me from his latest trip to London." He rubbed his hands together, and I followed him. "He knows how I feel about vintage guitars, and he found me the perfect slide guitar. I've been itching to show it to someone who will appreciate it for what it is."

I laughed and patted him on the back. "You're not going stir crazy out here in the middle of nowhere?"

"Are you kidding? I get to play host to all of our best friends. I don't have to deal with LA traffic. Ain't gotta cook. This is heaven up here."

"I guess it would be," I said, thinking that I, too, might like a little break from the rat race. "What about the rain?"

He shrugged. "Hasn't gotten to me yet. We went down south for a bit when it was snowing. Lydia likes the cold, so she booked all the time. Worked out good. Sometimes the damp fucks with my joints, though. Getting old is a bitch."

"Whatever," I said, rolling my eyes. And then I realized we were at the two-story house they'd converted into the main studio space when Morrison and Lydia bought the place, and Leland was going up the steps. "Oh, uh, aren't they working in there?" As much as I was tempted to flirt with disaster, busting in on Boone's studio time was probably not a great move.

"Yeah, it's fine. It's just in the control room." He held open the door for me and waited.

Fuck. Now it would be weird to beg off.

What could I do but accept his invitation?

I walked in and he let the heavy door close behind us. We stood in the foyer of the old house and through a set of glass French doors, I could see Morrison sitting behind the board with his headset on, having some sort of...seizure? He had his hands pressed to the earpieces as he jerked his head and his whole upper body, his track-pants legs flailing about, rolling his chair side-to-side

"Oh shit, I heard what they were working on last night. This album is going to be all kinds of sick." Leland opened the door and gestured for me to follow.

Beyond the control board, Boone was playing and singing his heart out, his long curls bouncing on his shoulders, his eyes closed. I couldn't look away. Not even when he opened them and stared at me in surprise.

Leland put a hand on Morrison's shoulder, making his partner jump. He stood and hugged Leland, bouncing up and down and pointing his finger at the band. He flipped a switch, and the control room was blasted with sound.

The sound of Boone's voice flooded me with heat. I thought I might black out when he rested his hands on the mic stand and sang a high note that made the hair rise on my arms.

His giant blue eyes were focused on me as he finished the last note of the song. When it was over, he smiled at his band-mates, nodding at them. When he looked back at *me*, his expression was wide-eyed, as if he'd just gotten caught doing something naughty. Or that was just the salacious thoughts in my head.

"Boone, that was fucking brilliant," Morrison said over the mic, jarring me from my little fantasyland. "I'm out of my head over here."

Boone took a dramatic bow, and his eyes connected with me once more.

"I ran into Butler, and I wanted to show him my new toy," Leland said to Morrison, reminding me we were not here to gawk at Boone Collins.

Leland stepped over to the rack of guitars and pulled out his new shiny. "Morrison already has my heart, but damn, would you look at this beauty?" The guitar was a rare Lectraslide, and he proceeded to run his fingers lovingly along the strings. "I've always loved these. I can't believe you found one."

Morrison shrugged. "I knew you'd love it. Plus, I thought it could come in handy if Boone agrees that this song we've been working on needs slide."

"If Boone agrees to what?"

Boone stepped out of the studio and joined the three of us. The twins pulled out their cigarette packs and basically snuck out like a couple of kids cutting school. But Boone didn't seem to notice. He was staring at me. Again. Making me realize that I was imposing on his studio time.

TEN

B oone

I did my best not to show that Shane's appearance had rattled me. Flirting with him earlier was a ballsier move than I thought myself capable of, and thinking about what I'd said? My hands shook as I reached for the mic and put a little more oomph into the last note on this new song than I'd done previously.

"Damn, Boone," Annie said when the song was over. "Way to show off for your mans."

I didn't say anything because, well, it was all out there. My band knew I'd developed an unhealthy amount of attraction to the surly man.

Shane had walked in with Leland and I'd nearly lost my focus. His eyes were so dark under his heavy brows, and they seemed to bore right through me. He had that crease between his brows that I never could tell whether it was pissed or pensive. Then Morrison had gone bonkers, hugging on Leland, all while Shane stared daggers into me. I felt naked in front of him, as if he saw all of my flaws, all the work I did to appear to have my shit together.

I so didn't.

But I was trying. God, it was hard, but I was trying.

I worked myself nearly to death as the leader of my band, but that had never been as hard as my current battle with diabetes. Food tracking, exercise, medications, managing my blood sugar. Thankfully, Annie and Brandon were totally on board when I suggested we all work on getting healthy without telling them why. They'd given up booze, and that meant the world to me that we could support each other. They still smoked, which they were headed out to do now, since I'd called for a break, but I couldn't expect them to give up *all* the fun.

It really, *really* sucked giving up all the fun.

When they were out, I checked my app to see if my blood sugar was okay, and it wasn't. I tended to go dangerously low while performing or working out, and was still trying to figure out how to keep that from happening. Not sleeping the past couple of nights hadn't helped either. I turned and went back into the studio to grab a peanut butter protein bar from my backpack and was just about to open it when Morrison's voice came over the com.

"Boone, come check this out."

I dropped the bar back into my bag and entered the control room. Shane's presence hit me like an electromagnetic pulse. My chest tightened and I opened my mouth to speak, but I started to list to the side, feeling dizzy all of a sudden. I reached for the chair and tried to smile and hide the fact that I was about to collapse.

"Hey, so I picked this up in London and it's a helluva slide guitar. I want you to listen to something. Leland is going to play the bridge on 'Over The Moon,' and why don't you grab that Strat there and play along with it."

I blinked a couple of times, not trusting myself to pick up a guitar when I likely couldn't remain standing much longer. "Can I hear him first?" I tried to think of an excuse. "I want to hear the parts separate."

"Oh, okay, well it's really the combination of the slide with the wah pedal on the Strat I wanted to try."

They all looked at me, and spots started clouding my vision.

"Great, why don't you two play it. I'll be right back."

I pushed away from the chair and stumbled a bit, offering a nod to Morrison, who looked at me strangely. He grabbed the Strat and launched into an explanation for Leland. I had to walk danger close to Shane to get to the door. I tried to smile at him, but I bumped him with my shoulder instead.

"Hey," he said, and I thought, *Great. He thinks I'm going to be a dick.*

I held up a hand. "Sorry, I'm... Excuse me."

I pushed through the French doors, hitting them a little harder than I meant, and one of them slammed against the wall, rattling the glass. Thankfully Morrison and Leland were too busy playing to notice—but Shane did.

He frowned at me as I tried to hurry up the stairs to the bathroom. And then, like I'd never climbed steps before, I tripped and caught myself with my hands near the top. I prayed Shane wasn't still watching as I hurried into the bedroom which I knew had a bathroom attached, ducked inside, and shut the door.

"Fuck," I said, my hands shaking as I attempted to scoop water into my hands...to drink? Or splash my face? I kind of did both, and then started choking as the water went down the wrong pipe. Intense, body-racking coughs blacked out the rest of my vision, and I sat down on the toilet seat.

Someone pounded on the door.

"Just a minute," I said with a weak voice, and then coughed even harder.

"Boone, open the door."

No. Shane. *God*, how humiliating. I couldn't let him see me like this. I reached for the doorknob, intending to lock it, but the coughing wouldn't stop and I fell to a knee just as Shane opened the door.

"Jesus. Boone! What the fuck?"

I waved my hand at him to leave, but instead he closed the door behind him and stared at me, wide-eyed as he helped me to my feet.

"Fine. Water, wrong pipe." I closed my mouth and tried to control the coughing, but my lungs weren't done punishing me.

Shane reached over and patted me on the back, a little harder than necessary, then he left his hand on my shoulder and the weight gave me something to focus on.

"What can I do? You want me to go get the twins?"

I shook my head. Yeah, my band knew I had to make some "lifestyle changes," and they'd seen me a little more tired than usual, but if they knew how terrified I was that I might space out or, worse, fucking collapse, they'd insist we slow down, that I take time to get well, and that wasn't an option. We had momentum going, and we had no time to rest if Stellar was going to remain relevant. I needed our band in everyone's faces, everywhere they turned, for as long as it took for us to get to that level I knew we were capable of.

"Boone, what's wrong?"

"Nothing, I told you. I choked on some water."

"Sure. And before? You just plowed into me for no reason?"

Why I had to default to asshole when I was terrified, I had no idea.

"Maybe it was your giant ego in the way." But I couldn't add the sarcasm necessary to pull it off. I coughed some more and held on to the sink to keep from falling. Suddenly, all I could think of was crawling into bed, how nice it would feel to pull the covers over my head and pretend this wasn't happening.

"I'm going to get Morrison if you're just going to be difficult."

"No! Please." I couldn't let anyone else see me like this. Shane hated me anyway, what did it matter what he thought? "I'll be okay, I just need—" I thought I could get downstairs to my protein bar, and then I'd be fine, like all the other times.

Instead, I fell into Shane's arms.

He grunted in surprise but took my weight with no effort. I looked into his eyes, intending to apologize—and that was all, folks. My legs ceased to function for a brief enough moment, and I finally got to experience what it felt like to be close to Shane Butler. Later, I would remember thinking that his lips looked even sexier up close, that the tendons in his neck would be perfect to nibble on, that he was *really* strong.

"Dammit, Boone," he muttered, and he managed to get an arm around my back and one of mine around his neck. "Let's get you to the bed and we'll figure out what to do."

I desperately wanted to fight him, but I had no smart words. He got the door open and he dragged me over to the bed. Morrison had mentioned that he kept a bed up here in case he or any of his guests worked late and didn't feel like trekking in the dark all the way back to the lodge. I'd be eternally grateful for his forethought.

Shane lowered me to the bed and lifted my legs onto it. I was about to thank him when he spoke angrily.

"Maybe you should lay off the shit. If I'd known I was giving up our time with Morrison so you could get high—"

"I'm not—" I could see why he thought that. My eyes

filled with traitorous tears, and I channeled my disgust with myself into my words. "Will you bring me my bag from downstairs?"

"Why? So you can take more?" He grabbed my arm and pushed up my sleeve before I could yank it away, and he seemed surprised to not find evidence of his accusation.

"My bag. Please, Shane. Then you can go back to hating me with the fire of a thousand suns." I turned my head, hoping he wouldn't catch the tear that escaped.

He started to protest, but I rolled over onto my side and tried to remember the meditation I'd learned from my nurse practitioner.

Finally, I heard his heavy steps pound down the stairs, so I pulled out my phone. My blood sugar was now even lower at 67. *Shit*. My heart thudded, and I prayed he did what I asked. In the meantime, I berated myself.

Thirty years old and you can't even take care of yourself.

You're an embarrassment.

You're fucking everything up.

"Here." He tossed my duffel onto the bed and stepped back. "I'm only staying to make sure you're not going to OD, but you can bet your ass I'm going to—"

I pulled out the protein bar and with shaky hands, I attempted to peel the wrapper down, only I couldn't get a grip as my fingers were wet with my tears. I tried using my teeth, which was a waste of time, and I was about to throw the damn thing across the room when Shane took it from me. Gently.

"Here," he said softly, pulling out his Leatherman tool and cutting the wrapper open. He peeled it down and handed it back to me.

I might have said thanks, but I sniffled at the same time so I'm not sure what sound came out. I took a bite, my stomach roiling at the taste in my mouth, and deliberately chewed slowly to make sure I didn't choke on it, since I still felt that tickle in my chest like I might start coughing again.

"You want me to get you some orange juice? Or like a Sprite?"

My eyes shot to his. "Please, don't say anything. They don't know."

"What? That you're diabetic? What's the big fucking deal?"

"No," I said, holding up a hand so I could finish chewing the next bite. "My band knows I'm having some health issues, but they don't know it's this bad. Only my gran. I can't tell them."

"What the fuck, Boone? You're sick. Why is that such a big fucking deal?"

"It's a big fucking deal because I *can't* be sick."

He chuckled and shook his head, crossing his arms over his chest. "I'm glad you're such a control freak you think you can stop a whole-ass disease."

"I'm sorry, who's the one that still plays all the instruments on his band's demos to make sure it sounds perfect?"

Shane stood taller. "I write our songs. Just want to make sure I have it all worked out before I teach everyone else. It's not like I don't take their feedback in rehearsal. I'm not a *total* dick."

I took another bite of the protein bar, worried that I would top off this strange encounter by vomiting on his shoes or something equally vile.

"I see you trying to deflect here, but seriously. How long has this been going on? Have you seen a doctor?"

His questions sounded almost...concerned? "Why do you care?" As soon as I asked him, I realized how juvenile I sounded. I was merely curious why, after all these years of hating me, he would even ask?

"Why are you being so defensive?"

I groaned. "I saw the doctor when we got back from tour a few months ago. I'm trying to follow the plans, but when I'm working, I get caught up. I guess I didn't eat enough today."

"Yeah, you look like you've lost even more weight than since the induction ceremony."

He noticed? "Aw, it's like you *do* actually care." My assholery knew no bounds.

"Fuck off, Collins."

"Sorry. I'm a mess."

He shrugged and leaned against the doorframe, avoiding eye contact. "Whatever. You need anything else?"

"I'll be fine. Can you let Morrison know I'll be down in a bit?"

He nodded, still looking away from me, and the crease between his brows was deeper than ever. He went down the stairs, and I tried to collect myself. Ugh, why couldn't I talk to him like a normal person? I let my eyes drift closed for a bit and pleaded with my higher power to stop the room from spinning.

The next thing I knew, I woke up in the dark in an unfamiliar bed. My lungs were screaming for my inhaler, so I sat up and looked around, willing my eyes to focus.

And there was Shane Butler, sitting in a chair, his head bowed as if he were praying. My bag sat at his feet.

I needed my inhaler or else I was headed for a coughing fit that would surely wake him up. I attempted to slide out of bed, but the wood frame creaked. Then the floor crackled under my weight as I stood.

Shane remained motionless, looking like some sort of sentinel, only there was no way he'd willingly protect me from anything. He was the last person I wanted to appear weak in front of, and I'd made a total fool out of myself with him. I stood in front of him, wishing I could snap my fingers in front of his face and make him forget what had happened.

"Everyone's gone, if that's what you're worried about."

I gasped as he spoke and jumped clear off the floor, which was the catalyst for the asthma attack I'd been trying to stave off. I started coughing and crouched down to reach into my bag. I fumbled with my inhaler then took two puffs and tried holding it in as long as possible before I exhaled.

ELEVEN

S hane

"Asthma too? Damn, you really need to take care of yourself before you end up another dead rockstar."

He seemed small as he stood there taking shallow breaths. It reminded me of when we were kids, thrown together only because our grandparents knew each other, not because we chose to be playmates. He would follow me and my friends around, laughing at our jokes even when my friends told him to get lost. He was a persistent little fucker even back then.

"Ouch," he said, and he started to back up, but I reached for his arm. He flinched, like I was going to hurt him.

"Boone, hey," I said, jumping to my feet. I reached for his arms again, but then thought better of it. I shouldn't touch him without permission...again. Even after what he'd said earlier. "I'm sorry, I shouldn't have, I'm—"

He smiled, and I forgot that I shouldn't be talking to him

like this, so close to him. This time the smile wasn't that fake shit he did for everyone else. This one reminded me of our chat in my van, which was the first time we'd really talked... maybe ever. And dammit, it was that interaction that cemented my obsession with this guy. Who was he if he wasn't the asshole I'd always thought?

"I told you, Shane, I *want* you to."

"Why? I mean, why me? Why now?"

He shrugged one shoulder and lowered his chin, looking up at me with those fucking deep blue eyes, and my heart raced like I'd just had five shots of espresso.

"Maybe if you touch me, it'll mean you don't hate me."

His perfect voice cracked when he said that, and he followed it up with a pained expression.

He was so perfect. All of him. And I'd been awful to him because I couldn't stand that he was so perfect. Why, though? Why had I held on to these feelings for so long? Why hadn't I just reached out and touched him before?

"Shane?" His nervous laugh jarred me from my internal battle. "Do you want...*me?*"

Of course I did, that's why I'd been such an asshole. Didn't he see that? Did he really think I hated him?

If I touched him, though—

"Goddammit, Collins," I whispered. I grabbed his biceps and pulled him close, probably a little too forcefully, but any second my resolve was going to snap like a rubber band and the sting when it hit was going to fucking suck. I knew this was going to hurt, and I did it anyway.

Boone tilted his head up, and like this? He was even more sensual than when he sang, and I hadn't thought that was possible, that there was even more passion in him than what he gave to his audiences.

And what did I have to give *him?*

"Yes, Butler?" His eyes flared, and he laughed.

He'd imitated my much deeper voice, and I couldn't help but chuckle.

He sighed. "You have such a nice smile, Shane. Like the sun, it's too powerful to look at for long, and like an eclipse, it's so rare."

I rolled my eyes, but I stroked the backs of his arms with my thumbs, up under the sleeves of his v-neck shirt. My thumb ran over the bottom of his glucose monitor, and my heart swelled for him. He was dealing with so much, and yet, he seemed totally lucid now, here, in my arms. "You gonna be the poet now? Come on, be straight with me."

His smile faded, and that made me even more nervous.

"Fine. I love your smile, but when you scowl at me? Give me that 'dammit Collins' look? I want you to fuck me."

I gripped his arms tighter as molten heat consumed me.

"Fuck, Boone. You can't be serious."

"Hmm? That I want you to fuck me? I'm *dead* serious, Shane. And there happens to be a bed right here." He looked over his shoulder and when he turned back, he pressed his pelvis against me. There was no ignoring the heat he was throwing off, the bulge in his pants. "Tell me why we shouldn't?"

I gave no retort, no argument against what he was suggesting. I knew that if it went wrong, it would go WAY wrong. Getting closer to Boone could have catastrophic effects. But the bottom line? If this *didn't* happen, my obsession with Boone Collins would continue to grow, would devour me, and I wouldn't make it back in one piece.

I ran a finger through the hair next to his ear and lifted it away. I leaned in close, feeling him shiver as I spoke. "What's off limits?"

I gazed into his eyes, waiting for his response.

The dreamy look on his face faded for a moment and in a sober tone, he said, "Don't pull my hair. Please. That's all."

"Done." There was a story there, but as he placed his hands tentatively on my waist, under my shirt, I didn't want to break the spell, the magic he'd woven around us with his request.

"You?" He slid his hand under my shirt, up my back and then around to the front, brushing his thumb over my nipple.

"Don't pull my hair either."

It got the desired effect. He laughed and it became a moment not so full of tension. He reached both hands up to my head and ran his fingers over my baldness.

"I love this," Boone said, moaning. "So sexy."

My cheeks heated under his compliment. Losing my hair had been hard. It felt like everyone was looking at me all the time, the people closest to me would peer at my thinning hair, wince, and avoid commenting on it. Shaving it allowed me to take ownership of the situation. Thank God I didn't have a fucked-up head shape.

He turned us around and pushed me down to sit on the bed, leaving his hands on my shoulders. "I dreamed about having you alone, but now that I do, I don't know where to start." He let out a nervous laugh, and his touch became a little more hesitant. "I should tell you that even though I'm experiencing some health challenges right now, which you unfortunately had to witness, I'm healthy in all the ways that matter."

"Thank you for saying that," I said, running my hands up the back of his thighs and over his ass. *That ass.* It filled my big hands in such a satisfying way. I loved the weight, the curve, the firmness covered in soft corduroy. I loved that the fabric barely covered the globes, that if I could see us from behind, his crack would likely be visible over the top like the most enticing game of peek-a-boo. "But I wasn't worried. And I know what you said, but we can take this however we want.

We've gone from nearly coming to blows to talking about sex, so whatever happens..."

Boone crawled onto my lap and wrapped his legs around my hips. "Two extremes of passion. I like this one better."

"I like this, too. Come here." I had to know. I slid my fingers around his neck and pulled gently, urging his succulent lips down to mine, and *fuuuuuck* me did he taste sweet, even after sleeping. The slow sweep of his—

"Oh!" I breathed when I felt the metal on his tongue.

"Yeah," he said. "I really like metal. Kind of bought into the whole lifestyle." He pulled off his shirt, and I made a shocked and totally horny kind of groaning sound.

"My God, Collins. You should come with a warning label."

I traced his nipples, and he squirmed under my touch.

"And what would it say, this warning label?"

I looked down between us. "Contents under pressure? Flammable? I don't know, but *damn*."

He tilted his head to the side. "Is that good? I don't even know what you're into, what you like."

I took one of his hands and placed it between us, letting him feel just how much he was affecting me. "Any questions?"

He smiled, but then it slipped and he seemed unsure. "Can I kiss you again? God, I'm like, nervous all of a sudden."

"I don't want you to be nervous. Are you feeling okay?" I asked him, brushing his hair back from his face. It felt like silk between my fingers and it smelled so good, *he* smelled so good. Some sort of expensive hair products probably.

"Yeah. I'm okay. I'm just not very good at seduction, I guess."

"You're perfect," I said, and I decided to show him that I didn't give a shit about how he performed. I went for his collarbones first, needing to kiss him, nibble him, suck on him. He shifted against me as I gave him the first hickey. The second one I left on his right pec, after I tugged on his nipple. I couldn't help it, he tasted good all over and I got a little overzealous.

He really had lost weight, though. Gone was the slight roundness to his face and his midsection. I'd always thought he looked good with the weight. Made him seem fierce. Knowing that he'd likely lost weight because of his health worried me, made him seem vulnerable, though I wouldn't dare say that. His ass felt so good in my hands, and he was the perfect height sitting like this where I had access to his throat, which I nearly marked in my exuberance.

"You keep sucking on me like that and not only am I going to come in my pants, but everyone is going to know what we did."

I leaned back and frowned at him. "Does that bother you? Folks knowing you were with me?" I had to talk myself down from letting my thoughts go screaming into a negative direction.

"No," he said, pressing a hand to my chest. "No, Shane. I'm, fuck, I'm *honored* that you would want to be with me."

I looked away. "No need for all that. But if you're having second thoughts—"

"God, no." He placed his hands on my face, forcing me to gaze into his eyes. "Shane, I've wanted you for so long. I'm just waiting for you to tell me to get lost."

I wrapped my arms around him and rested my head on his shoulder with a sigh. "I really am a dick."

He threw his head back and laughed, then climbed off of my lap and over to lay on one side on the bed. "Not any more than I am. Maybe that's why it's good we're doing this." He smiled, but I could sense that uncertainty below the surface.

I turned to face him and stretched out on the bed. It was good he'd woken me up when he did. My back had been starting to cramp in the damn chair. I reached for his hand and brought it to my lips to kiss. "It *is* good."

He ran his thumb over my bottom lip, and I sucked it into my mouth, making him arch up off the bed, and that was all the talking I wanted to do. I stretched out over him and let him pull my shirt off. Our pants were unfastened next, and we were down to our underwear in a flash.

Boone cried out when I wrapped my hand around his length.

"Jesus, here too?"

He chuckled as I ran a finger over his Prince Albert. "The gift that keeps on giving?"

Fuck me.

His hands shook when he wrapped them both around my cock. And we kissed. The whole time.

As we stroked each other, our bodies trembling, bucking, vibrating, I tried not to let my thoughts move ahead to next time, as in, "Next time I'm going to suck him until he comes in my mouth. After that, I want to sit him back on my lap, so I can watch him as I stroke him inside and out until—"

"Shane," he sighed, and his hands fell still. "What's wrong? Do you not want—"

"I want to make you come," I said, kissing him deeply. I could concentrate better without him touching me.

He made a sound of protest, but then he moaned and gripped my shoulders tighter, his hips bucking, his cock thrusting hard into my hand. He pulled away from the kiss, squeezed his eyes shut, and he sucked in a breath as his body tensed. He let out a moan as he came that was so fucking sexy, I had to press down on my own erection to keep from coming in my shorts.

Boone lay there, his skin illuminated by the security lights outside the window. He panted hard, and I was mesmerized as I watched him. What a fucking picture. His face was relaxed, his lips parted and wet. I could have kept kissing him all night, but I wanted to...watch him.

"That wasn't exactly what I thought was going to happen, but I'm certainly not complaining." He huffed out a breath and stretched his arms over his head.

"What do you mean?"

He rolled onto his side and laughed, brushing his hair out of his face. "I thought...never mind." He reached for my dick, but I caught his hand. "What? What's wrong?"

"Nothing's wrong," I said, but he continued to stare at me.

"So that's it?" He sat up and flicked his hair over his shoulders. "You just...*that's it*?"

"No," I said, sitting up to face him. "No, just...for tonight. Was it not good or something?" His change of mood hit me like a blast of cold water. Was I wrong to—

"I don't get you," he said, his voice shaky. He climbed out of the bed and started searching for his clothes.

"Boone, wait."

"No, it's fine. I thought maybe we were finally through with this, but I guess not."

"Through with what? Boone, come here."

He'd yanked on his pants, but I'd grabbed his shirt. I didn't want him to run out of here in a snit. He planted his hands on his hips and exhaled.

"Through with me not being good enough for you. I wish I never would have—"

"Whoa," I said, standing from the bed. "That's not at all... Look, I don't jump right into anything with anybody. I have to... What's wrong with taking it slow?"

He opened his mouth and snapped it shut. "Slow?"

"Yeah, you know, in case you regret it in the morning."

I knew I fucked up as soon as I said it.

"*Regret?* Shane, I've wanted this for a long time. The only thing I'll regret is not getting to touch you."

We stood there, facing each other, both with our hands on our hips—and I had a sudden flash.

Either this was it, and we'd never be intimate again, or this was going to be us, moving forward, always at odds, everything an event between us. Always fighting until...he left. Or told me to get out. I was very familiar with both of those options.

"You should get some sleep. You want to stay here, or you want me to walk you back to the lodge?"

His eyes flared. "That's... *Really*? Thanks, but I can walk myself back just fine."

He shoved his feet into his boots, grabbed his bag and stormed out of the room past me, cussing the whole way.

I still had his shirt wadded up in my hand.

"That could have gone smoother." I took my time getting dressed, and by the time I got outside, set the electronic lock on the studio door, I could see Boone stomping up the steps of the lodge, his hair flying in the cold breeze.

He had to be freezing his ass off. His beautiful ass. And I'd been allowed to touch him. He was fucking majestic, every damn inch of him even better than I'd thought he would feel. I thought for a millisecond that perhaps now he'd be out of my system, but no. As he yanked the lodge doors open, letting them slam behind him, I knew there was no way he'd ever be out.

It was probably for the best that he walked away before either of us fell too hard into this thing.

He was wrong. I could never think I was too good for him. He was *so* much, so much larger than life, so overwhelming. And falling for him scared me more than I would ever admit. He would demand more from me than I was ready to share with another person.

It was better for him to think I wasn't into him, because he would break me if I let him.

TWELVE

B oone

I'm too old for this shit. That didn't slow down the tears at all, but it did motivate me to grab my notebook and start writing. I sat in my bed and wrote until my fingers ached, purging all of my anger, my humiliation at being rejected by the one man I never could seem to please. Stupid, stupid. I should have just been able to walk away with my head held high, forget how cherished I felt for those few moments that I thought he wanted me for real. I wanted to touch him, hold him. I'd been so hopeful when he covered me with his body, when he kissed me, and when he was so tender. So gentle. I hadn't known he was capable of that.

And then he'd rolled over and the moment was gone.

I'd felt cold to the bone, embarrassed, and that infuriated me. At least the only other person in my life who'd made me feel ashamed like this, I'd never had to face again, but Shane was going to be a constant presence in my life, especially now that our grandparents were dating.

"Fucking hell, Collins. You are killing it at being a grownup."

I wiped at the tears and prayed I'd still be able to read my writing in the morning. But then, it was morning already. I'd been at this for hours.

The knock at my door reminded me of my purpose. We were there to record songs for our next album, the one that had to be even bigger than the last, if we had any hope of fully conquering the rock world. I refused to be a flash in the pan, that one guy's grandson.

"Boone, it's breakfast ti—oh. You're...up?" Annie looked at my still-made bed and frowned. "Or you never went to bed?"

"Hey, sorry. Let me grab a quick shower. Look this over." I tossed my notebook at her and trotted to the bathroom, taking a quick shower, crying again when I realized that my hair smelled like Shane's cologne, which meant I needed to wash it if I was going to function. Smelling like him would keep me on edge all day, and not the kind of edge I needed.

I got out and wrapped my thick hair in a towel, knowing I'd be going out with it wet if I intended to get breakfast, and when I looked in the mirror, I paused.

"Oh, God." Shane had left two bright purple marks, one on my collarbone and one on my pec. It had felt so good at the time, but now it just made me angry all over again. How dare he mark me like this if he had no intention of—

"Forget it. Get yourself together, Collins. What would Papa think? Or what would Gran say?'

Then I remembered what she said before the induction ceremony: "chin up, tits out."

That made me bark out a hoarse laugh. I didn't bother shaving. Might as well look as messy as I felt. I drew on some eyeliner, hoping it would disguise my post-crying-jag eyes, and I wrapped myself in the bathrobe before heading back out to face Annie.

"Jesus, Boone. What the hell happened to you last night? Morrison said you weren't feeling well and went to lay down for a bit. We came back from our break and he ushered us out, said you were done for the night, and now I find you in here with *this*?" She pointed at the notebook, her eyes wide. "What's going on?"

I put on my best brave smile and followed Gran's orders. "Nothing. I was just having a bad night last night, but I feel better." I didn't, but she didn't need to know that. I didn't bother checking my blood sugar, I knew I needed to eat fast. I pulled on a pair of boxer briefs and then stood before the closet, trying to decide what to wear. Definitely not another v-neck, thanks to fucking Shane. I grabbed my black skinny jeans that were actually baggy now and yanked on a red-plaid button-up, turning to face Annie while I finished the buttons.

"Do you have music to go with this? Because this just might be the most incredible song you've ever written."

I blinked back tears, smiled at her, and took a deep breath.

Screw Shane Butler. I may not be the man of his dreams, but I'd written some phenomenal lyrics. Maybe I'd record it some day. Maybe he'd hear it and maybe not, but if he did, he'd know damn well it was about him—and that I was fine without him.

Only, breakfast turned out to be a cafeteria scene from a '90s teen movie.

Shane's band was there when I arrived, but Shane wasn't. Probably a good thing, although that didn't keep his guitarist, Dean, from smiling knowingly at me. That shook my confidence a little. I tugged at the collar of my shirt, making sure I'd buttoned it up high enough that Shane's stupid hickeys were covered.

I gestured for Bran and Annie to go ahead of me as I stopped to fix some tea first. I'd strained my voice yesterday and, well, the lame-ass crying session made matters worse. Morrison always kept the best selection of teas and local honeys for us, so I figured I'd start there. I was just carrying my mug over on a tray when I felt someone behind me.

I nearly spilled scalding tea all over me.

"Good morning." His fucking velvety voice gave me goose bumps.

"Shane," I said, my only greeting. My hands were shaking as much from my fucked-up blood sugar as from my proximity to this infuriating man.

"Did you rest last night—"

"Hey, Boone. I made the avocado spread you liked so much last time. Can I get you some?"

Felix, Morrison's chef, was the only guy I trusted to feed me food that wasn't the tried and true stuff I grew up with. Gran had catered to my picky-eater habits, much to Papa's chagrin, and as a result, I had a hard time stepping out of my comfort zone. I needed to, now that I was diabetic, but I didn't much like it, unless it was something made by Felix.

"Yes, please. With your homemade sourdough? I'm in heaven."

Felix added a heaping serving of potatoes and a fried egg and then placed the food on my tray as he winked at me. "Anything for you. Hey, Shane, can I get you the avocado spread, or would you rather—"

"That's fine, thank you."

Shane followed me over to the utensil and condiment cart and glanced at my plate. "Should you be having that many carbs?" He kept his voice low, and it was just the two of us, but his words raised my hackles.

"You don't get to comment on my food, Shane. It's none of your business."

"It is too." He sucked in a deep breath and let it out slowly, making himself busy with the salt and pepper shakers. "You forget how I found you last night."

"And I'd appreciate it if you would keep that to yourself," I snapped.

Shane set his tray down and turned to face me. "My grandfather is diabetic. I've been cooking for him for years, so I know what the recommendations are, that's all. It's manageable if you—"

"Thank you, but I can take care of myself."

I tried walking away, but I heard him say, "Sure. Sure you can." My hands tightened on the tray and I walked into the corner of a table in my rush to get away from him, banging my hip bone. My carefully constructed appearance of self-control wasn't going to hold if he kept showing up. I set my tray down a little hard at the table next to Annie, and she jumped.

"Geez. What—oh. Was he being a jerk?"

I shook my head and concentrated on eating and keeping the tremor in my hand at bay. "No. It's fine." I didn't need my band getting all protective over me. Annie had no qualms about speaking her mind. She was also the queen of revenge schemes. I'd been grateful for her when my previous relationship ended badly and she helped me fill his car with mouse traps. It was epic.

I listened to her and Bran talk about running into Dean and Tucker last night. "They invited us to go into town with them, but Rose wanted to color my hair. Doesn't it look cool?"

I glanced up at Annie and sighed. "I'm sorry I didn't notice. I'm out of it. I love the color."

She'd put blue highlights in her black hair, and they really popped under the lights in the mess hall. She and Brandon both had curly hair that they wore in organized chaos most of the time. Their father was Japanese and their mother was Black, so their hair required extra care.

My reddish-brown mop was still a nice color so I didn't mess with dye, but who knew? Someday I might want a change.

"I promised Rose a manicure. Maybe tonight? You guys want to join in?"

They enthusiastically agreed, we finished eating, and that should have been the end of breakfast, but as we stood and headed over to dump our trays, we had to walk past their table. Shane was staring at me, and I was trying to *not* stare at him while *actually* staring at him, and therefore I missed Drew standing up and I walked right into him, which caused him to bump my tray, which smashed leftover avocado into my chest, and he spilled his travel mug full of hot coffee all down the front of me.

"Damn, Boone! I'm hella sorry, man."

I stood there dripping while Annie hurried to take my tray, Shane jumped up, and Drew tried to clean my mess while apologizing all over himself.

"And you're sick and all, I feel bad, let me get that—"

"I'm fine!" I said in a louder-than-called-for voice—and everyone grew quiet. And stood there. Gaping.

Hoping to diffuse the situation, I turned to Annie. "You guys go ahead without me and I'll meet you in a few minutes."

They nodded and scurried out the door. Felix came out with a mop and bucket, and I just wanted to disappear.

"Here, let me," I said to him, but he waved me away.

"No harm done, Boone. I got this."

"Thank you. I'm so sorry." I didn't know what else to say, so I turned and tried the whole chin out, tits up, cocksure walking, despite coffee dripping from my still-wet hair, my shirt sticking to me. Except, Shane followed me.

"Are you okay?" he asked as he ran to catch up to me.

"Yes. And thanks a lot for telling them I was sick. What the fuck, Shane?"

"I'm sorry. I guess Morrison told them you weren't feeling well last night, and that I stayed to make sure you were alright. That's all."

By the time we reached the lodge, I was sweating on top of wearing my breakfast leftovers and Drew's coffee, and I was ready to lose it.

"You don't have to come in. I can take it from here," I said as I pushed open the doors.

"Come on, Collins. Can we talk about this?"

I turned to face him. "About what? Your bandmate bumped into me? Or the fact I'm wearing my breakfast? Unless you have anything else to offer, I'm going to chalk this up to an accident, change my clothes, and get to work." I started for the stairs and exhaled loudly when he followed again.

"I meant last night. I don't know what went wrong but I was hoping we could be civil about it—can you quit running from me?"

We'd reached the top of the steps and my room was just a few yards away. I was almost to safety. I pulled out my key, had it in the lock, pushed the door open—

And Shane put his hand on the door.

"I want to go back to us being able to be around each other without bickering, Boone, and I think you do, too."

"I..." Shane was in my room, and I needed to get undressed. "Fine, we'll be civil. It seemed clear last night that you have no interest in anything more with me, so you might want to leave."

"No."

I sighed and started unbuttoning my shirt, slowly. I flicked my hair back and stuck my chin out—or was it tits?

Which part was supposed to stick out?—and tried to look confident.

Shane leaned back against the now-closed door and folded his arms over his chest.

"Suit yourself, but these clothes are coming off."

Shane didn't move.

Fuck. Fine, then it was put up or shut up time. "You are one confusing man, Shane Butler." I finished the buttons and pulled off the flannel.

Shane covered his mouth with his hand. "I didn't think they'd be that...dark." He tried not to smile.

"Yeah, well, I bruise easily, so thanks for that." I wasn't mad about them, not at all. I was mad he hadn't put one where everyone would see it. And wasn't that immature on my part?

"I shouldn't like seeing you like this, but I do."

"What? Covered in avocado, coffee, and hickeys?"

He nodded. "I like you messy. Not trying to act like you've got it all under your thumb. Not trying to be perfect."

"I'm not perfect," I muttered, but new warmth sparked in my heart. If he saw me like this, and he didn't run... "But last night?"

"Last night I wanted to get you out of your head and help you relax. It wasn't supposed to be about me. But the hickeys? I wanted to be able to see them and know I put them there."

That shut me up. When had anyone wanted only to please *me*? People usually wanted to be seen with me, wanted to say they'd been with me as like a conquest, but that's not what he was saying.

"I couldn't...wasn't ready to give you more." He dropped his arms and put his hands behind his back. "I'm sorry if I didn't make that clear."

It dawned on me again how gentle he'd been with me, how I'd been the aggressor in the scenario. He'd been aroused, but if I'd slowed down enough to pay attention, I would have seen that he wasn't pulling away, necessarily.

"I'm sorry if I rushed you."

He nodded and shifted his weight against the door. "You should let me rinse your clothes so they don't stain."

When I didn't move, he walked towards me, and all I could do was gape at him. He was much bigger than me, and not just taller. He was built solid. I used to be bigger, but it was fat. I didn't work out. Didn't care. I hadn't realized just how much weight I'd lost until he put his big hand on my waist and squeezed.

"Let's get you out of these." He went to work on my fly and slowly, gently, peeled my wet pants down, taking my weight as I leaned on his shoulder and lifted one leg and then the other so he could pull them off. From his crouched position, he looked up at me for permission as he placed his hands on the waistband of my boxers.

I smiled and sucked in a breath. His thumbs slid along my hipbones, which tickled, and I squirmed a bit as my semi-erect dick sprang free. He pulled the boxers off, put his hands back on my hips and looked up at me for...permission again, maybe?

"What...what's changed?"

"I got out of *my* head."

And then he pressed his lips to the underside of my crown, licked over my piercing, all while his eyes never left mine.

Suddenly, I wasn't cold anymore. I didn't care that I was sticky and smelled like coffee, or that he was fully dressed, kneeling before me. His mouth was so hot, his lips so soft, and his tongue was so, *so* good. I'd never had anyone suck me off like this, like I was the last ice cream bar in the freezer in the middle of a heatwave. It was as if he intended to lick every last drop and savor the sensation.

"God, Shane," I breathed. "You make a man feel desired, you know that?"

He moaned in answer and gripped my ass tighter with one hand, taking more of me with each dip of his head. He'd closed his eyes now, and his free hand gripped the base of my cock, working me with such strength, I swayed on my feet. The hand on my ass shifted, and he dragged his pinky over my hole, causing my legs to buckle.

Holy hell, he was going to destroy me.

Words fell from my lips, or maybe just sounds, I didn't know for sure, and I reached for his head, cradling it, caressing it, trying to show him how much I loved what he was doing, the pleasure he was giving me.

"You...should...stop, if you don't want—"

He pulled off with a pop. "I want it."

I gasped when he sucked me back in, grabbing my hips and squeezing my ass. He moved faster, and I fought the urge to thrust, mostly because he was...it was...so *good at this.*

"Then take it," I whispered. "Take all of it."

I gasped as I came a few moments later, wave after wave of heat crashing into me until I couldn't take it anymore, and then it continued. It dragged on and on, and he sucked me through it all, his eyes rolling back in his head. I gripped his shoulders to keep from falling, and I tried to pull out, but he wasn't quick to let go.

"I'm going to fall on my ass," I finally said with a laugh, and he pulled back, licking his lips and moaning softly. In one quick motion, he scooped me up and carried me to the bathroom.

"You need a shower," he said, setting me down. He got the water ready and reached for a towel. "Let me go get your clothes."

"Hey," I said, stopping him with my hand to his cheek. He

was frowning again, but it was...softer, somehow. He took so much care with me while taking care of me... How was this the Shane Butler known to the free world as the Metal Menace with growling vocals, a percussive guitar style, and a dark, quick wit?

I stood on my toes and kissed him, groaning as I tasted myself in his mouth. It was the hottest thing ever, and I wanted more.

"We have to stop," he said, pressing his forehead against mine and breathing heavy. "I don't want you missing time with Morrison, and I've got a lot of work to do with my band today. But tonight?"

"Oh, um, I promised Rose a manicure. After? Later?"

"I'll find you," he said, giving me one last kiss. Then he smacked my ass. Hard. And I liked it. "Get in the water. I'm going to rinse your clothes out and then get out of here before I bend you over this counter."

I growled at him. "Fuck, Shane."

He chuckled as he pushed me inside the single stall and shut the door.

I tried to be quick with my washing but I was still feeling loose and hazy. I started to hum a melody I'd been thinking of last night, as I wrote down the lyrics to a song that had a whole different meaning this morning.

Shane came back in, rinsed my clothes, hung them on the rack, and then washed his hands. He opened the door and looked me up and down.

"I'll find you later." He leaned in, and I kissed him once more, tempted to pull him into the spray so, oh darn, he'd have to strip down too.

"Do," I said with a dreamy grin.

One more glance and a satisfied grunt, and he shut the shower door and then the bathroom door.

"That just happened." A bubble of laughter exploded into

full-on hysterical guffaws that racked my body until I couldn't breathe.

How had we gone from nearly coming to blows to not being able to keep our hands to ourselves? Whatever had happened, I was quite pleased with this new development.

Thirteen

S hane

Despite my lack of sleep the night before, my interludes with Boone, and the fact that I'd forgotten my coffee in my haste to chase him down, I was on fire the rest of the day. We rehearsed the first five songs for the album before lunch, with Lydia sitting in to provide feedback, then after lunch, we worked on the next five until she thought they were pretty strong. But her comments were a little lukewarm for my taste, so when we broke for dinner, I asked her to stay back for a few minutes.

"What do you really think, Lydia? Please."

Lydia Pride was one of the best producers in the business. Though Morrison was the final producer on all of the Wicked Soul records, Lydia was a good coach. I valued her opinion as much if not more than Morrison's, especially since I knew she would be brutally honest with me, whereas Morrison would continue to dress up what I gave him until it was good enough, but maybe not as good as it could be.

Lydia pushed her chair back from the control panel and sighed. "Do you feel like this is growth for you?"

My first instinct was to clap back. My spine stiffened involuntarily, and I had to press my lips together to keep from spouting off angrily. I wouldn't do that with her, not when she was prodding me to be better.

"I thought so until you just asked me that question." I ran my hand over my head.

She smiled and folded her hands over her midsection. "Shane, you have so much fire in you—much more than the guys in your band, by the way—but I feel like...you're keeping a lid on it. You only allow enough heat to keep the fire burning, but what if you blew the lid off and burned the whole shit down? What would happen then?"

I opened my mouth to speak, and my throat closed as I choked back that well-guarded vault of emotion I kept under wraps for the protection of everyone around me.

"I don't know."

She tilted her head. "You spend so much time trying to make sure that everything is controlled, everything is at the level you approve of...that's got to be exhausting. I know you compose all of Wicked Soul on your own, and I personally think it's made your band lazy. Have you ever let the guys in on the writing process?"

I shook my head. "Once." I laughed humorlessly. "They knew that was the deal going in."

"That it's your way or the highway?"

I leaned forward and rested my elbows on my knees and looked at the floor. "It's worked for us."

"What if you let them in? What would you think about having a group chat with the band? All of you. I'd sit in on it if you think that would help. Hear what they have to say about where you guys are as a band now. What do you think?"

"Like group therapy or some shit?" I shook my head. "That seems a little extra?"

She laughed. "I'm no therapist. I'll kick your ass before I give you a hug. But maybe if your bandmates felt like they had a little more ownership in Wicked Soul, a little more responsibility, they'd help you take this music to the next level."

"You think I can't do it on my own?" I didn't mean it to come out defensive, but was she saying I *couldn't* do it on my own? I couldn't be great my way?

"I think *you* can do it. You can continue going the way you are with Wicked Soul, putting out albums, and remaining a respectably talented band. You might even be great. But I think *you* can be greater. Drew is a decent bass player, and Tucker? He's a fucking monster on the drums. But he's playing these prescribed fills and shit. And you and Dean harmonize well together, both on vocals and guitar, and yet you don't use it as much as I think you could. But that's one producer's opinion." She held out her hands.

"One of the best producers in the business."

She smiled and did a little bow. "Thank you. Now, how about we meet up tomorrow morning? Don't tell the guys. And don't worry, I won't let this be a free-for-all." She stood up and turned off the board. "Have some fun tonight. Try to relax. I'll see you in the morning."

She smacked me on the shoulder—her version of a hug, I guess?—and I pretended she hadn't just shaken my whole foundation with her questions.

Do you feel like this is growth for you?

The more I thought about her words, the more anxious I grew. Normally in a situation like this, I'd grab my guitar and fucking play until my fingers bled. But tonight? Tonight I wanted Boone, and in the state of mind I was currently in, that was probably a bad idea. But I had to know. I had to know what he thought. About me, about this thing between us...

My band's future and my heart's future seemed to both be on the line right now, and I didn't like it one bit. I was on the edge of a steep cliff with my mountain bike and as soon as I shifted my weight, I was either going to have the ride of my life, or break everything.

By the time I left the rehearsal cabin, the lights were off in the recording studio and the kitchen was closed, so I made my way back to the lodge. I could hear laughter as soon as I climbed the steps. It sounded like there was a rowdy party going on, but once I got into the lobby, I saw who was responsible for the sound.

Rose, Annie, Brandon and Boone were in the bar, the screen had karaoke lyrics going, and Brandon was currently up on stage singing "Do You Really Want Me" by Salt-N-Pepa. Boone was painting Rose's fingernails and bobbing his head along to the song.

"Oh hey, Shane!" Rose waved me over with the hand she was trying to dry. "Dean and the guys took your rental into town to go bowling. He said to text him if you wanted to come out. They waited for you, but they didn't want to miss their reservation."

Boone glanced up and smiled at me. My heart fluttered at first, and then seemed to stutter.

"You can take one of our vans if you want to join them," she offered, and then her eyes widened as I lowered myself into the empty seat next to Boone.

"Thanks," I said to Rose. Then I leaned closer to Boone and asked in a low voice, "This okay?"

He beamed up at me. "You want to go next?" he asked,

holding up the polish brush and pointing toward the screen. "We've got the karaoke machine on random so there's no telling what might come up."

"Thanks," I said. "I'm good." Really, I wanted to zone out and not have to think, and Boone and his friends kept me entertained for the next hour, at which point, Boone poked me.

"You know, we'd all feel a lot better if you took a turn singing. For all we know, you're sitting there quietly judging us."

"I'm not," I protested. "I wouldn't."

But he was laughing, so I let out a breath and sat back in the chair. It was odd to me how close they were, the three of them. I'd never been cozy with the guys in my band, nor in the bands I played in before Wicked Soul. I was there to do a job, or so I told myself. I'd seen what getting close with your bandmates could do, and I didn't want to give anyone that much power over me.

Boone had finished painting everyone's nails but mine. I kinda wished I would have taken him up on the offer, if only to have him touch me. I was twitchy and my skin felt tight thinking about tomorrow morning. I needed to get out of my head.

"Fine, I'll sing."

Boone's eyes widened and he clapped his hands. "Shane's up!" He turned to me and placed a hand on my arm. "You sure?"

I laughed and nodded. "Hit me."

I took the microphone from Brandon and stepped up onto the small stage. Then I saw the song that popped up.

"Oh, no."

Brandon and Annie whooped with joy, and Rose burst out laughing.

The '90s ballad "I Can Love You Like That" by All-4-One

cued up, and I cringed. Annie and Rose jumped up and started slow dancing like junior high kids and the whole thing felt...right.

I hammed it up, which I think surprised all of them, but I kept my gaze on Boone. I even did some choreography—yeah, my metal-slinging ass could dance—and the others laughed, but Boone? He stared at me with stars in his eyes as if he were swooning over me. It only fed my momentary lapse of coolness, and I hit all the high notes, all the stylings and then some, until I had to gasp for air. When the song was over, I got high fives from Rose, Annie, and Brandon, and Boone just pressed a hand to his chest and shook his head as he laughed.

This was happening.

"I hate to be that one addict, but I gotta smoke," Annie said, looking between us as I took my seat next to Boone once more.

"Oh, me too, definitely," her brother said, getting a clue.

"Got one for me?" Rose asked as she followed them outside, waving to us as she caught up to them. They went out the door giggling and singing my song.

"That was wild, Butler," Boone said as he packed up his manicure tools. "You went for it."

"When one is challenged by the karaoke gods, one must push thyself into greatness."

Boone chuckled and rested his chin in his hand, his smile fading. "How did today go?" he asked me. "You seem, I don't know. Off, maybe?" He slid a hand onto my thigh and leaned closer.

I wanted to be able to trust Boone, but this was all so new. "Rehearsal went. We have the songs down. But then Lydia and I talked after."

He leaned back a little. "Uh-oh. I've had those talks with her."

I looked down at his hand. His nails were painted silver

and he wore several beaded bracelets, some wooden and some gemstones. I placed my hand on top of his. Our fingers were the same length but his hands were thinner. Mine dwarfed his. "She wants us to have a big pow-wow in the morning...wants me to, I don't know, open up, ease up on needing control."

"Ouch." Boone tucked his hair behind his ears and his gaze was so intense, I started to panic.

"Hey, maybe you could paint my nails."

He seemed to figure me out. He stood up and tugged on my hand. "Why don't we do it in my room?" He picked up his bag with his polish and supplies with his free hand.

I was happy to let him take the lead. I didn't want to have to make any more decisions tonight. And wasn't that something? Me giving up control to Boone Collins, of all people.

We climbed the stairs slowly, and Boone sang a few bars of my silly song.

"You sing it better," I said, placing my hand on his lower back.

"No way," he said, putting his arm around me. He fit snugly under my arm, and he slid his hand under my shirt. It felt so damn good to be with him. I didn't even care that anyone could see us, I didn't care if anyone else knew what was going on between us. I'd take all the teasing if it meant him looking up at me with those blue eyes.

We got to his room and he fumbled with his keys. I leaned forward and nuzzled his hair. He smelled like—

"Native from Target. Strawberry Vanilla Taffy. Come on in," he said and held the door open for me.

I burst out laughing, caught sniffing him. Then I looked around.

"Wow. You've, uh, done some redecorating since this morning?"

All of his clothes, his guitars, everything was spread out on every surface.

"Oh. Yeah, well. I was trying to decide what to wear, and—"

"I don't care." I pulled him in for a kiss like he was the only air left in the world. He and his friends had kept me from breaking apart tonight, but now I needed more.

Boone backed us up to the bed and dropped his bag on top of a pile of clothes, and though I really wanted to keep kissing him, he deserved better than for me to only half focus on him.

As if he sensed my mental sparring, he pulled away.

"Why don't we sit at the table and you can talk while I paint," he said, and he bent down to grab his polish bag. "As different as we are, Shane, I can tell you're upset, and I know *I* need to get shit out before I can let it go."

"Yeah," I said, my shoulders slumping. "I never really talk about this stuff, though, except with Pops."

Boone pushed me down into a chair at the little table in his room, and he pulled his hair back, using a hair tie from his wrist to make a low ponytail, just like Pops wore.

"Alright then," he said in a thick British accent, "fire away, lad. Tell us about it, love. Oh wait. That's my Papa. I don't do a good Irish accent." He laughed and sat down across from me. He reached for my hand and inspected my nails. It helped that he wasn't looking me in the eye. He pulled out a file and began shaping each one. Thankfully I didn't bite my nails anymore, so they didn't look terrible.

"There's a reason for everything I've done in my career," I said, though whether I was justifying my actions or thinking out loud, I had no idea. "When I decided to form a band, I hired these guys based on their talent and knowledge of their instruments. That was it. I'd been writing songs for a long time. I started with Pops, you know. I moved in with him when I was a teenager."

"What about your family?" he asked, still not looking in

my eyes. He finished filing my right hand and moved on to the left. "I remember meeting your mom when we were little. She seemed...intense."

I smiled. "Mom *is* intense. And intensely against me being a musician. I'm just as stubborn as her, so when she didn't back down, I left school with my GED and moved in with Pops. He immediately connected me with as many folks in the music industry as he could, and I began what was basically an internship. I worked in studios, I got a job at Guitar Center doing repairs, I took lessons with anyone who would teach me, I roadied for Brothers' tours. The whole time I was making a mental list of how I'd do things when it was my turn."

"Sounds fair," he said, finishing the left. He pulled several colors of polish out of the bag and gestured with his hand. "Which color?"

My gaze was immediately drawn to a dark teal that reminded me so much of his eyes...

"That one."

"Not black?" He seemed genuinely surprised.

I shook my head. "I do have more than one side, Collins."

He chuckled and started to shake the bottle of base coat. "So what did Lydia say that has you questioning everything? Right? I mean, that's what it seems is happening."

"Yeah. It's funny, because it's the same shit that *you* once said in an interview that pissed me off."

"What?" His head shot up. "What did I say? Wait, you actually listen to those?"

I shrugged. "Sometimes. You said you thought I could do more than I was doing with Wicked Soul."

He pressed his lips together. "Oh. Yeah. That. So, what did she say?"

I was glad he didn't deny saying it, but I wanted to know more. Maybe not now, while I was in the middle of this whatever-the-fuck kind of crisis, but I valued his opinion more than I ever thought I would.

I was coming to realize that despite our vast differences, we hailed from the same rock lineage and, as a result, we'd had to face similar struggles to make names for ourselves as part of that legacy, as well as prove we were able to stand on our own.

I sighed, trying to release some of the tension in my shoulders. His touch was light but firm and I tried to concentrate on that contact.

"She asked me if I felt like I'd grown with this album. And for the first time, I don't know."

Boone nodded without looking up. He made deliberate strokes on my nails with the brush, leaning in close to observe his work. "She thinks all artists have room to grow and get better."

"Right, but...I guess I always thought that was for *me* to decide, you know? I didn't want to accept that anyone else might know what was best for my band. That doesn't mean I don't ever listen to feedback or that I'm not willing to take advice from Morrison, but—"

"Isn't that the definition of growth, though? Accepting that you don't have all the answers?"

"I guess, but what about you? You *are* Stellar, for all intents and purposes. Do you collaborate for Stellar?"

"We do. I might come in with the bare bones for most of the tracks, but Annie and Bran always make them better. Bran is way better at arrangements than I am, and Annie, frankly, has a much more extensive vocabulary than I do, and she often tweaks my lyrics to make them flow better. We're more of a democracy than not. But at the end of the day, the responsibility to be great lies solely on me."

He blew on the first hand and moved on to the second.

"I think the difference between us, Shane? Is that I was always told I *could* and *would* make it. I had total support from my family from the beginning. Sounds like you didn't, and that would make it hard to trust people with your art, for sure."

I watched him expertly apply the second coat on my left hand...and it dawned on me.

"How was I so wrong about you?"

He looked up, his blue eyes unsure, his vulnerability sucking me in. "What do you mean?"

He let go of my hand, closed up the polish bottle, and reached for the top coat. I wanted to snatch his hand back. *Don't let go.*

"You're so real, Boone. I thought you were only your stage act. Your little snotty comments, all a show. I had no idea that you...that you'd understand. And it was wrong of me to assume that everything was handed to you."

He laughed. "Compared to you, it was. It's true, I never had to live the shitty-apartment-off-Sunset life. I didn't have to spend years playing in bars before I got noticed. Nepotism is a thing, man. But I fought so hard to be taken seriously...*still* fight. I don't want anyone to ever question whether I've earned what I've accomplished."

"Which is why you don't tell people you're sick."

"The focus is on the music, the performances, sales, charts. That's what counts."

"Boone." I leaned in and tried to put my hand on top of his, but he pulled his hands back.

"No. You'll mess it up."

"Sorry." Even with nail polish, he was a perfectionist. He used a series of tools to clean up any potentially stray marks— there weren't any—and then he picked up my hands and blew on the nails gently. I couldn't stop staring at his perfectly shaped lips. Makeup artists used liner to get the effect he was born with. Unbelievable.

"Boone, I'm serious. You need to tell them. You need to take care of yourself—"

"Shhhh," he said, standing, and then he pressed a finger against my lips. He moved to my side of the small table and knelt between my open thighs. "Don't touch anything. These need to dry."

He went to work on my fly, and I scooted my hips back with a jerk. "What are you doing?"

Without looking up, he pulled my cock out. "I'm not done taking care of you."

"Boone," I said, intending for it to mean *stop, no, it's not necessary*, but it came out more like *oh, please, please do that, yes.*

He took his time exploring with his tongue, that fucking metal ball driving me wild as he dragged it across my hypersensitive flesh. I reached for his hair, but he caught my wrist without losing a beat.

"Hands on your thighs and don't fucking move them. If you mess up my work, Butler, you're in trouble."

Oh, I was in trouble, all right.

He gazed up at me with those deep, deep blues as he hollowed his cheeks and my legs started shaking so bad, I could barely stay in the chair.

"I want you to come in my mouth, Shane. Make me a mess."

His words hit me like a lightning bolt, and I came with a surprised shout, doing exactly as he asked. He flattened out his tongue, closed his eyes, and let me make a mess of his pretty face, the visual almost as intoxicating as the sensation. The orgasm hit me so hard that when I finally relaxed, I was slumped over in the chair, barely able to form thoughts, much less worry about my band's future.

"God, that was awesome," Boone said as he wiped his face

with his fingers and sucked one into his mouth. "You were so neat, too. Didn't even get any in my hair."

That made me laugh, and I reached for him, brushing his hair back. "I like you messy, Boone."

He laughed, then pushed up on his knees and kissed me. "Good. I like your mess." He stood and took my hand. "Come lay with me."

I stood, tucked myself back into my drawers, pulled off my shirt and pants, and let him lead the way, dropping his own clothes onto the floor as he went.

Yeah, he was a mess. I was becoming quite fond of his mess.

Fourteen

B oone

I lay on the bed with the compound lights shining through the window with a big fat smile on my face. Next to me, dead asleep, was a perfectly sated Shane Butler with perfectly manicured hands. One of them was splayed on his bare chest, the light catching the sparkles in the teal paint, and the other was tangled in my hair. I didn't mind it since it was him, and his nails were dry.

We'd had such a great talk. I couldn't believe he'd opened up so much to me, that he'd finally *seen* me, not the spoiled brat he'd thought I was. Not that he was totally wrong. I *could* be a brat, and an insufferable perfectionist, but so could he. I hoped we could work around those things, because I really *really* liked being with him like this. The fact that he knew about my health challenges and hadn't freaked out, that we were in similar positions with our bands...it was almost too good to be true, to have someone like him.

I dared to hope that I might even be close to having that musical partner I'd always dreamed about.

God, what would it be like to play and sing with him? Oh fuck, or to *write* with him? I giggled out loud, and then covered my mouth when he stirred in his sleep. I didn't want him to leave. I liked pretending we were a couple.

Annie and Brandon were happy for me earlier when Shane joined us. They'd already let me know that they liked Shane, but if he hurt me, they'd implement the most egregious revenge plan ever. I appreciated their support and hoped it wouldn't come down to that because the Thompson twins— no, not *the* band, *my* band—were brutal in their attacks. I wouldn't want them on the hunt.

I couldn't stop staring at Shane. He even frowned in his sleep. But watching him orgasm? I'd never felt such satisfaction in sex with another person. I always worried about my performance, but with Shane, I was more worried about pleasing him, helping him relax. I knew he was concerned about tomorrow, but I had a feeling it would be a really good thing for him. Lydia knew what she was doing. She'd protect him.

My phone buzzed, and I looked at the clock. It was nearly two a.m. I picked up my cell and saw a notification from the app for the flight charter company I'd bought shares in. Seemed the trip I'd booked for Gran to come up on Sunday had been canceled. Huh. I'd call her in the morning. She often went to bed late, but two in the morning was late even for her.

Shane mumbled in his sleep and turned toward me, and it was way too much of a temptation not to touch him. I ran my thumb over the crease between his brows, and his eyes opened.

"Sorry," I whispered. "I didn't mean to wake you."

He grunted and pulled me into his body, sliding his knee between my thighs. Sweet Jesus, he felt so good, and pressed up against his chest was where I wanted to spend every night. I couldn't stop smiling.

"Don't say it's morning time," he mumbled.

"It's not," I whispered, kissing him. "Go back to sleep."

He sighed. "Stay with me, Boone. Right here."

I looked up at him, and he still had his eyes closed. Was he talking in his sleep?

He slid a hand down and grabbed my ass, pulling me in tighter to him, and he groaned.

I definitely did not mind the sleep-groping or the sleep-talking, but the sleep-twitching was something else. At first it was like a puppy dreaming, hands and feet moving, but then a few times he tensed up, and one of those times, his hand that was still tangled in my hair yanked on it—hard.

I sucked in a breath, and when he didn't let go, I tapped on his chest. He mumbled and rolled over, loosening his grip, thankfully. I curled up to his back and sighed.

I hadn't known he had his back completely tattooed until that night. I hadn't gone that route with my art. I'd only enjoyed the piercing needle as far as body modification was concerned. Shane's strong back was covered with a vast black and gray mural like something out of Ancient Greece with a quote in the middle of a stormy sky. "To Live Alone is the Fate of All ~~Great~~ Wicked Souls." It disturbed me. Was that him being flippantly pessimistic, or did he truly believe that? I drew over the letters with my fingers and thought that, no, I didn't want his fate to be alone.

I wanted him for my own.

I finally dozed off for several hours, waking when I felt Shane move next to me.

"Don't wake up," he whispered.

I grabbed his hand to keep him from leaving and pulled him down for a kiss.

"No matter what happens, Shane, you're not alone." I wanted to say more, but I knew he needed to get in the right headspace for his meeting. I squeezed his hand and let go, gazing up at him from the bed.

He stared at me with his head cocked to the side. "How was I so *wrong* about you?"

I grinned up at him and rolled onto my back with my arms over my head, letting the covers slide down below my belly button. "I have no idea, but I'd love to be wrong with you again."

He shook his head, leaned down to kiss me, then bent farther, slid the blanket off my hip and laid another love bite on my hip bone, causing me to bow up off the mattress.

"Fuck," I cried out. "That feels good. I love it."

"Let's do this again." He pulled on his pants and shirt, then turned for the door. When he opened it, he looked back and his scowl had returned. "Thank you, Boone. See you later."

I waved as he shut the door, and then I moaned, sinking into the bed. I stretched my arms above my head and wiggled my toes. I had time to rest, but I was vibrating with energy. I was concerned for Shane, but also needed to focus on my purpose here. We were done rehearsing and it was time to start laying tracks down.

Morrison was thrilled with the new songs, but my voice wasn't cooperating yesterday. The plan today was no singing, just instrumentals, and there were a few guitar parts that I wasn't completely solid on, including this guitar part on "Over The Moon" that Morrison suggested I add slide to. I hadn't done a lot of work with a slide and it just wasn't coming out the way I wanted. Probably I would have Morrison track that part...or maybe... Would Shane do it? Would he agree to play on a Stellar record?

That thought had me springing out of bed. I tripped over my shoes on my way to the bathroom, did my business, and then grabbed my guitar. I lost track of time and nearly missed breakfast. I called Gran on the way but got her voicemail.

"Hey Gran, I saw the flight for tomorrow was canceled. Everything okay? Call me. Mwah."

I hurried up the steps and found Annie and Brandon finishing up their breakfast.

"Good morning, good mo-orning," I said in a singsong voice.

Annie turned her head slowly and raised an eyebrow.

"Okay, Debbie Reynolds. I thought you weren't singing today." Her eyes widened when she looked at me.

"Oops," I whispered. "Sorry I'm late."

Brandon was finger-drumming on the table. "Not late yet, but you better hurry. I think Felix is closing up."

I rushed over to grab food, which was scrambled eggs and bacon with some sort of biscuits that looked delicious. *Perfect.* Felix greeted me cheerfully, then his smile fell.

"Uh, you've got..." He pointed to his neck, but before I could ask, Leland shouted for me.

"Hurry up, Collins. More is ready for you."

"Got it! Be right there."

I said thanks to a bewildered-looking Felix and hurried over to my band.

As I sat down, they both stared at me.

"What?" I asked with a mouthful of eggs.

"Uh, Boone?" Brandon had stopped mid finger-drum. "Did you sleep with a vacuum cleaner last night?"

I frowned and shoved more food into my mouth, anxious to finish and get on with our day.

"Unless Rose was right and there really is a ghost in the

lodge," Annie said, picking up hers and Brandon's trays. "Or a vampire."

I shook my head. "I'll be done in three minutes."

They nodded at me, elbowing each other. "We'll see you in the studio."

"Yeah, you and your—"

Annie yanked Brandon towards the door, cutting off whatever he was going to say.

I sat like a happy camper eating my breakfast, songs running through my head. Today was going to be a great day.

My great day lasted until I went into the bathroom upstairs at the studio. The one where Shane and I had our first run-in, I guess. After I washed my hands, I snagged one of Morrison's packaged toothbrush/paste combos. I looked in the mirror... and spit the paste out, getting it all over my shirt.

Oh my.

Shane had somehow managed to add another silver-dollar-pancake-sized hickey on my throat, and now breakfast made sense.

What was it with this guy that he got so overzealous? And why did I like it so much?

I rinsed my shirt, but the toothpaste wouldn't come out without a major scrubbing, which stretched out the waffle-weave material. I went back into the bedroom and dug through the closet and dresser, which Morrison had told us the first time we came here were fair game, and prayed for a turtleneck, or at least a flannel.

Most of the clothes were giant-sized, not for a men's medium like me. I didn't want to feel like a little kid in my grandpa's clothes, so the only option was a women's cut, slim-fit, long-sleeved boatneck shirt, which left my throat exposed, as well as the original hickey on my collarbone.

"Well. This is a statement."

I shook out my hair, knowing it would definitely not cover the marks, and I marched down the stairs with my...shit...chin out and tits on display?

Frickin' British-isms. I'd grown up around them, seeing as both grandparents were raised in the UK. You'd think by now I'd get them right.

"Sorry I'm late," I said as I opened the door to the control room.

Morrison and Leland had their heads together and they both turned and looked at the same time.

"Hey, Boo—oh," Morrison said.

"*Someone's* boo. Damn," Leland said with a laugh. "You do realize someone been gnawing on you."

I tossed my hair. "Whatever do you mean?" I rolled my eyes and they both laughed, and I hoped that was it. But no. Leland was full of humorous quips about my love bites. In fact, I wasn't aware there were so many songs about hickeys, but do you know that Leland *was*? And he sang every one of them before lunch?

"I think the Judas Priest one is my favorite," he said to me as we packed up to go to the mess hall. We had guitars and drums tracked on two songs, and after lunch the plan was to add in some keyboards to one of them. I'd originally written the melody using Gran's piano, and so I was hoping to recreate it.

"Wonder how things are going with Soul."

My ears perked up at Morrison's musing.

"You think things are going to go *well*? With his temper?"

My hackles rose. It wasn't my place to stick up for Shane, but I wanted it to be. I didn't like hearing Leland criticize him, even if what he said was true.

When we sat down to eat, I asked, "Hey, Morrison? What

would you think if I asked Shane to play that slide part on 'Over The Moon'?"

The two producers looked at each other and then back at me.

"I think he'd kill it. I don't know what he'll say, but I think it's a good idea." Morrison stroked his chin. "You know what, you should also see if he'll sing the harmonies with you."

Leland looked between the two of us. "That would be… that would be *fire*."

"Yeah, your voices really complement each other. Let's talk to him after—"

Leland cleared his throat, gave a quick shake of his head.

Morrison's eyes flared, and he gave me a weak smile.

"Sure. After. Uh, you guys almost done? I'm gonna head back, I want to work on that piano part some more."

"Yeah, let's do it."

I wasn't sure how I could concentrate on my own music while my heart was worried and hurting for Shane. I had a bad feeling and I couldn't shake it. So I channeled it instead. And I played my ass off. Leland and Morrison sat with me and helped me tweak a few parts, but then I played that shit all the way through until I was fucking crying, it was so damned pretty. I wanted it to be pretty for Shane. I wanted to create a piece of music that showed him how much he'd made me feel, how honored I felt that he would share space and time with me, let himself be vulnerable with me. The lyrics were a start.

What can I say
   What can I do
   It's all Feuds and Interludes between me and you
   We say what we don't mean
   We mean what we don't say
   We fuss and we fight then we just walk away

Metal Menace, all growls and sharp words
You pull me in close while you hold me at bay
Your lips soothe my ire and leave bruises behind
Frustration sensation at war in my mind
Can we meet in the middle
Without weapons or rage
Or are we just destined for tabloid front page
Can you ever see me as more than my faults
Can I ever fit perfectly
In your world of vaults
Our rivalry runs deep as our bloodlines and bones
But we can rise higher above the unknowns

FIFTEEN

S hane

The three men I'd worked with as closely as you possibly could for the past seven years, the ones who I'd carried with me, shared my music with, were breaking up with me.

"When were you going to tell me?"

Dean looked at the others and continued acting as the band's spokesperson.

"We talked about it. I guess after we wrapped this album. Man, we want to do something more commercial. You know, go back to pop punk. That's what's selling now, not this dark, heavy shit."

I opened my mouth to speak, but why? It appeared I'd walked into a mutiny. Did Lydia know when she'd suggested this sit-down? Did Morrison? What about Jeff, our fucking manager?

"Look, Shane, we've made good music together. We've had a great ride. But if we want to remain relevant, we need to make a change. Look at MGK. Hell, look at Bring Me The Horizon. One gave up rap for punk, one gave up the metal scene for I don't even know what you call it, other than pop."

They weren't telling falsehoods about MGK and Oli and company. I actually thought both of those diversions worked for those bands.

"I'm not a pop punk singer."

My band looked back at me expectantly, as if they were waiting for me to figure out the a-ha moment.

"Ah. You weren't intending for me to sing."

They squirmed in their seats and finally had the decency to look uncomfortable. Good. I could be mature and still not make this bullshit easy for them.

"Shane," Dean began. I was probably closest with him, both in age and experience. "It's business. And it's creative differences. You want to keep playing the hard stuff, and that's fine. You should do that. But we want to make a change. And if that's not what you want, hey. Wicked Soul is your IP. We're not going to fight you on that."

Glad he was smart enough to— *Wait.*

"You already talked to a lawyer."

He nodded.

"So that's it? All three of you?"

"Actually," said Tucker. "I got asked to tour with Demi Lovato. She's doing this whole rock thing. Pays good." He shrugged. "I don't really care what I'm playing as long as I'm getting paid, and we ain't getting paid as much as we did after the first two albums."

I rubbed my hands together. "That brings us to the fact that we're still under contract. The label expects one more album at the very least."

Drew shrugged. "You've already got the music. You play most of the instruments anyway. Record it. Hire a touring band. That's all we've been to you."

That...*ouch*. That hurt, but I couldn't argue with him.

"I'm sorry you feel... I'm sorry if I gave you that impression. You all mean more to me than a contract."

They had the decency to accept that as truth and not throw it back in my face, but it was obvious that my feelings toward them didn't matter anymore.

"And Rocktoberfest?"

They all looked at each other and back at me. We'd been asked to play after last year's event, and part of this trip up to Bolder Breed was so that we could rehearse. We'd planned to play new music at that show, kind of a kickoff to album preorders and our first single hitting the airwaves. It was six weeks away.

"You'll figure it out," Dean said. "You always do." There was no malice in his voice at least. There was that.

"I guess that's it then." I stood and walked toward Dean. He looked nervous as I approached, but when I stuck my hand out, he relaxed. "I wish you all the best."

Dean took my hand, stood, and we shook. There was no bro hug after, like we usually did.

Lydia had been quiet the whole time, I guess figuring that she didn't need to step in as long as no punches or chairs were being thrown.

I shook hands with Drew and Tucker, they all thanked Lydia, and then they were gone. Off to the airport and back to LA. They'd been packed before we even met this morning.

"Wow." I slumped back into my chair.

Lydia whistled and dragged her chair closer to me.

"That was not at *all* how I thought this would go down. Don't get me wrong, I had a feeling y'all might not stay together. But to quit? Just like that? And pop punk? Seriously? They're not going to be the new Green Day. That ship sailed. Nostalgia only gets you so far."

"Did you know?" I folded my hands between my spread knees and stared at the floor, my eyes burning with tears I would not shed.

"That they were going to quit? Hell no. Not at all."

That made me feel better. I trusted Lydia more than most. It would suck if I found I couldn't trust her, either.

"I've worked my entire career to avoid this kind of shit, to not end up alone like Pops. What the hell for?"

"Shane, you can't be an island in a band. It has to be solid, with interconnecting and dependent parts, you know? A brotherhood, or the gender-appropriate equivalent."

"But I *am* an island! My band just ditched me like I'm fucking Captain Jack Sparrow."

Lydia kicked my foot with her boot. "Does that make me Elizabeth? Shall we get drunk off pirate's rum?" She chuckled, but the last thing I wanted was to get shitfaced.

I wanted something—someone—better.

"I know this sucks, and I know you're going to freak out when it really hits you, but this is actually a huge fucking opportunity. Your band did you a massive favor."

I frowned and sat up straight. "How do you figure?"

She spread her arms out in a grand gesture. "You have a clean slate. You are no longer limited by what *they* can and can't do. You can completely reinvent Wicked Soul, or you can blow the fucking lid off and be fucking Shane Butler. You can do whatever you want!"

I smiled at her enthusiasm. I could tell she was building to something.

"If you hadn't pushed me to confront them, I'd still have a band, maybe. And a mediocre album. Do I have you to blame? Or to thank?"

She bent over laughing. "I guess you could see it either

way. Or you could see that you have three brilliant producers at your disposal, ready to work with you on this reinvention."

I thought about what else I might have that I didn't before we came up here.

Do I have Boone?

"If you don't mind," I said, giving her the eyebrow. "I think I'll take the day to let this all sink in."

She clapped her hands together. "Splendid. Unice is coming in this afternoon anyway and after she unpacks, I plan to whisk her away to the spa and then take care of her other needs, if you get what I'm saying."

If I thought Boone and I made a strange pair, Lydia and her much-younger pop-star girlfriend had raised more than a few eyebrows when they went public with their relationship. Unice was wildly talented, and I'd heard Lydia had pulled a similar stunt with her, offering her an opportunity to make changes in her professional life. Personal too, it turned out.

"I need to call Pops. And I need to find Boone." I was thinking out loud, and obviously the second item piqued her interest.

"Boone, huh? Rose said you were hanging out with Stellar last night. You guys squash whatever beef you two had?"

My cheeks burned when I thought of what Boone and I had been up to. Any beef that may have been there evaporated the second I kissed him. He was too precious for that.

"Life is short," is what I ended up saying. "There's enough shit in this world. I don't need to make more. We're cool." I wondered if I was pressing my luck to take her further into my confidence.

"Cool?" She grinned at me. "A little birdie told me Collins has been strutting around here grinning like a loon with some new decorations on his neck. You have anything to do with that?"

"Am I in trouble if I say yes?"

She shrugged as she stood and straightened the cabin, putting my former band members' chairs away. "Not if it's consensual. Not from me." She narrowed her eyes at me. "Boone's good people. His grandparents raised him right, thank goodness, because he went through some shit as a kid. I knew his dad, motherfucking scumbag. Excuse my language. And I'll never forget the damn pictures of Boone when his mom was found dead. He was alone with her for hours, Shane. Those guileless blue eyes, staring into the cameras through a curtain of curls as he was led out in front of the damn paparazzi, daring the whole world to feel his pain just for a minute. I still *see* that pain in him sometimes. I know he's a grown-ass man and all successful and shit, but I'll never forget those eyes. Thank God for John and Vera Jean, right?"

"Right." And that was another reminder. Boone had suffered so much loss as a child. I used to think of him as spoiled because he had his grandparents to care for him, but losing your parents like that, for the whole world to see? I might not talk to mine, but at least they were alive. Someday I hoped to mend fences with them. Seemed like I was about to have a lot more time on my hands. Maybe it was time. "Oh, hey, I heard you offered Bolder Breed to the Collins Foundation for the fundraiser. That was really cool of you."

"Least I could do for Vera Jean and Bruce. It's going to be a blast—"

"And Bruce? What does Pops have to do with it?"

She blinked at me. "Oh, haven't you talked to him? He and Vera Jean are doing it together. I'm so excited. They've got big plans."

I stood there like I had a fucking cramp in my brain. Way too much information coming at me. They had *plans*? Why the fuck was I hearing this from Lydia and not Pops?

I needed to call him. I needed to find Boone.

"So let's regroup tomorrow morning, sound good? I'm

happy to be here for you to bounce ideas off of, you know, whether it's a Wicked Soul album, a solo project, or...who knows, a Butler-Collins collaboration. I'd love to get you two in here and write with you. See ya later."

Why did that last one sound like it was god-blessed fucking meant to be?

SIXTEEN

B oone

I was rushing out the front doors of the lodge as Shane was coming up the steps.

"We have a situation," I said as I came to a halt before him. Then I got a look at his haunted face. "Wait, what happened? Shane?"

I put my hands on his face, not caring who saw us, and he closed his eyes.

He leaned into my hands. "I was coming to find you."

"What do you need?" Because whatever he was going through, I would let him set the pace.

He took my hand and looked around. "Mind walking with me?"

I looked back at the doors. I was supposed to go eat with the twins. "Let me text Annie and Bran. Lead on."

I pulled out my phone, hurriedly tapped in a few words,

shoved my phone in my back pocket and took his hand. He didn't speak as he led us down the steps, and instead of heading toward the studio, he hung a left and took us into the orchards. It had been a cool August so far up in the Pacific Northwest, and the ground was wet because it had been raining off and on all day. The water dripped from the trees around us as we walked and the quiet was peaceful.

I wanted to ask him a million questions but I knew he'd talk when he was ready. Holding his hand was already so exciting, I wanted to squeal and skip through the apple trees that weren't quite ready to harvest but smelled so good, but I held it all in—along with my alarm over the grandparent situation.

"I'm sorry, I'm trying to figure out how to say all this."

Oh. There was an "all this." Fine. Whatever he needed, I was going to be there for him, because one thing I'd learned about Shane was that he really didn't let folks in. I doubted he had anyone in his life besides his Pops. If he trusted me, I'd prove trustworthy.

"Whatever you need, Shane."

He let out a huge exhale and pursed his lips, shaking his head. "First off, my band just quit."

"*What?!*" My shouts interrupted the stillness and a couple of crows squawked and flew out of the trees near us. "That's insane! How dare they! What the fuck? They're *nothing* without you. What do they think—"

"Hey," he said, his lips split into a satisfied smile. "I'm surprisingly okay about it."

I stopped walking and stared at him. "Really? Are you sure?"

He shrugged and tugged on my hand to keep us moving. "Yeah. I am. Somebody told me recently that I was better than my band."

I ducked my head. "Wow. Yeah, I did say that. But it's not like I meant to manifest this shit to happen!"

He laughed. He actually laughed! His world had just shifted violently and he was laughing.

"Are you sure you're okay? You need to lie down or something?"

He shook his head. "Nah. I'm good. I need to regroup. I need to talk to Pops. I need to call my manager, the label, all kinds of other shit, but nah. I'm going to take today to walk through this orchard, holding your hand, and not even think about it."

I stopped again. "You're really not okay. Shane—"

"I am. Honestly? I feel free. Lydia kind of instigated this whole thing, the talk with the band and shit, and now that they're gone, it's like a *weight* is gone. When Lydia asked me yesterday if I thought I'd grown, I think it set off a spiral where I'm like, nope. I'm stuck. These guys were hired guns, not true partners. I guess I finally realized why Pops stuck around with your grandpa and the other guys."

"They made beautiful music together." I smiled at him. Could it be that he was in the same space as me? "Shane? I wanted to ask you... You know that slide part Leland was talking about?" He nodded, a slight frown bending his brows. "I wondered if you would play it. On our album. And I wondered if you would sing the harmonies with me. Would you even consider it? I know it's not your thing—"

"Yes, Boone. I would love to."

He pulled me close to him and rested his hands on my waist.

"Really? We're not too...how did you say it, too much like candy?"

He squeezed my waist, letting his hands roam south a bit as he groaned. "I like it. I like the way you taste. I want candy."

He slid his fingers under the waistband of my pants and I sucked in a breath as he crushed me against him.

"Never knew you had such a sweet tooth, Butler," I whispered as he went to work on my neck. I clutched at his shoulders and gasped. "Maybe you need to watch that."

"I'm watching my intake, I can pace myself, but I want more."

"Fuck, it's yours." My phone vibrated in my pocket, clearing my head enough to remind me of why I'd been looking for him. "Shane, sweetie. It's our grandparents."

"What about them?" He kept kissing me like that, up my throat, along my jaw, behind my ear, and I could barely breathe.

"They're here. *Now*. They got into Portland last night and they're staying at a hotel. Together."

He pulled back. "Together? Shit. That was fast."

"Yes. And they want us to come into town and meet them tomorrow night for dinner before they come here and work out all the stuff for the show."

Shane rubbed a hand over his mouth and thought for a minute, but he didn't let go of me, thankfully.

"All right." He barked out a laugh and, once more, I was ready to have him sit down. I wished I had smelling salts. His expression was so stunned, I worried he'd keel over any minute. Although, maybe I was projecting what *I* would be like in the same situation.

"All right?"

He nodded and smiled at me, using that hand to smooth back my hair. "Yeah. I can keep my hands off you for a dinner."

I frowned. I hadn't thought about that, the fact that our grandparents had no idea what we'd been up to. Maybe he wasn't ready to tell them. "Oh. Sure, okay. Yeah, you're probably right."

"Right about what? I just mean I'll need to behave myself and not give into the desire to maul you for a few hours. Jesus, I really did a number on your neck—"

"Forget about that. What...what should we tell them about us?"

It was his turn to frown, but then he had a playful smile on his face. "Well, definitely not how much I love that ball on your tongue."

"Shane. I'm serious. Are you ready for other people to know about us? Especially our grandparents?"

He pulled me closer, and I started to shiver, maybe from the cold, but more likely from my fear that this was the end of any possibility of a partnership with Shane.

"Why, are you worried? You think Vera Jean will object?"

"God, no, Shane. She adores you."

He smiled. "That's nice. I've always admired her."

He was acting so weird. So un-Shane-like.

"Shane! Focus. What are we doing?"

"I can tell you what I'm *not* doing. I'm not freaking out. It's weird that I'm not freaking out, but I'm not. That goes for my band, and it goes for you. Us." His smile fell. "But Boone? I'm kind of floating unmoored here. I hope...I hope this wasn't just an experiment for you. I don't fuck around with people. If you're not serious—"

"I'm serious as a goddamned heart attack, Shane. I'm still waiting for you to send me away, though."

"Why do you keep saying that?" He rested his hands on my hips. "Why do you act so confident one minute, telling me what you want, what to do, and so damned skittish the next?"

I pulled away from him. I needed some space if I was going to admit some shit.

"You called me perfect. I've been called that before. Let's just say perfect gets old real quick for a lot of people."

He reached for my hand but I took a few steps away, over to one of the trees. I ran my fingers over the bark on the trunk and looked up at the *perfectly* shaped fruit. "Soon these apples will turn from this current shade of green to shiny red and yellow. They'll be harvested, sent out to stores, and some choosy shopper will pluck them from a pile thinking they're perfect, but once they get them home, they'll start to see the imperfections and wish they would have picked another one." I turned back to face him and took in his confused expression. "That doesn't stop me from trying to be perfect*er*, but yeah, usually people decide real quick that they should have picked a better apple."

"They were ignorant then. Nobody's perfect. That's a helluva weight to put on yourself, Boone." He shoved his hands in his pockets. "But is...Is that how little you think of me?" he asked after several beats.

My eyes flared. "What? No, Shane—"

"You think I give a shit about how beautiful you are? How talented you are? I keep asking myself 'how did I not see you?' Because you are so much more than who you show the world. You let me see the real you, and *that's* why you're perfect in my eyes. You're messy. You're a mood swing waiting to happen. You are a brat. You're bossy."

I didn't back up as he approached me, calling me on my bullshit. He ran a finger down my cheek and lifted my chin.

"If that's your idea of perfect—"

"You have a brilliant mind." He pushed me up against the tree. "You are so thoughtful. You're flexible, adaptable to situations I can barely stand, and you handle everything thrown at you with grace—"

"Except diabetes. God, I need a smoke—"

"You drive me crazy," he whispered, leaning down to kiss me. "You're so goddamned seductive I can barely think. You taste like heaven. You make me want to get all deep up inside you and never let go."

I shuddered under his touch, under the brush of his lips against mine as he spoke.

"Fuck, Shane. What—"

"I don't care who knows, Boone. Do you?"

He pulled back just enough to stare into my eyes. I had a feeling he was just as nervous hearing my answer as he was to admit that.

"No. I told you. I'm honored you'd want to be with me. I continue to be gobsmacked by this development—you and me—but I'm honored."

"There's nothing honorable about the things I want to do to you," he admitted in a husky voice.

"I think you made that clear with all the hickeys."

He breathed a laugh before pressing his lips gently to mine. "Don't break me, Boone. Please. If we do this...don't break me."

I put my hands on his face. "I would never. Shane—"

He went all in with his tongue then, probably to keep me from answering him. I got the sense that the last admission was not one he'd been ready to make to me.

I needed to be so careful with this man.

He lifted my leg up to hook on his hip and he ground his hard cock against mine. God, I didn't care if anyone was watching, I wanted him to fuck me right there. I wanted him to fuck away all the bad in my past as he thrust so deep inside me, like he'd promised to do. I wanted him to replace all of my painful memories of sex with new ones, good ones. He was the right man to do it.

I hadn't given my heart or my body to anyone in a long time, and never like this. If he thought I could break him, he had no idea how thoroughly he could destroy me.

SEVENTEEN

S hane

My heart thudded in my chest as I realized how much I'd revealed of myself to Boone. It wasn't that I hadn't been close to people before, but never another musician, never one I respected like I did Boone. I'd chosen safe men in the past, ones who couldn't touch my core, the part of me where creation came from, where I held in all of my truths and fears. Boone had already clawed his way in, and I'd thrown the doors open for him in response.

The truth was that I wanted him to be a safe space, but that didn't mean he would be. Well, it was out there now, my fucking scaredy-cat truth. We'd see what he'd do with it.

My grandfather's actions in his life were clearer to me now. I didn't know whether he ever had feelings for John Boone more than as a best friend, but I wondered if maybe he might have. It would explain why he'd tolerated all of the heartache, if only to get close to this type of harmony with another person. I didn't doubt that he'd loved Vera Jean, continued to love her after all these years, but if John was anything like Boone, so vibrant, honest, and compelling... queer or not, their relationship made a bit more sense to me now. Not only did I want to fuck Boone, but I wanted to make music with him—which, to me, was an even bigger revelation.

I didn't make music with other people. I played in bands, but that wasn't the same thing. Letting someone in on my creative process was too intimate, too close. The only person I'd ever written with was Pops. My talk with Lydia yesterday had been a huge step, and she'd been so careful with me. Probably I wasn't the first hotheaded, control freak, megalomaniac songwriter she'd ever dealt with.

Damn, that made me sound even more like my mother. Maybe I owed her, not quite an apology, but a little empathy.

Boone shivered and curled up against my chest. "You want to take this someplace a little warmer?" His teeth started chattering, and he had goose bumps all over his chest where I was currently exploring.

"I'm sorry. Yeah, let's go." I pulled him against me, hating any separation. What the hell was I going to do when it was time to leave here?

"Let me text Gran and tell her we'll see them for dinner tomorrow." He pulled out his phone and then shoved it back in his pants with a grin. "We may need to stop at REI, though, so I can get a fuckton of turtlenecks. Gran will give me so much shit about these love bites. Do you know Leland sang every song about love bites ever written all day today?"

He wasn't mad, though. He was smiling so wide and there was a bounce to his step that made my heart unclench a little. Maybe this would be okay. Maybe I didn't need to be so afraid.

"Hey, Boone." What the hell, why not just welcome him deep inside my terrordome. "I had an idea."

"Tell me," he said, looking up at me with a blissed-out gaze that had me wondering what he'd look like when I finally got to bend him over a surface. That booth we'd sat in last night in the lodge would be a good height.

"Shane?"

"Sorry. I was just thinking of how hot you looked when we made that mess last night."

"Cold or not, you keep talking like this and I'll perform an encore right here, right now."

I laughed, pulling him against me and kissing the top of his head.

"Good to know. Seriously, though, I know I've got a lot to contemplate, but there's one thing I'd love for us to work out together."

"Elevated Splits? Or Folded Deck Chair? I would need to stretch out real good first, but we could probably— Oh, did you mean something else?"

My jaw hung open and I'd stopped walking. "Elevated *what*?"

Boone gave a dismissive shrug and grabbed my hand to drag me forward. "You know, like I'm in the splits on top of a counter or something, and you—"

"You can do the *splits*?"

"Hmm? Oh yeah. I took ballet for a while. Gran had this thought that I might use my vocal talents on Broadway someday instead of that 'rock 'n' roll rubbish.' Of course she loved Papa's music, but she had bigger plans for me." He sure mimicked her British accent perfectly. "Ballet has its perks. I can also still put my leg behind my— What?"

I reached down to adjust the monster in my pants, straining to get out and do whatever Folded Deck Chair was with Boone. "You can't say these things. Seriously, how do you...where...who decided on these names?"

"Oh," he said, all nonchalant as he kept walking beside me with that pep in his step that made his curls bounce on his shoulders. Damn, I had hair envy more than ever. At least he didn't mind me playing with it. I wanted to have it spread all over me like right now. "I've read a couple of books about sexual positions," he was saying. "There are a couple of good websites too. I'm happy to show you. We can try whichever ones you want, I'll do my best—"

"Whoa, whoa, Boone." I pulled him to a stop at the edge of the orchard and held his arms. "When we fuck? It's not a performance. You don't have to do anything except tell me what you like and don't like and be there a hundred percent with me, okay? Sex doesn't have to be acrobatic or choreographed to be great. It just has to feel good."

"Oh." He smiled at me but it was unsure again. "I just want you to be happy with me."

"I'm wild about you, Boone," I said, cradling his face in my hands. "But I wanted to ask you...are you guys playing Rocktoberfest?"

He blinked up at me in confusion. "Like, in the desert? Black Rock City? No. We've never been invited. I always assumed we weren't hard enough for them, or maybe they had an issue with the gay thing—"

"Are you kidding? Do you know how many of those bands like dick? I mean, seriously."

"Sounds like a party." I could tell he was teasing, but he also seemed confused. "Why do you ask?"

I cleared my throat and stood up straight, dropping my hands. "Well, since my band just broke up with me and we're scheduled to play, I'm kind of in a bind. But also...how cool would it be for Collins Butler to play a set of the old guys' songs at Rocktoberfest?"

"Butler Collins," he said.

"What? No, it should be your name first."

He shook his head. "It sounds better with your name first. It's the alphabet, people expect things. Besides, you're older and more established. So wait, you mean play California songs?"

"Yeah." I laughed, of course he'd have a whole thesis about the name. "And John Boone's solo stuff and Brothers, maybe a song or two of ours."

"And 'Paisley'?"

I grinned. "I would love to sing it with you. I think the thing that bugged me the most about the ceremony was that I wanted to be the one sharing the mic with you, not Pops."

Boone burst out laughing and threw his arms around me. "I think it would be a blast!" But then he straightened and cleared his throat. "I'd have to ask the Thompson Twins though."

"Why? *Wait!* Is that seriously their last name?"

Boone chuckled. "They're not *The* Thompson Twins, but they're *my* Thompson twins. I wouldn't want to make any commitments without them. They're my band, my best friends."

"Let's ask them to play with us. You guys sounded great at the ceremony. You mind letting this old metalhead tagalong?"

This time, Boone hopped up into my arms and wrapped his legs around me and he laughed as he kissed me. I spun him around, rejoicing in his reaction. I loved how he let his feelings out so freely. I was beginning to realize just how much I had to learn from him.

"I would fucking love to play with you, Shane Butler. Let's make some beautiful fucking music together."

. . .

Our excitement waned a bit when we sat down after dinner with Annie and Brandon, who faced us with arms crossed identically over their chests.

"Would this be a one-time thing?" Annie asked. "Because I'm not sure I'm ready to commit to a polyamorous gig moving forward."

"A poly-*what* now?"

"Look what happened to Fleetwood Mac," Brandon said.

"No one is suggesting—"

"And The Mamas and Papas," Annie said. "What would we be? Mama and the Three Papas? I'm not into the reverse harem thing. Uh uh. I don't think so."

"Wait—"

I looked to Boone for assistance, but he was just staring blankly at the twins. *Awesome. Way to throw me to the wolves.*

"And no offense? But I've seen all the leather Wicked Soul wears, and that shit chafes," Brandon said.

"No one said anything about leather—"

"And if you think I'm going to ride on some gay orgy bus cross country or, like, play some Taylor Swift break-up anthems every time you two fight—"

"That's going way too far." Before I could argue any more, the three of them burst into laughter. Boone fell on the floor and Brandon started snorting repeatedly.

"What the hell?"

Annie shrugged at me and examined her painted nails. "Just making sure you can handle us, Butler."

"Taylor Swift!" Boone cried from the floor, where he was rolling around, holding his stomach. "You should have seen your face!" He held out his hand for me to help him up and then he plopped into my lap and put his arms around my neck, lightly massaging my head. "I do like you in leather pants, though."

I grabbed his hips, ready to push him off, but he held me tight and Annie gave me a big smile.

"All right, all right, you had your fun."

"It's all fun and games 'til someone gets hurt, metal boy. Just remember. We have a reputation for enacting excruciatingly painful revenge. You hurt our Boone, you suffer the consequences. Dig?"

She held out a hand and I half expected it to have a buzzer on the palm that would zing me when I touched her. I took her hand and fought not to wince when she squeezed it with more force than a five-foot-eight, buck-thirty-pound mixed girl should be able to muster. Brandon was a bit beefier, with an impressive Afro, but not even as tall as Boone. We were going to make an interesting picture on stage...that is if they actually agreed to do it.

"So are we doing this?" Boone asked. "Rocktoberfest?"

Brandon looked at his sister and then to Boone before leaning back in his chair with his arms crossed once more. "For starters. We'll see if you can keep up." And with that, he leaned too far and fell over backwards in the chair.

Boone scrambled up and Annie started shouting at him.

"I'm all right, I'm all right, geez!" He scrambled to his feet and back into the chair, trying to look like nothing happened.

"None of this works with a broken drummer, Bran," Boone said as he sat back in his chair beside me. He rested his elbows on the table next to mine and leaned his head against my shoulder.

"Four on the floor, Thompson," I said to him, shaking my head.

He gave me an incredulous look and then nodded with a sigh. "Yeah, all right."

"Now. Schedule," Boone said, looking to all three of us. "We're booked up here three more weeks. I'd love it if we could finish recording these tracks over the next week, work our asses off, so we can start rehearsing with Shane. Does that work for everyone? Shane? Does that give us enough time?"

"Yeah," he said. "Plus, I've got to unfuck my situation, call my lawyer and all that." I ran a hand over my head, and Boone put his arms around me.

"I'll help," he murmured. "However I can."

Somehow, I knew he would.

"Yeah, and if you need some muscle, you know," Annie said, cracking her knuckles, "we gotchoo. In certain cases, we rent out our revenge services."

"I'll keep that in mind."

Eighteen

B oone

No lie, it was fun watching Shane squirm under the Thompson Twins Treatment. I'd been ready to step in if it got out of hand, but he hadn't needed it, though he made it clear when we got back to my room that he was also skilled at serving up revenge...hot.

I might have given him some ideas when I mentioned I was flexible, but when he had me naked and spread out on the bench at the foot of the bed in my room, I knew I was in trouble.

"Now that I've got you here, I want to look my fill for a while. What's wrong with that?"

I held on to the footboard, under strict instructions not to let go, and waited as Shane stood behind me making hungry sounds, walking back and forth, looking at my ass on display.

"Mmm mmm mmm," he said over and over.

"I know I said I could do the splits, but if I stay here much longer, things will cramp."

He came up behind me, and I heard his knees crack as he knelt down. He brushed my hair off of my shoulders and pressed kisses down my spine, on my shoulders, and when he got to my ass, well, my legs were shaking and not from strain.

"This ass...so underrated."

Panting, I tried to turn and look at him but he clicked his tongue against his teeth. "Uh-uh."

"Shaaaane," I whined, and he chuckled. He ran his hands over my ass and I whimpered. "Please?"

"I'm serious. We all know you've got one of the best voices in rock, you're a phenomenal front man, but I don't think the press has paid quite enough attention to your posterior asset. I mean, *dayam*."

I managed to bounce said asset enough to get him to swear some more.

"And it's all yours, sweetheart, if you would just— *Ohhhhh...*"

He ran his fingers between my glutes and moaned softly. "Don't rush me, *sweetheart*. I'm enjoying myself. You don't have any tattoos, I just realized that. Any reason?"

"Nothing's felt permanent enough to me so far. And now, with diabetes, apparently the ability to heal can be compromised. I'm nervous to test that theory."

"I'd love to design a back piece that does you justice. One that accentuates all your curves."

This time I did peek at him. "Design? Are you a visual artist too, Shane?"

"When I have time. I designed mine."

I blew my hair out of my face. "Makes sense. You'd want to have control over what went on your body."

He frowned. "It's not like that—"

"No, I mean it in a good way. You have a great ear, you

know how things should sound and you're great at it. It would make sense that you'd know exactly the right design to go on your back. It's quite a statement, I was admiring it while you slept."

"Thank you," he said. I heard him stand up, kick off his boots, pull his zipper down, and then drop his pants on the floor, his belt buckle clanging on the tile. "You can rest now."

I rolled back on my hips, pulled my legs into my chest, and turned to the side. I'd felt quite exposed, but when I saw his smoldering dark eyes and satisfied smile—and got a load of his fully naked anterior and his fully erect cock—I was pleased with my efforts.

"Any more requests?" I asked him, licking my lips. "I'm happy to take care of you."

He held out his hand. "Come here," he said. I took his hand and turned to face him, taking my own minute to admire his physique.

He didn't have a six pack, but his external obliques were cut nicely and he had a wide chest. His arms were toned and he was *strong*. *So* strong. Thick thighs supported an ass like you might see in a pair of sportsball pants. He was much less hairy than me and his taupe skin was so lovely.

His face, though... so many contradictions. His deep brown eyes were so intense with a nearly permanent furrowed brow, he could be mistaken for cold, and I kind of loved that when we were alone, his features would soften so that his kind and vulnerable side would appear. His eyebrows would raise in concern, his lips would part the slightest bit when he experienced pleasure, and his lids would drop. And his smile... I hadn't thought he could possess such a sweet, sometimes bashful expression. He'd opened himself to me in so many ways that had nothing to do with sex. But since that was on the menu, I was going to look—and take—my fill.

"You work out, don't you? Like a lot?"

He shrugged and pulled me to standing. "Not hardcore or anything, but yeah. Strength training gives me more energy. I used to think it was all about running until I puked, but that's not what's best for me."

"Running sucks. Working out sucks. Why can't I be like our grandfathers? Drink, smoke, get up on stage and work my ass off, repeat."

Shane laughed. "I think Pops would give that plan the thumbs down, and didn't John pass away from lung cancer?"

I knew there was a bit of a scolding there, but he was gentle. I sighed. "Yeah, you're right. Sorry, I know I sound like a whiny bitch. I just need to let it out sometimes. I'll get used to my new normal. Eventually."

He pulled me into his arms. "You can always vent to me, Boone. I get it. Pops had a really hard time with it too."

I rested my chin on his sternum and looked up at him. "You sure you want another damaged rockstar on your roster? Seems like you have your hands full."

He laughed. "We're about to both have our hands full if our grandparents are serious about this relationship."

I sighed. "You know, now that I've quit having a fit about it, I'm actually happy for them. Gran has been awfully lonely since Papa passed. She doesn't show it, but when I'm gone on tour, I worry about her." I stroked the back of Shane's head, loving the feel of his scalp. "And finding this...with you? Why would I stand in the way of her being happy?"

Shane gazed at me with those deep brown eyes, dark as coal and so intense, but now, with us standing in the dim light from the windows and the bedside tables, his usual grim countenance had softened, and instead of his frequent scowl, his expression was almost peaceful.

"Honestly, hearing him go on and on about her all these years, there was a part of me that was a little envious. Love and I haven't been on the same page for some time, and I think at first I was selfish about it, like come on, old man. He'd been married twice, and though both times he kinda got screwed, he wasn't always the best partner. Meanwhile, I tried to do everything right and it didn't seem to matter."

"You don't have to do everything right with me, Shane. We're both going to fuck up, you know? But if we remember this, how this feels…"

"Yeah. It feels good. Scary good."

"So good. Scary, but good."

"Let's not stand in our own way," Shane said, stroking my hair.

"Let's not."

And something shifted right then, the two of us standing in an embrace, naked, tentatively embarking on something big that was alternately terrifying and the greatest thing to ever happen to us.

Shane held me closer, and I rested my head on his shoulder, and though there was no music playing, we swayed together, our bodies moving to the rhythm of our souls searching the other out, filling in the holes, bridging the chasms left by hurts of the past, building a terrace upon which we could stand together as more than new lovers, more than partners in song, more than grandsons with legacies to uphold. And when he kissed me, it stilled all of the quivers and tremors threatening to weaken my resolve.

"Are you ready to take me to bed? I'm asking fully understanding that you might not be, and that's okay with me."

Shane frowned at me for a moment, and then he stepped back. "Fully understand *this*, Collins. You give me that ass, I'm never gonna *not* want it. Don't give it to me unless you want it to be mine."

Fuck me. "That is the sexiest thing I've ever heard." I was breathless, my brain about to short out. "Don't take it unless you intend to keep it," was all I could think to say in response.

Shane groaned and reached down, cupping said ass, squeezing it and pulling me to him so tight our erections were trapped between us, straining against each other.

"I want it," he said, biting down on the tendon of my neck. "Please, Boone."

"Take it."

I don't know what I expected when I made the offer, but it was not the tender and sweet lovemaking that commenced. Shane prepared me so carefully, murmuring in my ear as he stretched me enough to take his thick length.

"This feel good, baby? You good? You okay?"

"So good," I said over my shoulder as he tended to my ass. "I'm ready, Shane, please...*please*."

He only took his hands off of me long enough to roll on a condom. He caressed my back and hips, murmuring to me how much he craved my body and wanted this closeness, and when he pressed against my opening, I shuddered and then relaxed my muscles, welcoming him in, taking him so deep, deeper than either of us thought he could go.

With my hips in the air, my legs splayed, my cheek pressed against the mattress, he thrust in slow, stroking deep inside me, and he moaned softly each time. He ran his nails down my back with one hand and gripped my hip with the other, pulling me back to him, and when he started to shake, he gathered me up close to him and turned my chin so he could look in my eyes.

He didn't speak, but his gaze said everything. Right before he came, I saw fear there.

"I've got you," I whispered. "Let go..."

He cursed as his body seized up and his grip tightened everywhere, stealing my breath for a moment, but not long enough for me to panic before he let up. He reached down to stroke my cock as he continued to have aftershocks, and when he thrust in deep once more, it was enough.

"God, *Shane*!" I cried. I fell forward onto my hands as I convulsed, covering his hand and the sheets with my load. I could barely hold myself up, I was so wrung out, and do you know? He took care of me. He cleaned us both up, lay a clean towel down in the wet spot, and then pulled me to him, kissing my forehead before commanding me to sleep.

"I'm not going to be able to walk tomorrow," I muttered against his chest.

He kissed the top of my head. "Then I'll carry you. Sleep."

NINETEEN

S hane

I'm not too proud to admit that I cried after Boone fell asleep. The whole night was too heavy not to, with all these *feelings*. He'd *seen* me, he let me be myself, he didn't judge, he let me in and seemed as genuinely moved as I was by what was happening between us. He said he'd be mine, and I believed him. Mostly. Although lying in the dark, sobbing quietly while trying not to disturb him, I ran my fingers lightly over his gorgeous pale skin and wondered how the fuck the planets had aligned to let this supernova go off in my hands.

What would happen in the light of day? Would he roll over in the morning and give me that blissed-out smile? Would he open those big blues wide and say it was all a mistake? Would it be awkward, us tripping over each other to get some space?

Would he be upset?

Fuck, Shane, get it together. He's not like them.
He's just as sensitive as you.
I stroked his hair and he stirred against me.
"Switch." He rolled over and held out his arms. God, how had he known I'd needed to be held like that? I went gingerly into his arms, not wanting to squish him, and as soon as I settled with my cheek on his chest, he rubbed his lips on the top of my head and sighed.
"Can this be every night?"
I wasn't sure I heard him right, and when I went to speak, he let out a snore. The cutest fucking snore I'd ever heard, all high-pitched and shit. I wanted to look at him, but he had me trapped.
Good. I was where I wanted to be, come what may in the morning.
What I *didn't* expect the next morning was a lot of cursing prior to getting smacked in the face with a pair of jeans.
"Goddammit, Butler," he muttered. "I swear to God!"
"What did I do now? I'm not even awake yet."
Boone screamed, slipped on a t-shirt on the floor, and fell onto his ass. Hard.
"Babe! Are you all right?" I scrambled out of bed and over to his side, getting my feet tangled in my pants from the day before, and I caught myself before I face-planted in his lap. I looked up at him to apologize...but he was beaming.
"You called me babe."
I laughed and got to my knees. "I did call you babe. Are you okay?"
"I'm great now." Then his smile fell. "No, I'm not, actually. Shane!"
"What's wrong?" My heart was thundering. It was too early for this.
"Rocktoberfest! We have to come up with a set list like *now* so I can be sure I know all the songs! I don't want to make

any mistakes! I was looking for my notebook, which I'm pretty sure I'd left on the bed before you brought me back here and seduced me—"

"Whoa, wait a minute—"

"But I had this nightmare right before I woke up that we were right in the middle of 'Paisley' and I forgot the next chord and I couldn't catch up to you and you were mad and—"

I pulled him into my arms and kissed the top of his head. "You're fine, we have plenty of time—"

"And I was naked onstage and everyone saw my hickeys." He lifted his head and gave me a wicked grin.

"Really? This early in the morning, you're gonna mess with me? I haven't even had my coffee yet."

"I really did have a dream about Rocktoberfest, though. But my hickeys were gone by then."

"I can make sure you have more."

This led to tickling and kissing and wrestling and laughing until we couldn't breathe. It was all fun and games until Boone started to cough.

"Shit, I'm sorry. You need your inhaler? Oh, man, is your glucose monitor okay? I didn't mess it up, did I?"

He smiled at me. "I'm fine. But I really should get to work."

"Okay. If I can find my clothes, I'll get out of your way."

"Shane?" He stopped me with a hand to my chest.

"What's wrong?"

"Nothing...did you have a good time? With me? Like, was it all right? Last night?"

I brushed back his hair and kissed him until he melted against me.

"It was incredible. Perfect. I'd love to do it again."

He exhaled with so much relief, I frowned.

"Were you actually worried? Come on, Boone! Last night was—"

"I just needed to hear you say it. It was one of my best nights. Being with you. Thank you."

He sounded so unsure, I couldn't believe it. How could he think I didn't feel the same?

"It was one of my best, too, babe. It was perfect."

His eyes flared. "Babe." His cheeks flushed and he spun around in a circle. "Okay, what's on your agenda?"

"Welp, a whole lot of business stuff. But hey, if you need me for that song—"

"Oh, please. I'd love that. If you have time. And then dinner? I'll have to find something to cover my neck."

I rubbed at my mustache. "I'll still know it's there." I glanced around at the room. He'd pretty much wrecked it before I came in, but we'd done more damage. "Never trashed a hotel room before. Guess being with you means really living that rock star life."

He shrugged. "See if you can keep up."

We split up after a few more kisses, a frantic search for my left shoe, and more kisses. Boone would say he needed to get into the shower, but then he'd grab me again, suck my bottom lip into his mouth and tease me.

I could get used to this.

I found Lydia at breakfast with Unice, and she and I made a game plan. First up, hire a new manager, then fire Jeff. That was easily done when she contacted *her* manager, Arthur Frye, who was a partner with the firm where Jeff worked. She laid out the tale and told him Jeff had conspired against me. Turned out Dean had already told Jeff the band wanted to quit, and he'd suggested they wait until the album was done so he'd get his cut. Jeff knew I'd be pissed when I discovered we were double booked with Stellar and he'd still let it happen.

Lydia found all this out from Rose, who'd heard Drew and Dean talking about it while she was taking a smoke break. Arthur assured me he would handle Jeff, which Lydia told me meant Jeff would be finding new employment. Arthur set me up with his protégé, Audra, and I immediately liked her.

"Don't worry, Shane," she assured me. "We can unfuck this situation." She said she'd draw up an agreement and send it over and then we could have a longer talk.

Lydia and I spent the rest of the day listening to my demos together and talking over which ones had promise and which ones I should scrap. We were in complete agreement. There were only three that made the cut.

"I want to take advantage of this clean slate," I told her. "I want to try some new ideas."

That led to us jamming together for hours, and by late afternoon, we had the beginnings of two new songs.

Boone opened the door around four and peeked inside. "Sorry to interrupt."

"Not at all," I said, gesturing for him to come in as I got a load of his outfit. He was wearing a tight, almost sheer black button-up shirt with the top two buttons undone and those low-rise flared rust-colored corduroy pants. To finish off the outfit, he wore the pair of sparkly gold Converse high-tops he'd worn to the Rock Hall gig. Damn, he looked hot. He sidled up to me kind of shyly, smiling at Lydia.

I grabbed his hand and pulled him to me for a kiss, which made his cheeks all kinds of pink.

"This is quite a development," Lydia said, hugging Boone. "I thought hickeys were, like, a middle school thing."

The collar came up high, but my love bites peeked out when he moved. I liked it.

Boone blushed again but I pulled him against my side. "Can't help it. I get carried away with him."

Boone's eyes widened as if he were shocked I'd be so open. He had a lot to learn if he thought I would be closed-lipped about how I felt. Maybe with the press, but with friends and important people, he deserved my honesty.

"I just wondered if you were ready to meet Gran and Bruce?"

"What time is— Oh man, I lost track of time. Yeah, babe. Let me pack up."

He smiled nervously and waited by the door. "I'm sorry to interrupt—"

"No, no," Lydia said. "Don't keep them waiting on my behalf. Can't wait to see what you guys put together for Rocktoberfest. I've heard it's pretty wild out there in the desert."

"We're open to suggestions," I said to her. "I gotta let the promoters know about the change. Audra said she could handle all of that. She's awesome. Thanks for setting me up with her."

Lydia clapped hands with me and pulled me in for a bro hug. "You got it, Butler. Nice work today."

My heart felt so much lighter, and a lot of that was thanks to her. "Thanks for everything, Lydia. Seriously."

She gave a bow and twirled her hand at me before waving to us and heading out the door of the cabin.

"I'm sorry if you weren't done—"

"Come here," I said, standing from my stool. I held out a hand to him, and he took it. He stepped close to me with a timid smile. "Goddamn, you look good."

He tucked his hair behind his ear and ducked his head. "Yeah, well, Gran is still going to have a coronary."

"I'll take full responsibility." I leaned down to kiss him, and he gave a soft sigh that made my belly go liquid. All I wanted to do was get him back into his bed— "Oh, hey," I said, lowering my voice. "Are you feeling okay?"

He stared at me blankly. "What do you mean? Yeah, my asthma's been fine. My blood sugar was a little high this morning, but that's not abnormal for me. Oh, you mean—"

"Yeah," I said, feeling a little awkward. It's not like I was some hung beast or anything, but we'd gotten pretty intense last night, and I knew sometimes things—parts—were angry the next day.

He raised an eyebrow. "You mean am I suffering any after-effects of being splayed out like a spatchcocked chicken and used heartily by one Shane Butler? Is that what you mean?"

I exhaled and planted my hands on my hips. "I see that smart mouth of yours has been working up to this moment, so please. Enlighten me." I had to press my lips together to keep from laughing.

He crossed his arms and kicked out a hip. "I'll have you know that no amount of stretching or CBD cream could come close to dulling the ache from doing the splits without properly stretching. Which is my fault, I really need to do better from now on."

My eyebrows shot up. "Anything else bothering you?"

He licked his lips and looked me up and down before kicking his chin up. "No, actually. Someone took really good care of me, so besides being the slightest bit tender, I'm perfectly fine."

"Good." I stepped closer to him and ran a hand over his ass, cupping him gently. "That's good to know. I take care of what's mine."

Boone looked up at me with those hypnotic ocean-blue eyes and his lids fluttered. "God, that's hot," he moaned. "But seriously. I feel mostly great. Just, ah," he said, his gaze darting away. "I thought about you all day. I don't want things to be weird or anything, but I wanted you to know." He offered a nervous smile. Again with the skittishness.

"You've been on a constant loop in my head. Every call I made, every song I played, I wondered what would Boone think, or how would Boone sing this, play this... Is that weird?"

Boone beamed. "Not at all." Then he shook himself. "We should probably get going. Did you need to—"

"Yeah, let me run up and change real quick. Want to meet me in the bar? I'll grab keys from Rose—"

"Oh, I did already. Need help carrying anything?"

"Nope. Just going to lock up. Let's go."

He paused a second and put his hand on my chest. "You sure you're okay?"

I put my hand over his and breathed easier than I had in a long time.

"I'm great, Boone. Really. Now let's go be the grownups. I'll tell you everything on the way."

TWENTY

B^{oone}

I was ready to jump out of my skin at the prospect of having dinner with these two seventy-agers and the fact that Shane was being so calm, despite his professional life falling apart. I asked him to drive because I was liable to run us off the road in the studio's van, as jittery as I was.

Shane was a surprisingly careful driver. He didn't speed, he didn't tailgate, but I was still waiting for him to go off the rails a bit. He looked damn good in the black slacks and black dress shirt he'd put on. I loved the leather, but I could barely keep from drooling at sharp-dressed Shane. I'd been paying more attention to his hands on the wheel and watching his lips move than I had what he was saying.

"Anyway, I'm looking at this time at Bolder Breed as an exploration, see what moves me, see what I feel like. I don't know, you know? I don't know if I want to hire a band before doing final recordings, or just Dave Grohl this shit and play it all myself and go from there. Lydia and I decided on three of the songs I'd brought in, and we're re-working some of the riffs from the others. She's brilliant, you know? Have you ever —hey, you all right over there, babe?"

"I'm fine! I'm just listening to you. I can hardly believe you're talking to me about all this."

Shane frowned and checked his mirrors before reaching for my hand. "Believe it. If you let me, I'll talk your ear off."

I smiled at him but it was strained. Thankfully, he wasn't able to really pay attention. As he focused on the road, I tried to make my fake smile genuine.

"Talk away. I'm all ears. And I'm happy for you, I am. Did you get everything squared away with a new manager?"

"Yeah, actually. Her name is Audra. I love her already."

"That's great."

He grinned at me as he made a right turn. "Enough about me. How did your day go? You know, I like this. It's been a long time since I had someone to share the events of my day with, and none of them were musicians. Well, besides Pops. Sometimes it was tough to talk to him about music things when they were going good for me, because he wasn't having the best luck in his career at the time. He's always supported me, though. No matter what."

"Of course he has. He's so proud of you," I said. "I get the sense he's not too fond of me." I immediately hated that I'd said that. God, I was so nervous.

"He likes you, Boone. He's just...he's old school. He'll ride your ass before he'll compliment you. He thinks you sing even better than John, and that's a huge compliment. For him, the sun rises and sets with your grandfather."

"And my grandmother." Now I was flitting around the subject that really had me jumpy. Gran always texted me back right away, she was always there when I needed her, but these past couple of weeks since she and Bruce had been spending time together, it seemed as if her replies came later and later, or not at all, like today. This whole canceling the flight I'd booked for her, changing plans at the last minute…that wasn't like her. I had no idea what we were walking into and that had me jumpy.

I fully realized that I was a thirty-year-old man who shouldn't need his grandmother at every turn, but ever since Papa died two years ago and I got sick, she'd been my rock. I wasn't sure I was ready to share her with Bruce, but that wasn't up to me.

"Right," Shane said, and his brows drew together, a look I was quite familiar with. "Guess things are going to be different, huh?"

"Yeah. It's hard to imagine."

Telling Shane my worries, showing him my tender underbelly, was a terrifying prospect. How could someone like him —someone who *hadn't* curled up in a ball and wailed about his band quitting, when I would have at the very least gone on an epic bender and probably ended up in a diabetic coma— want to hear my petty bullshit? How could I even consider leaning on him when he had such bigger issues to deal with?

I knew already, after this short courtship, that I couldn't bear to see disappointment in his gaze. I wouldn't impose. I'd just have to get over my Gran issues myself and be worthy of his attention. I'd spent my whole life trying not to be an imposition on anyone. I'd done my best since becoming an orphan. If I was good enough, people would love me. It was as simple as that. I didn't want their pity, I wanted their respect, and I planned to work harder than ever to earn it from Shane.

A few minutes later, Shane made the turn onto SE 13th Avenue in the Sellwood District and looked for parking near Gino's. I hadn't spent a whole lot of time in Portland proper, and I was glad he was driving. And parking. He even made parking sexy.

"Man, how'd you get so good at parallel parking? I couldn't park a golf cart in these spots, much less this big van."

He grinned. "What did you call it? The van life? I got used to parking that thing. Anywhere you go in LA, you're likely to have to parallel park, right?"

So capable. "Yeah, well, I'm that brat who will hire a driver or book a Lyft if the place I'm going doesn't have valet parking. It makes me anxious." I bit the inside of my cheek. Why did I have to open my mouth? I should just sit and look pretty tonight before Shane really figured out what he'd gotten himself into with me.

"Makes sense. There's enough angst trying to drive in LA, much less worrying about parking. If it stresses you out, you should let someone else drive. I love driving. Traffic and that stuff doesn't bother me. I'm happy to be your personal Lyft anytime." He turned and winked at me as he put the van in park. "We're here, Monsieur Collins." He leaned over and presented his gorgeous lips for a kiss, but my dumb ass hesitated.

"Hey," he said, reaching for me once more. "What's wrong, Boone?"

The way his face got all soft when he looked at me was too much. It was so much easier when he was the Metal Menace. This sweet side to Shane Butler had me unsteady, and I knew I needed to get it together before we went inside.

"Nothing. Thank you for driving." I reached for the door, but he put a hand on my arm.

"Boone, talk to me."

"I'm just—" My phone beeped and I checked my glucose monitor. "Wow, a little low. Let's get inside. The sooner I get some food in me, the more human I'll be. Sorry."

"Don't apologize. Wait for me. I don't want you to fall."

He hopped out his door and walked around to open my door, which was probably a good thing since my legs felt like jelly.

"Thanks," I said, pushing up on my toes to kiss his cheek.

That warm smile was back, and he stared at me for a moment before he put his hand at my lower back and gave me a little caress.

"My pleasure. And hey, I'll follow your lead with the grandparents, okay? Whatever you want to do. I know this is a big deal for you. John hasn't been gone that long. It's probably weird seeing her with someone else, even if it's Pops."

My breath caught and my eyes burned. He knew exactly what to say. God, this was too good to be true. I blinked back the fucking tears and chinned and chested the fuck up. I didn't dare speak though. I didn't trust my voice.

We went inside and Shane stood beside me as he let the hostess know we had a reservation. When she went to check on our table, he slid his hand along the waistband of my pants. He leaned close to my ear and spoke in that low voice that made me break out in goose bumps.

"Goddamn, Collins. These pants are fucking glorious on you. I've never seen a man wear pants as well as you do."

Heat rushed to my face and neck, and I avoided turning to look at him for fear I'd combust.

"Keep that up and you'll see me *not* wearing them later."

I reached behind my back and squeezed his hand as the hostess returned.

"Your party has already arrived. Follow me."

We strolled through the crowded restaurant and more than a few people did double takes as we passed them. A few even whipped out phones and took pics of us together.

"The interwebs are going to implode," Shane muttered, "in three...two...one."

I turned to laugh at what he said, and then saw some very

excited fans holding back their squeals as they tapped furiously on their phones.

"You didn't happen to mention to your new manager today that she may be fielding a bazillion calls for comment tonight, did you?"

"Did *you* call Dickie?"

I laughed loudly, throwing my head back. "Should we give them a show?"

Shane shook his head but he was grinning. "Watch this." He placed his hand at my lower back and bent to whisper in my ear. "We might regret this later, but I'm having way too much fun to stop now."

I turned and gazed up at him, fluttering the eyelashes just a bit. I placed a hand on his chest and pressed up on my toes to whisper back. "I'm not wearing any underwear. Any more fun and it won't just be the hickeys showing." I kissed his cheek for good measure.

We turned the corner and were faced with the sight of our grandparents kissing in the booth.

That cooled our ardor.

"Gran," I said as we approached the table.

She pulled away from the kiss and didn't even blush, didn't seem concerned about being caught.

"There you boys are. Come. Sit." She patted the seat next to her, which meant there was only space for me and Shane would have to sit next to Bruce. That made me sad. We were a new development, of course, but I guess I'd pictured us sitting next to each other, holding hands under the table in solidarity.

I glanced at Shane, and his scowl was back.

I slid in next to Gran and hugged her, kissing her cheek as Shane and Bruce hugged. I extended my hand to shake Bruce's, and he looked at it in surprise for a minute before he awkwardly shook it like he might an overzealous fan's. Shane, of course, had to show me up by being totally cool when he took Vera Jean's hand and graciously held it in both of his as he bowed to her. Man, he was good at this.

"Boys, we have news," Vera Jean said. She barely waited for our asses to hit the seat before she grinned and linked arms with Bruce.

"By all means," I said, thinking we had some pretty big news of our own.

The septuagenarians turned to each other and grinned before turning back to face us.

"Bruce is moving in with me."

My face was about to break under the strain of holding up my smile.

"Wow," was the clever response I came up with. I glanced at Shane, but he just turned a concerned expression on his grandfather.

"That's right! I'm selling my condo, Shane, and I'm donating all the proceeds to the Collins Foundation. It feels good to do something in John's name."

"Pops?" Shane leaned a little closer and said quietly, "That's your nest egg. Are you sure?"

"Never been surer," he said, turning to smile at Vera Jean, who had such a starry-eyed gaze when she smiled back at him.

Shane looked to me with his eyebrows raised, as if he was struggling with what to say as well.

"When?" I finally asked, not sure I wanted the answer.

"I signed a contract with an agent two days ago and the movers are packing up my stuff tomorrow." He leaned his elbows on the table and said the next specifically to Shane. "Life is short, son. Why wait?"

Shane held his gaze for a moment, and then faced me. "That's very true." He kind of shrugged with one shoulder and waited for me to respond.

"Well, maybe I should get the agent's number," I said with

a laugh. "Guess I'm going to be in the market for a new home." Sure, the laughter came out a little manic, but it wasn't the worst response I could have made.

"Oh, dear boy, there's no rush. Whenever you're ready." Gran patted my hand, and I swore I felt my cheeks crumbling like one of those dry skin commercials. Any second now my face would be a pile of rubble on the table.

Twenty-One

S hane

I had to do something, but what, I had no clue. Boone was about to crack and I couldn't stand to watch it happen.

"You sure you want movers, Pops? I can come help as soon as I'm done up here, which could be anytime."

Bruce frowned at him. "What happened?"

I didn't want to make this about me, but perhaps the deflection would give Boone a moment to recover.

"Dean and the guys quit. Tucker's going to play drums for a pop star, and Dean and Drew are going to attempt to recapture their emo youth playing pop punk."

"Jesus Almighty," Bruce breathed. "Can't say I saw that coming. You talk to Jeff?"

"Actually, I didn't. My new manager Audra let him know his services were no longer needed, and Slade fired him. Seems I walked into a bit of a minefield and Jeff knew about it, but it's all good. I'm working with Lydia, trying to decide which direction I want to go. I've got to set up an appointment with the label to discuss my future with them. In the meantime..." I smiled at Boone, who'd gone from fake smiling to lost puppy in the span of a few moments. I nudged his foot under the table, and he snapped out of it. "I've enlisted Boone and the twins to play Rocktoberfest with me. Instead of a Wicked Soul set, we thought we'd play the old tunes. You know, California, Brothers... What do you think?"

"Oh, Shane, that's wonderful!" Vera Jean said. "I'd love for you two to make music together. And that brings us to the other thing we wanted to discuss with you. The Collins Foundation benefit. We'd like you both to perform, of course, but we've lined up Blackened to be the house band this year, and we're going to invite a bunch of old friends to perform with them. We've already asked Lydia, Morrison, and Leland, and we're going to ask Aldous Archer and Ozzy if he's feeling up to it. Bruce is going to organize the rehearsals, and I'll handle the invites and the usual details. It'll be an extra-special occasion." Vera Jean put her hands on the table, and Bruce took them in his.

"It'll be our engagement party," he said softly.

I watched Boone's face morph into horror as he noticed the giant rock on Vera Jean's ring finger.

"Congratulations," I said, but my inflection was off, and it sounded as if I was asking if the congratulations were merited rather than bestowing it on the happy couple.

The server appeared just then with a basket of bread and asked for our drink orders. I watched Boone push his hair back with a shaky hand.

"Actually, yeah, can we get a couple of cranberry juices and can you bring out an appetizer of, what, uh..." I looked down at the menu. "Bring us some mozzarella sticks and wings, please? As soon as you can?"

Boone had gone as white as the tablecloth, and Vera Jean patted his arm.

"Boone?" she asked quietly.

"I'm...congratulations." He gave her a closed-lipped smile.

She nodded and turned back to Pops. He gazed into her eyes and they kissed once more.

"I'll be right back," Boone muttered, and he stood from the booth. He caught himself on the edge of it to break his fall and then stumbled down the hallway to the restroom.

Vera Jean's gaze followed him and for a moment it looked as if she thought to follow him.

"I'm going to go too. It was a long drive out here."

She opened her mouth to speak and then smiled at me knowingly before turning to smile at Pops.

I trotted after Boone and found him just inside the men's room, leaning against the wall and trying to get his breathing under control.

"Babe," I whispered. I locked the door behind us and took him in my arms. "How much of this is your blood sugar and how much is from those fucking bombs they just dropped?"

He stepped back and held up his phone. His glucose monitor showed him at a dangerously low level.

"Here's what we're going to do," I said, brushing his hair away from his now sweaty face. "We're going to go out there and you're going to eat. Once we get a little food in you, you should feel a little better, but if not, you just say the word and we'll go, okay? I'll take you back and—"

"I swear, Shane, I'm not doing this on purpose. I tried...it was a shock, but I swear I didn't mean to make a scene. I'm sorry."

Tears poured down his face as his whole body started to shake. He hugged himself and started to slide down the wall, but I caught him.

"Do you need to go to the hospital? This is bad, babe."

"No, please, just help me get it together. *Please*, Shane."

"It's going to be okay, everything's going to be okay. Just breathe with me, baby. Just breathe." I held him against me, wanting to scream from the helplessness.

There was a knock on the door.

"Mr. Butler? It's your server. Ms. Collins said you might need the juice?"

I opened the door and took the glass of juice from him. "Thanks," I said, closing and locking the door again. "Here, Boone. Drink some of this."

He reached for the glass with both hands, and I held it for him as he brought it to his mouth. He took a couple of sips and then he started coughing. Before I could ask, he pulled his inhaler out of his pocket and took two puffs. Once he stopped coughing, he leaned back against the wall and reached for the glass again.

"You're doing great," I murmured. "So great. You're going to be okay." My words were calm but I was freaking out. This was too close. I thought to myself, what if he'd been alone? And then my chest cracked open.

He *was* alone.

Vera Jean's relationship with my grandfather was absolutely perfect for them, and they deserved all the happiness, but Boone had isolated himself from everyone else, including, to an extent, his bandmates, who had no idea how sick he was. If he moved out of Vera Jean's, he would be on his own whenever they weren't on tour. I know he was determined to do this all by himself and not let the world know, but *I* knew, and I would not abandon him. I would stand by him, take care of him if he insisted on pretending he had it all under control.

I *wanted* to take care of him.

"I'm sorry, Shane—"

"Don't ever apologize to me for being sick," I said in the calmest voice I could muster. "But you let me in, so whether you like it or not, I'm going to take care of you, Boone. You're not going to go through this on your own, okay? Don't even try to be stubborn about it, because I'm more stubborn than you."

He chuckled against my chest. "You are pretty stubborn."

"Damn right, I am. I take care of what's mine, remember? And you're mine. I *want* you to be mine."

He finally looked up at me, and my previous conversation with Lydia came back to me. Those eyes. I had no clue whether or not he'd ever had therapy to deal with the trauma from his childhood, but there was no doubt that the scared little boy who'd watched his mother die, who'd spent hours with her afterward, alone...he was still in there. And he'd had the rug pulled out from under him just now, sorta like I had the day before, although my situation was a lot less traumatic. I was going to be fine. I was going to make sure Boone would be fine too.

"I hate that you're seeing me like this," he said, reaching for a paper towel to dry his face. "Once upon a time, I could handle my shit."

"You still can," I said. "Taking care of you doesn't mean doing it all for you. You'll lean on me when you need to, and together we can figure out how to get you stable. Diabetes is hard to manage, especially by yourself. Lean on me, Boone. Let me take care of you."

"Goddammit, Butler," he said. "This would all be so much easier if you still hated me."

"But I don't. I never did. And it's not going to be easy, especially since those two out there are trying to age us before our time."

I knew that would get a laugh from him. "I found a gray hair! The morning after their date. Can you believe it?"

I shrugged and deadpanned, "I wouldn't know about that."

That was what he needed to let go. He threw his arms around my neck and held on tight as he took several deep breaths.

"I don't know how this happened, but thank God for you, Shane."

"Well, don't thank Him yet," I said, pulling away from him. "We still have to get through this dinner. I might clobber Pops with a damn mozzarella stick if he keeps making eyes at your gran."

"Seriously, how are we the adults?"

"I don't know. I am pretty mature, though."

"Right," he said with a snort. "You're the eldest." His smile slipped. "I feel like there have been a lot of bombs at that table already tonight. Maybe we don't tell them about us yet. And please don't take that as anything other than my messy ass can't handle any more drama tonight."

"You know I like you messy. Don't worry about it."

"You'll still call me babe?"

I kissed him once, just enough to take him out of his head and hopefully get us through the rest of this meal. "You ready to do this, babe?"

He smiled—not that face-breaking fake one he'd had plastered on—and took a deep breath.

"I am now."

When we made it back to the table, the hors d'oeuvres had arrived and our grandparents looked admonished. We took our seats, and I hated that I couldn't sit beside him without making a big fuss.

"Did the server find you?" Vera Jean asked, and she gave Boone a pointed look. It was obvious that she was trying to help him save face.

"He did, thank you." And then he turned to Bruce. "I'm newly diabetic, and I'm having trouble getting my sugars managed."

So fucking brave. I couldn't believe he'd just admitted that to the man he said he worried didn't like him. It was a rare moment that Boone allowed himself to appear vulnerable, and I knew how difficult it had to have been for him to make that admission.

Pops's expression melted to one of sympathy. "I feel your pain. I don't think I would have been able to get mine managed without Shane's help. He took over planning all of my meals, got me exercising. I finally got in shape at sixty-nine years old, thanks to him." He patted my shoulder, turned back to Boone and, bless him, he spent the rest of the meal talking about tips and tricks that helped us get his diabetes under control. This allowed Boone to eat his salad and salmon and get himself under control.

Vera Jean kept looking over at him, and I was glad to see her paying closer attention to her grandson. She'd pat his hand, move his hair back from his shoulder, or give his back a gentle rub. I hoped they were able to have a good conversation in private about all of these changes.

"So where are you staying?" I asked Pops.

"We got a room at the Crystal Hotel."

"Did you need me to come pick you up tomorrow?" Boone asked Vera Jean.

"Oh, thank you, dear boy, but we drove up here. That's why I canceled the flight, which, thank you for setting that up."

"You drove? What did you drive?" I asked them. Pops's car was old. I hated the idea of him driving at all, much less in that old hooptie.

"We brought the Corvette," Vera Jean said with a sneaky grin. "Bruce had it serviced and it drove like a dream."

Boone and I looked at each other in shock. Oh, seventy-agers. They were going to make us both old before our time. Thankfully the server came up at that moment, and I handed him my card. We needed to get out of here before this conversation went further south.

"Great," I finally said. "Well, Boone and I should head back." I stood up, feeling my hold on the Metal Menace slipping. "Boone has an early day tomorrow."

"I hope your sessions are going well?" Vera Jean asked Boone as he leaned over and kissed her cheek.

"Good. Yes, thank you."

"We'll see you boys tomorrow," Pops said, standing and giving me a hug.

"Be safe," I said to him, giving him a raised eyebrow.

He grinned bashfully. "Sure thing."

I fought the desire to roll my eyes. I needed to get Boone in the car and get him back to the lodge. I needed to hold him. It would go a long way toward making everything okay again.

We made it out to the parking lot, gave more hugs and kisses, and we went our separate ways. I walked beside Boone and then opened his door to the van. He gave me a small smile and climbed into the passenger seat. He turned to me and sighed.

"She didn't comment on the hickey."

"Hard to notice when she's sucking face with my pops."

He exhaled out his nose and nodded.

Fuck, I hated to see him so sad. I handed him my phone. "Play something."

He tapped the screen and frowned. "What's your password?"

"Boone."

I put the van in drive and pulled out of the parking spot. I glanced over at him when I realized he hadn't started the music.

He was holding the phone against his chest with his eyes closed.

"You good?"

He nodded, but he didn't speak.

A moment later "Still Remains" from Stone Temple Pilots came on. Only one of the most beautiful love songs ever written.

"Perfect," I said as I pulled onto SE Tacoma which would lead us toward the 205 Interstate and back to Bolder Breed.

"It's always been a favorite," he murmured. "Hits harder tonight."

My heart bottomed out. Sweet Boone. He was so sad, and I had no idea if I could be enough for him, but dammit I was going to give it my all.

We were mostly quiet the rest of the drive home. He'd queued up more similar songs, many lesser-known songs that were brilliant. How did I not know we vibed so well together? How had he been under my nose this whole time, and I was too busy letting my ego keep him in a blind spot?

No more. My eyes were open. My heart was ready.

I parked the van and turned to find him snoozing in the seat, his knees pulled up to his chest. Like a child curling up for safety.

I tried to open and shut my door quietly, and when I opened his, he sat up with a start, letting his legs down as he looked around, confused.

"Come here," I said, ready to carry him.

He smiled sleepily. "Thanks for driving." He held my hand as he stepped down and came to me as I pulled him in close. "Stay with me?"

"I was hoping you'd ask," I answered, kissing his forehead. Together we climbed the steps to the lodge, and then the stairs to his room. At his door, he unlocked it and stepped inside. He pulled his clothes off and climbed into bed with his back to me.

He'd told the truth. He was sans boxers.

I stripped down to mine, crawled in next to him and touched his back.

"Spoon, please?"

"I was hoping you'd ask," I said again. I curled up to his body and wrapped my arms around him, loving how he snuggled against me and sighed.

"Shane?"

"Yeah, babe?" I nuzzled the back of his neck through his hair and sighed happily.

He didn't answer right away, as if he was trying to think of the right thing to say.

"I don't know why you're still here, but I'm so fucking grateful it scares me."

"Get used to it." I felt the pull of sleep and kissed his shoulder before settling in to what had become my favorite place.

He exhaled a shaky breath and whispered so low, I'm not sure he intended me to hear. "I don't know if I can."

TWENTY-TWO

B oone

I was grateful the next morning that Shane was gone before I woke up. He left a note saying he'd gone to the gym and to text him when I wanted him to come work on the song. He signed it with a little heart that looked a little squiggly, as if Shane wasn't used to drawing them. So cute. It was just as well. I needed the space to gather my wits.

The previous night had been a trainwreck.

Our grandparents were shacking up.

They were engaged.

I needed to leave the nest, which had been the only place I'd ever felt safe in my life.

I needed to grow the fuck up about my new normal and stop pretending like it wasn't happening.

I'd been so afraid once I'd realized in the bathroom at the restaurant that my blood sugar had gone so low I was about to keel over, but then Shane was there with juice and the comfort of his embrace. The doctor had warned me that until we got things under control, I could experience something called dysglycemia, and last night I'd realized that it could hit when I was least prepared to handle it alone.

I had to be ready to ask for and receive help from the people I trusted.

That's why I decided I needed to let the twins in on what was going on.

"I hate everything."

Okay, not everything. I loved being with Shane, even when things were falling down around me. My fucking Gran had a new honey, and though I was mature enough to know she still loved me and that I should give her the space to enjoy herself, I was kind of in shock about how quickly she'd jumped into this.

Though I was asked from time to time about my parents and everything that happened when I was a kid, I never allowed myself to go there. I had a prepared statement, one Vera Jean coached me on as a child.

"My parents had their issues. I'm grateful I had my grand-parents to take care of me." I refused to answer questions about what I remembered. I did remember. I remembered every second from the moment I found my mother on the floor in the bathroom to the moment the fire department broke down the door. I remembered holding Mommy's hand in the dark thinking at least this time she wasn't crying, or bleeding, as she would be after fights with my father. She'd been so still though. So cold.

So no, I didn't ever speak about that experience, but it was always lurking close to the surface of my consciousness. It haunted me in my sleep. It drove me to work so hard using the talent I'd been born with to become a master at my craft so people couldn't ignore me, perform so *well* that people wouldn't leave.

I needed to get past the feeling that being with Bruce meant my Gran was leaving me. I didn't doubt Bruce was head over heels for my Gran, and I knew he would do his best to take care of her, so my discomfort was really my own. I'd become too dependent on her, and it was time I took care of myself.

Which had me worrying about Shane. I had to be careful not to put too much on him. He had his own issues, and I didn't want this blossoming relationship to get marred by codependent behavior.

Listen to me and my big words. Okay, really I wanted to spend every night in his arms and let him take care of me. He was so good at it. Who'd a thunk?

We were in a bubble up here, though. We both had careers to worry about, and his was at a major crossroads.

I could only control so much, so right now, I was going to go down and meet my bandmates and tell them the truth. And eat, so last night didn't happen again.

Before I hopped in the shower, I checked my phone and found a lengthy text from Gran.

Dear Boy, I know last night was hard for you in many ways. I hope you are feeling better this morning. It was kind of Shane to take care of you. I'm glad the two of you seem to be getting along better. I love you very much.

P.S. Love bites are tough to cover up. I never found a good concealer that would work. Perhaps a nice scarf next time?

. . .

I burst out laughing as my eyes filled with tears. Despite the radical changes in my life, she would still be there to impart her wisdom, and how like her to not embarrass me but to let me know she cared, and that I hadn't gotten one past her.

I'll keep that in mind.

Her response came a moment later.

May I assume it was Shane?

Of course she'd know. I was so moony-eyed around him.

You were right. He's a good one.

I barked out a laugh at her response.

Of course I was right. He comes from good stock. Take care of each other.

I knew she'd be happy for me. I owed it to her to be the same.

I found Annie and Bran sitting in the mess hall, heads bobbing together as they watched a video on Annie's phone.

"Boone! You gotta see this. It's video of Blinding Light

playing at Rocktoberfest last year. We've been doing our research. Come sit."

"Yeah," Brandon said. "We're already making a schedule of who we want to see! Friday is F-Holes and Flightless, and Warrior Black is playing. This is going to be so rad."

"Let me grab food," I said, my heart pounding. God, I didn't want to tell them. We had the perfect thing going. We were best friends. We got along great. Would they start treating me different? Ugh, I hated this.

"Morning, Boone," Felix said as I approached the counter. "What can I get you? We've got waffles, and I made some pastries—"

Chin and chest up and out, motherfucker. "Whatever would be good for a Type 2 diabetic who's trying to get his blood sugar under control." I gave him a smile that didn't quite make it to my whole face.

"Oh, shit, Boone. I had no idea."

"Yeah, because I haven't told people yet. But I'd love some help."

"Sure, sure. No problem. Okay, let's get you some eggs… how do you like them? Right, you like them fried. And here's some fruit, and do you want some sausage? This should give you some good energy to keep you going today."

My eyes burned, and I blew out a breath. That wasn't so bad. "Thank you."

"Yeah, man. Anytime. My parents are diabetic, and I've had to overhaul their diet. It's an adjustment, but eventually you won't even notice. If you want, I can make up some meal plans for you for when you leave, some ideas based on what I know you like."

"That would be great. Thank you."

He grinned. "Sure. Here you go," he said, sliding the eggs on my plate. "Take care, drink lots of water, and take some of those oatmeal muffins with you for later. They're not too high in carbs and they've got four grams of protein. Oh, and here, take these nuts."

I'd been so worried about people fussing over me, but Felix was all business. He wasn't pitying me.

"Thank you, Felix. I'm not good at this."

He shrugged and gave me a knowing smile. "Of course you're not. Your lifestyle is the antithesis of taking care of yourself. This is what I do for a living, and I love to feed people what they need to make their bodies work *for* them rather than against them. I'll get you those meal plans, okay?"

"I'm so grateful Morrison has you up here. Thank you again."

"Who do you think got *his* ass in gear?"

I laughed at his attitude. He'd made it easy for me to accept his help. Maybe I'd been stupid not to tell folks.

I took my tray over and set it down across from the twins. They looked up with raised eyebrows.

"Good morning," I said, and for the first time ever, I was nervous to talk to my bandmates.

"How did it go last night?" Annie asked. She put a hand over mine. "Was it weird?"

I sighed and picked up my fork. I made myself take a bite of eggs before I spoke. "It was, but probably not for the reasons you think." *Here goes.* "I have something I need to tell you both."

They leaned back together, their hands on the table in the same exact position.

"We went too far with Shane, huh? Damn, I'm sorry," Bran said.

"It was the Taylor Swift comment, wasn't it? Or the orgy bus visual. I figured the Metal Menace would be able to take it."

I grinned at them as I chewed and swallowed more eggs.

"No, you were perfect. It's *me* that's not... I fucked up, guys, and I owe you an apology."

They looked at each other.

"What is it?"

Deep breath. "You guys have been so good about the drinking, and I appreciate that you were willing to—"

"Are you breaking up with us?" Bran asked.

"What? *No!* What the fuck!"

Bran shrugged. "I just thought maybe it's in the air, since Shane's band broke up with him."

"No, it's not you, it's me—"

"You *are* breaking up with us," Annie said. "Shit, Boone, I thought—"

"*I'm sick, okay*? And I should have told you, but I didn't, and I made it weird."

"You're sick?" Annie's voice was quiet. "What...what's wrong?"

"I saw the doctor when we got home from tour. I hadn't told you guys, but I'd been feeling really shitty. I passed out a couple of times and—"

"Are you *serious*?" They both shouted over each other. "When? We were with you—"

"In the bathroom at that pub in Liverpool. And in Boston when we came back from Europe. In my hotel room. I'm diabetic, and I have something called dysglycemia, which makes my sugar drop really low, and since I hate to eat before we perform, and then I don't drink enough water, it got bad. I'm on medication but it's not under control yet. I'm trying."

They both stared at me, not speaking. And staring. And not speaking.

"You're okay, though? I mean, you're going to be. Right?" Annie asked, her voice shaky.

"Eventually. I'm not very good at this but I'm trying."

"But you're okay though?" Bran asked.

"Yeah, mostly."

They sat frozen for several beats as I waited for them to say something. Anything.

"Okay." They looked at each other, Annie nodded, then they turned back to stare at me. Bran threw a piece of potato at me and it pinged off my forehead.

"What the—!"

Annie threw a grape at my chest.

Bran threw a strawberry that landed in my hair.

"Come on, you guys—"

"How dare you?" Annie threw a muffin, which was dense, and it hit me in the eye.

"Ow, *fuck*. I'm sorry!"

"And you didn't say anything?" Bran threw an ice cube from his juice. "You could have fucking died, asshole!"

"Guys! Wait—"

And then all I could do was put my hands up as they pelted me with more ice cubes.

"Whoa! What the—"

Shane came in then and caught me as I nearly fell backward off the bench, trying to get away from the vicious twins.

"I told them," I said as an ice cube hit me in the lip. "Motherfucker, that hurt—"

"Wait! Are you saying Shane knew before us? What the actual *fuck*, Boone!" At that, Annie stopped with the semi-playful throwing and stormed out of the mess hall.

Bran watched her go, and then threw one last piece of pineapple, which hit me in the nose and splashed in my eye. It burned like hell.

"I'm sorry," I said, as Bran rushed out after his sister.

"That could have gone better," Shane said. He had a napkin and was trying to clean off my face. I stopped his hand.

"No, they're right. I have to go after them," I said,

squeezing his hand. "Tell Felix I'll clean this up." And I dashed out the door while I shoved the rest of the sausage in my mouth.

Bran and Annie were standing by the fountain outside the lodge, arguing with each other.

"Guys, wait, please. Let me explain."

"I don't get how we're supposed to be your best friends, and you tell your booty call before us," Annie said, then crossed her arms over her chest.

"He found me in the bathroom our first night here, when I went upstairs? He thought... Shit. He thought I was on drugs. I had to tell him. I needed his help getting the wrapper open on my stupid protein bar." This was not going well. I knew they'd be upset, but I didn't think it would be like this.

"Jesus," Bran said. "Why didn't you tell us? We could have helped you—"

"That's exactly why I didn't! I *hate* this, I swear. I hate having anyone know I can't handle myself. I don't like it one bit. But I had another close call last night, and I realized it's not fair, me not telling you. As ridiculous as this has gotten, I might keel over onstage and you won't have any idea what's wrong with me."

"Boone," Annie said, and her attitude melted away to concern. "If you're sick, maybe you should be resting. Take some time off—"

"No! We're on a roll, Annie. We need to stick to our schedule. Out of sight will mean out of mind, you know? We can't afford—"

"For you to get sicker," Bran said. "Come on, man. This is serious. Should we even be doing Rocktoberfest?"

"Yes, we absolutely should, and we're finishing this album. We're halfway done already and Morrison is happy with our progress. Let's finish it up and then we can rehearse with

Shane. I'll rest, I promise. I told Felix, and he's going to help me with food—"

"You told him before us too?" Annie narrowed her eyes. Man, I was in hot water with her.

"Just right now," I said, gesturing toward the mess hall. "Come on, please? Don't be mad. I'm trying to do this right, I swear."

"Doing it right would have been telling your best friends first, but whatever," Bran said. He tilted his head up and looked at the sky.

"You're right. I'm sorry." This was awful. Worse than I thought. "I thought once I got on medication and stopped drinking it would, like, go away. I've been exercising...some, not as much as I should, and, well, I try to sleep but it's hard." In trying to pretend this wasn't happening, I'd kept a big deal from my best friends. All I could do was hope they'd forgive me and not decide to leave me.

"Instead, you've been letting that hot man in there suck on your neck," Annie said, rolling her eyes. "Probably other things, too."

I opened my mouth to answer but all that came out was a snort.

"At least there's a good reason you quit drinking and smoking," Bran said with a sigh. "I thought you were just going through a phase or something, like that time you went vegan for a week." He turned to look at Annie with an eyebrow raised. "Guess we should quit smoking, too. If it can happen to Mr. Perfect Pants over here, it could happen to us."

She exhaled with a groan. "Fuck, I know. I thought we had at least until we were forty to fuck around. Guess we just found out."

"I'm sorry, guys. I really thought I could handle it and you'd never have to know."

"Do you have to give yourself shots and shit?" Bran asked, shuddering.

"No, at least not yet. I've got this," I said, pulling up my shirt to show my glucose monitor that I'd moved to my stomach. My arm was getting itchy. "It's read by an app on my phone. I'm taking medicine, but I need to call the doctor when we get back to LA because it's not cutting it. I don't know what's going to happen, but I'm going to follow doctor's orders, I swear."

Annie finally dropped her arms and she put a hand on mine. "I know it's scary. I'm sorry you've been going through this on your own. Asshole. You should have told us. We've always taken care of each other."

I put my arms around them and they returned the gesture.

"You guys are my world. I love your crazy asses."

Bran elbowed me in the gut, then apologized. "Guess I have to be careful. No more wrestling, huh?"

"I mean, as long as we're careful."

"God, you're both children," Annie said. "Is Shane at least being smart about this shit?"

I grinned. "He is. He knows how to take care of me."

"I bet he does," Bran said. He started with the *bow-chicka-wow-wows* and I jumped on his back. He spun me around, and we both went down in the bushes while Annie screamed at us to stop fucking around.

Shane appeared at her side while Bran and I cracked up. The two of them shook their heads at us.

"I hope you know what you're getting into," Annie said to him as she took off toward the studio. "Come on, dorks. We've got an album to record."

Bran gave me a double tittie twister and then ran before I could get him back.

"Bran, you butt munch. That's going to bruise," I said, rubbing my nipples. Shane reached down to help me up and then pulled some twigs out of my hair. "Great. They'll match my other ones," I said, smiling up at him. "By the way, Gran saw. She suggested I wear a scarf next time."

His eyes widened. "What else did she say?"

"That you're a good man. That you come from good stock."

He sighed. "Guess I should reach out to Pops."

"You probably should. Especially if you plan to leave any more marks on me." I gave him my most winning smile and he shook his head, but he was smiling.

"What *am* I getting myself into?"

I wrapped my arms around him. "Me later?"

He licked his lips and bent down to kiss me. "I was hoping you'd ask."

"At this point, you can assume."

"Oh." He seemed surprised by that. "I'll still ask, though. I'm all about consent. I got a rep to protect." He held up a paper bag. "I grabbed your muffins and cleaned up the mess from you hooligans."

He slung his arm around my shoulder as we walked toward the studio.

"Actually," I said, "your reputation is that you're the Metal Menace, a stubborn perfectionist control freak. You keep this up, people are going to think you're a nice guy."

He sighed. "We can't have that."

Twenty-Three

S hane

I continued to be impressed by Boone. Not only had he faced the music and told other people about his illness, but he lived up to *his* reputation of being a wonder in the studio. His relentless pursuit of perfection was a little dizzying, but it was incredible to observe. At times he took Morrison's place at the board and moved things around like he was the fucking wizard behind the curtain. Morrison and Leland gave him feedback, but they mostly just did as instructed.

When it became my turn to play the slide part on the guitar, Boone turned that focus on me and I was a little intimidated. He perched on a footstool in front of where I sat on the couch, with his knees up and his hair tucked behind his ears.

"How do you want me to play it?" I asked as I warmed up on my Les Paul. It was one Pops had given me and it was a favorite of my collection.

"Here's the part." He picked up his Strat and proceeded to play a more complicated riff than I was expecting. I loved watching his hands as he played, his graceful fingers gliding along the fret board with ease. I had a much more caveman style than he did. Not that I couldn't play quick or delicate, but I got a little more percussive, like Pops did. I guess I took after him.

"That's...wow. Okay."

"What do you think?" he asked. "I thought the slide would take it just a little bit further."

"I agree," I said. "But what if you simplified it a bit and added some vibrato here." I played through what he showed me, making a few changes.

He watched with interest, then he reached over and moved my finger on a string. "Try it again."

It was so natural for him to touch me, and so unusual for me to accept being corrected like that. If I wasn't already under his spell, I might worry about this change of heart in me.

He was leaning so close to me, his hair fell forward and brushed my fingers, which frustrated him. He pulled a hair tie off his wrist and did some complicated twisty thing with his hair, piling it on top of his head. He picked up his Strat again and played along with me, watching my fingers move.

"It sounds so much better when you play it."

"Maybe it's the guitar. You try it." I handed my Gibson to Boone, and he played a few scales.

"Man, your action is high on this. What gauge strings do you use?"

"Right now it's got an eleven set, but I changed these two strings to thirteens. I use this guitar specifically for playing slide. I've fucked around with it a lot to get it where I want it."

He grinned at me and noodled around a bit. Then he played the part again and his eyes lit up.

"It sounds so good," he said, playing it a few more times, and then he handed it back to me. "Now try it with the slide. I feel so clunky when I try to play slide. You do it."

"Clunky is not a term I'd ever think of to describe your playing," I said, laughing as I slid the metal slide on my ring finger.

He tilted his head and smirked at me. "Thanks. All right. Let's hear it with the slide."

"Yes, sir."

He barked out a laugh and then brought his knees back up as he watched me play.

"Yes," he breathed. "Again."

Once I played the part through three times, Morrison was ready to record. I put on the headphones and listened to the tracks Bran, Annie, and Boone had already recorded. I let myself get lost in the dreamy tune. It was one where you wouldn't expect to hear a slide used, but that was the genius of it.

I played my bit and then looked up at Boone, who had his hands clasped in front of his chin. He was grinning like a loon, bouncing in his seat.

"Yes, yes, yes! That was..." He made the chef's kiss motion, and as soon as I set the guitar down, he bent forward and threw his arms around my neck, sprawling onto my lap. I laughed as he practically tackled me and wrapped my arms around him.

Annie groaned, Morrison *aww*ed, and Leland laughed.

"All right, lovebirds. Shall we record the vocals?"

Boone climbed off me and pulled me up from the couch. "This is going to be fun."

"Yeah, well, no *fun*ny business in the booth," Bran shouted. "There are children present."

"I know you're speaking of yourself," Annie said. "I'm forty-six seconds older than you and I'm no child."

"I was talking about Leland, but okay."

Leland continued laughing. "Man, those two kill me."

Boone grabbed his tablet and pulled me into the vocals booth. He handed me a pair of headphones and bounced on his toes.

"How do you want to do it?" he asked.

"I mean, I usually like a little more room to maneuver," I cracked, knowing full well the mics were hot.

"Gross!" the twins shouted in unison.

"I promise, no funny business," I said, raising my hands. "Why don't you sing it through and then once I hear the part, we can decide on the harmony."

He shivered. "I can't believe we're doing this," he whispered. "I can't wait to hear what we sound like together."

We put on our headphones and Morrison played the track.

I was not ready to be in an enclosed space with Boone and that fucking voice of his. He closed his eyes and started off low and sultry with the first verse, and I broke out in goose bumps. Then he opened up when he got to the second verse, and I could hardly breathe. By the time he reached the chorus, there was so much emotion in his voice as he sang, my heart squeezed in my chest. I thought I couldn't take any more, but then the section where I'd played the slide part came on and he opened his eyes and smiled at me, a bit out of breath himself.

When the lyrics came back in, he belted out his soul, emotions laid bare, and he climbed to a ridiculously high note, his voice cracking the tiniest bit more from emotion than from strain, it seemed, and then it abruptly ended on a gasp from him.

"Holy fuck," I said when it was done. "Jesus, Boone."

"I know, right?" He laughed, but then he coughed a few times, and he left the booth to get his inhaler.

I tried to catch my own breath.

My God, the man was talented. Hearing such a raw song had me thinking back to what Lydia had asked me, whether I'd grown. We were about to find out, because these vocals were not only going to push me to my own limits, but I was going to be singing a song about fucking *longing*, in a tiny booth, with a man who had gone from my nemesis and rival, to my lover to—God—my fucking musical soul mate in such a short time, I thought I must be suffering from emotional whiplash.

Which had me inspired.

Before Boone made it back to the booth, I whipped out my phone, opened my notes app and typed in the thoughts going through my head and heart.

You're so close I can't breathe
   I never want to leave
   But what if I do something rash
   With this emotional whiplash
   Will you follow me down
   and follow me in
   whatever the flesh
   whatever the sin
   You're so close I want more
   Don't ever shut the door
   Let's do something rash
   In this emotional whiplash

"You ready?" Boone shut the door behind him and handed me a bottle of water as I slid my phone back in my pocket.

"Ready," I said, but I meant way more than singing a song with him. I wanted to take leaps I thought I'd never make with another person after the last two men I'd loved let me fall.

I was ready to take Boone into my arms, into my home,

into my life, and never let him go. I was falling wildly in love with this vulnerable fucking sprite who could turn on the seduction with a flick of his hair and force me to my knees with the quirk of his lips. He was magical like the fucking fae in a fantasy book, and I had no defense against the influence he had on me. I didn't want to fight it, even though my head was telling me to slow the fuck down, dial it back a notch.

He took a sip of water and his lips on the bottle were almost my undoing. I pulled him against me, and he chuckled as he dribbled a little water on my shirt.

"Oops."

"Boone, I—"

"You guys ready?" Morrison cut in. "Want to take it from the top, Boone? Or just that part?"

"Give us a minute," Boone said into the mic. "Want to try without music first?"

"You tell me where you want me," I said.

He wiggled his eyebrows and then he got serious. "Go where you want," he said. He cleared his throat and he sang the part. I focused on reading the lyrics the first time, then I hummed along with him. The third time, I came in under him.

The fourth time he sang it, I pushed myself and managed to climb higher than him.

"Holy shit, Shane!" Leland shouted, while Morrison tossed his headphones to the side, grabbed his head and stomped around the control room shouting, *"Fuck yeah, fuck yeah, fuck yeah!"*

Boone pressed his hands to his mouth and laughed. "Goddammit, Butler. That was fucking *hot*!"

I tried to play it off. I hadn't been sure I could even hit those notes. I couldn't believe I'd tried it in front of Boone.

"I'm not even sure what I did," I laughed. "Which one did you like best?"

"All of it! Fucking hell! More! Can we do it both ways and you can like wrap him all around me like a fuzzy blanket, with a little phaser on top?"

"On it!"

"I could kiss you right now," Boone said to me. "I love the way we sound together."

I loved the way we *were* together.

"Who'd a thunk?" I said with a laugh.

"Oh my God! I was just saying that to myself this morning. Right? Who'd have ever thought they'd hear Butler and Collins on a record together? Who'd a thunk, indeed."

We stood there grinning at each other like loons, and it was almost as if a partnership was forming tangibly between us, right there in the vocals booth.

"All right. Let's fucking do this!"

Morrison was still doing some strange sort of dance moves like a deranged disco zombie in the control room when we heard the music come through the headphones. I watched Boone closely. He began to sing the part and when it was time for me to come in, I did the lower part first, and his face lit up when he heard us together through the headphones. He was grinning so wide, he made me grin, which made it hard to stay on pitch. Once again, he had the slightest amount of strain on that ludicrous note and when he dropped it, he started coughing again.

"Hey, maybe we should take a break?"

He shook his head. "No, let me just drink some tea and honey. Bran? You mind getting me some?"

Bran gave a thumbs up and dashed out of the studio.

Annie was watching us closely through the control room window, and I couldn't tell what her expression meant. She'd been awfully mad when she realized that I knew about Boone's illness. I hoped we could be cool. In no way did I want to come between Boone and his band. I liked the twins.

They were fucking insanely good musicians and, once I realized they weren't really going to cause me bodily harm, they were hilarious. But I could see concern in her gaze. I needed to assure her that I had Boone's best interest in mind.

"Have your tea," I said, kissing him on the cheek. "I'm going to go use the bathroom."

He nodded, his smile a little less bright. He had a hand pressed to his throat.

"Hey, how's your sugars?"

He looked at his phone. "They're okay. I'll be fine after I have my tea."

I squeezed his hand and stepped out of the booth.

"He good?" Annie asked me as I passed her.

"He's frustrated about that note. I told him he should take a break—"

"And he didn't listen. Shit. Okay. Time to implement distraction maneuvers."

I frowned and watched as Annie walked into the booth and she and Boone talked. She led Boone out of the booth and over to where her bass was plugged in. I turned on the mic to hear them.

"I'm just not sure about that break. Can we go over it together?"

"Yeah, let's go."

He picked up another bass and the two of them played the part over and over until I realized that, holy shit, she was genius. By asking him for help on something I'd already heard her play flawlessly, she got him out of his head and forced him to rest his voice. I wondered how long she'd been doing this with him. I'd have to study under her tutelage so I could be useful. Boone wouldn't take breaks for himself, but for his friends, he would go to the ends of the earth.

"Oh, good, she got him to stop," Bran said as he returned with the tea.

"This happen a lot?"

He shrugged. "Sometimes. Especially the past couple of recording sessions. He pushes himself so hard, strains his voice, and ever since he started feeling bad on our last tour, we've had to conspire against him."

"Brilliant. Feel free to include me in any conspiracies going forward."

Bran elbowed me. "You're all right, Butler. Glad you two finally got over yourselves. Man, the amount of mooning he did over you..." He shook his head.

"Mooning?"

"You know, 'I don't know why he hates me so much! He's so talented!' Blah blah blah. He'd make us watch interviews to see if you said anything about him. Shit. I probably shouldn't have told you that part."

"It's fine," I said. "I don't know why I always got asked about him. I tried not to talk shit, but people always gotta push."

"Because it's juicy, right? Especially after the Rock Hall gig. He wouldn't shut up about you after that."

"Yeah, well, it was mutual."

"Good. It's nice to see him happy. I just wish he'd told us about his illness. Damn. That's scary shit. I knew something was wrong, but he'd just blow off our questions. He can be a moody fuck anyway, but when he doesn't feel good and his body doesn't cooperate, he's inconsolable."

"Thanks for the warning."

He nodded. "I better get him his tea before it gets cold. Thanks, man," he said.

"For what?"

"For taking care of him when he wouldn't let us."

Bran went into the sound room and handed Boone his tea. The three of them were super tight-knit. I was happy he had that. It made me want more, too. Whatever I decided to do next, I definitely wouldn't settle for less than true bandmates, people I could trust to have my back.

Guess that meant getting used to letting people in.

Fuuuck.

My phone buzzed in my pocket and I pulled it out. "Hey, Pops. You good?"

"Sure, I'm great, only I had to hear the good news from Vera Jean. You and Boone, huh?"

"Yeah, it just sort of happened. Hadn't had a chance to talk to you about it. I was going to talk to you about it tonight when you two get here."

"And we kind of sprang our news on you last night without asking about you."

"Yeah, you did," I said, glad he realized it. "But we understood."

"Well, it's going to make for some interesting holidays, then, innit?"

"God, don't make it weird, old man. Weirder than it already is."

"I'm only taking the piss. I'm sorry about your band, son. What are you going to do?"

"I'm not sure. Right now I'm hanging out in the studio with Boone."

"Those ungrateful bastards. I'm sorry, son, but yer much better off without 'em." I loved when his Irish came out. I could tell he was truly pissed off then.

"It's all good. Boone and I...we're talking about doing some more stuff together. He asked me to join one of Stellar's songs. Pops, he's brilliant. He's stunning in the studio. I'm more excited about this Rocktoberfest gig now that I'm playing with him and his band. We gotta decide which California and Brothers tunes to add to the setlist. What do you think?"

The old man chuckled. "I think it'll be perfect whatever you lot decide to play. Ye'll make this old man really happy."

And when it came down to it, that's all I wanted. To make him happy, and to make Boone happy. If that meant going beyond my comfort zone, so be it. The Metal Menace was on hiatus.

Twenty-Four

Boone

Adulting sucks, especially when it means listening to medical professionals.

After the frustrating end of the vocal session with Shane, I made the decision to listen to my body. I told everyone I needed to call it a day and that I'd call and make a telephone appointment with my ENT.

They were shocked. And relieved.

Shane stepped out to take care of some more phone calls regarding his band's implosion, and I immediately felt his absence.

"I hate this." I stood before my band feeling like I failed them. The twins swooped in and hugged me.

"It's going to be all right. We have plenty of stuff we can get done that doesn't require you to sing. We need to record the rest of the instrument tracks and then we can start learning the songs for the Rocktoberfest show."

"Good point." I still hated it.

My doctor called me back right away and I told her what was going on.

"I'm sorry, Boone, but you know what I'm going to say. Complete vocal rest for two weeks minimum. I'm also sending you a referral to my colleague up there to have them scope your throat. Let's make sure we're dealing with strain and not something more serious."

"*Fiiiiiine*," I groaned. "I'll get with my producer and rearrange the schedule." I'd never done it before and I hated to do it now, but the alternative was continuing this route and blowing out my voice, which wouldn't help anyone.

We agreed to chat after I saw her colleague and hung up. Then it was time to talk to Morrison and Leland.

"Makes total sense," More said. "I didn't want to push, but I think it's a good idea. We were going to take a trip to London to see my mum the week after anyway. Why don't we take the week off and regroup? You guys are welcome to stay and use the studio if you want. Butler told me y'all are doing Rocktoberfest with him. That's rad."

I thanked him and was able to breathe a little easier.

"Your grandmother and Bruce should be here soon to go over the gala plans."

"Great," I told him. "See you in a bit."

My bandmates were relieved as well.

"Man, am I really that bad?"

"Not bad, exactly," Annie started. "But you *are* human, Boone, and you tend to push yourself too hard."

"And in turn, the two of you, huh?"

They looked at each other and then back at me.

"Sometimes."

I blew out a breath and blinked away the burning in my eyes. "I'm sorry. You deserve better from me and you're going to get it. Why don't you two take off for a few days? Go home, go on an adventure...my treat?"

"And you promise you'll rest?" Annie asked, raising her eyebrow.

"I promise. Morrison said we're fine to take time off. Him and Leland are going to head across the pond for a week and we can finish up recording when they get back. We have use of the lodge and studio for rehearsing while they're gone. I'm going to see a doctor tomorrow in Portland. I'll follow orders, I swear."

"I have been wanting to go up to Seattle to the MoPop museum," she said with an eyebrow raised. "They have some cool exhibits going on."

"Awesome. I'm serious, it's on me. Go have fun. I promise I'll be better when you get back."

I could tell they weren't sure they could trust me on my own. I'd have to prove it to them. And to Shane. He'd been worried about me today, too, and I didn't want our whole relationship to be about me and my physical issues.

I sent the twins on their way to dinner and then to pack, and I went in search of Shane. Rose said he'd gone up to his room to change before the grandparents arrived, so I climbed the steps and went in the opposite direction of my room. I heard him playing acoustic guitar before I got to his door. I knocked before opening it, and my breath caught when I saw him in the window seat with his guitar. He'd lit candles and was watching the rain outside the window.

He looked up and smiled as I closed the door. I couldn't believe we'd gone from nearly coming to blows a few months ago to him looking at me as though I lit up the room when I walked in.

"Hey."

I walked over and sat next to him in the spacious window seat. "I come bringing news," I said, trying to speak softly.

He set the guitar down and turned to face me with one knee up and the other foot planted on the floor. He held his arms out, and I scooted over into his space. I was finally able to let go of the tension as he wrapped me up in his strong arms.

"I called my doctor and I'm on vocal rest. I need to go into Portland tomorrow and have my throat scoped."

He held me tighter and exhaled. "I'm so glad you made that call."

I'd rested my head on his chest, and I looked up at him. "I hate this."

"Did you know I had to have surgery? I had a node. Fucking sucked. Right after our first tour."

"I didn't know that," I said. "How scary."

"It was. The first doctor I saw told me, 'Your screamo days are over.'"

"So you got a second opinion," I said with a laugh. I knew Shane wouldn't take that sitting down.

"I did. I had the surgery and then I worked with vocal coach Mirabel Sanchez. Have you met her?"

I shook my head. "No, but I definitely recognized the change in your vocals after the first album. You got so much stronger."

"Thanks," he said. "She definitely helped. I'd love to set you up with her. You have an incredible instrument, Boone. I worry you're gonna push yourself too far."

I heaved a giant sigh. "You and everyone else. Apparently my band agrees with you. I gave them a few days off, that's the next part of my news. That, and Morrison and Leland are going to head to London and give me some time to heal."

"That's great that they could be flexible. I'm sorry, babe," he said as he smoothed my hair back. "I know this timing sucks, but maybe it doesn't have to."

"I was thinking the same," I said, sitting up. "I thought we could work on the setlist for Rocktoberfest, and when the twins get back, we can start rehearsing in the time we have."

Shane smiled. "Sounds great. I also have a favor to ask."

"What is it?"

Shane looked down at the guitar he'd been playing and he blew out a breath before he looked at me again. "Watching you guys in the studio today, getting to be a part of your process...I wondered... Would you write with me? You can totally say no—"

"Are you kidding? I would love that!"

He gave me a shy smile. "I don't know what I'm doing about Wicked Soul. Maybe it's time to let it die. But I do know that I'm inspired to make music. Between my sessions with Lydia and being with you...I feel energized like I haven't in a long time. I want to see what we can do together."

"I think we've already established we're pretty incredible together."

That was enough to make him chuckle. He kissed the top of my head.

"That's definitely part of it. But it's more than that. I wrote lyrics today, and I normally have to pull teeth to get something that makes sense off the bat. It just happened, though. And God, singing with you? Fuck, Boone. I've never stretched like that. I keep on doing the same things, but you had me practically singing opera in there."

"You sounded amazing. You saw Morrison," I said, laughing. "He lost his mind."

"I think we could go harder, deeper. I think we could make something that's exceeds everything I've done on my own."

I took his hands in mine and delighted at the excitement on his face.

"Then let's put our heads together, shall we?"

"After we deal with the seventyagers."

I sighed. "Right. Let's go."

Three Weeks Later...

And that's what we did. We hammered out the gala details, we firmed up a set list for Rocktoberfest, and in between sessions with the twins, Shane and I wrote a double album's worth of new Butler Collins music. Morrison and Leland came back from London, and we finished recording all the instrumental tracks for the Stellar album.

Thank goodness my throat was just inflamed and two weeks of rest did the trick. Shane kept me in tea with honey, and saltwater gargles in between. When we started back, we took it slow. He showed me some exercises I hadn't done before and they really helped. When we circled back and got to "Over The Moon," I hit that goddamned note effortlessly.

My doctor and I talked and adjusted my medication, which meant my blood sugar also leveled off and I didn't have any more cases of dysglycemia. I started going for runs with Morrison and didn't totally hate it.

Bruce and Gran continued talking with the Bolder Breed staff and soon everything was set for the Collins Foundation Gala. Bruce also looked at our setlist for Rocktoberfest and he made a few suggestions. The gala was set for March, and Bruce and Gran continued to work on the plans...for both the gala and their wedding.

I think Shane and I were still in denial about it, although Bruce did sell his condo and he moved in with Gran. I think we were both happy to not be there while they settled in. They didn't need us around being all weirded out.

We did some cohabitating of our own. I eventually moved my things to Shane's room, as he had that awesome window seat with a gorgeous view of the property, and there was a giant bathtub in his room, which we made use of.

Though we were sharing space, most of our time was spent on music. We'd spend all day in the studio and then go back to our room and jam or tinker with lyrics together. He made me go to bed at midnight every night and woke me at eight to start the day.

"Schedules are important. Taking your medicine at the same time every day is important. Eating meals at the same time—"

"Yeah, yeah," I'd say, and when he went to object, I'd blow him a kiss and he'd smile at me. I could get used to this.

Sleeping in his arms every night, though, did wonders for my peace of mind. I'd never lived with a partner before, and he made it so easy.

Now, he probably would have a *different* opinion on the peace and harmony of our living situation. He was mostly patient with the destruction I left in my wake. He was neat and I...well, we've established that I'm not.

We never fought. Not even once. I think it surprised everyone around us. By the end of the three weeks, we were finishing each other's sentences, he was choosing my food for me, and he even let me shave his head one night. In the bathtub. Together. Life was unbelievably good.

Annie and Bran seemed the most shocked, and though they didn't say anything to burst my happy bubble, I could tell they were waiting for the other shoe to drop. I should have been too, probably, but I was so blissfully happy I likely wouldn't have listened.

"So," Annie said at the end of our last scheduled day at Bolder Breed. Two new bands were scheduled to work with the producers the following week, and though Morrison and Lydia said we could stay as long as we wanted, that they had rehearsal space for us, the twins were getting restless. Bran had a girlfriend he wanted to get home to, and Annie missed her cat. "What's the plan?"

Shane and I looked at each other. We hadn't discussed much past our time at Bolder Breed.

"We have Rocktoberfest in three weeks. We should probably rehearse pretty much the whole week before, at the very least. And next week we have a meeting with our label to play the rough mixes, talk release dates, and schedule our tour." I looked to Shane.

He didn't have much on his agenda. After Rocktoberfest, he was a man without a country. We had the music we'd written together, but we hadn't decided what to do with it. There were two things...well, *three* that I had to decide immediately:

Did I want to jump into Butler Collins, record with Shane, and go on tour together?

Did I want to continue with my focus solely on Stellar? Where would Shane fit if I did?

And probably the biggest question I had was, where the fuck was I going to live?

This all seemed so big, and I couldn't go to any of my usual confidants to discuss my options because, well, they were all going to be impacted, no matter what I decided.

"Well," Shane said, his gaze darting around the three of us. "About that. Boone and I haven't talked about it, so I might be asking prematurely...but what would you two think about recording music with us? Boone and I have written a bunch of songs together, and I would love to have the Thompson Rhythm Section on them."

Annie and Bran looked at each other, wide-eyed, and then they did that twin thing where they communicated without speaking. I'd learned to decipher some of their language, and what I was picking up wasn't completely positive. This was such an awkward position to be in. I didn't want to force my new boyfriend down their throats, but I also wanted them to love him as much as I—

Wow.

I did. I loved him.

"That's...thank you, Shane. That's a huge compliment," Annie finally said. "Can we talk about it?" She looked to me with her eyebrows up. *Uh-oh.*

"Absolutely, and I know you guys are about to have a full schedule too. I just wanted to put that out there." He smiled at them with confidence. It seemed like either way was truly okay with him.

They nodded, looked at each other, then looked at me.

"I know you guys need to get home, though," I said. "Go ahead. We can regroup back in LA next week for our meeting. Sound good?"

They nodded, hugged us, and set off toward the lodge to pack and book flights for the following day.

And then it was Shane and I, and some big fucking conversations to be had.

Twenty-Five

S hane

Suffice it to say, my delivery could have used a little more planning and panache.

Poor Boone. We hadn't talked about the end result for the music we'd been working on. It had just been so fun for both of us to see what would happen, and I knew he was as excited as I was about it. But his allegiance needed to be with his band, and I got that. I didn't want to be clingy or anything, it just felt like I'd finally found my musical soul mate, who happened to come with a phenomenal pair of musicians and...now what?

The door closed after the twins and Boone set about cleaning up our trash from the day, which was a very un-Boone-like activity. I'd yet to see him clean something up.

"If I overstepped with Annie and Bran, I'm sorry."

He whipped around and walked over to where I sat on a stool in front of a music stand.

"Don't be sorry. *I'm* sorry. I probably should have planned for this conversation better. Those two are usually down for anything, but I think they're...worried."

"Worried?"

He tilted his head and ran a finger over my collarbone before pulling his hand away.

"Like, worried about what me being with you means for us as a band. They're pretty flexible, but I've never, you know, been with someone like I am with you."

I couldn't help it, I had to poke him a little. I took his hand and pulled him closer to me until he was standing between my legs.

"How are you with me?"

He bounced his knee a couple of times and tapped my thigh with his fingers.

"I guess I don't know how I am with you either. It's been pure fucking bliss these last few weeks, but the real world is about to come calling. I guess I don't know..."

I slid my hand around to his ass and pulled him flush against me. "What do you wish for us to be, Boone?" I smiled up at him as I ran my hand under his shirt, scoring his back with my nails.

His eyes fluttered closed and he swayed toward me. "Like this. Always. I want to sleep with you every night. I want to make music with you. I want what we have now to be us. I feel like I finally have my life where I want it, with my health getting better, my band sounding killer, and I finally have a partner who understands me and my music like no one ever has."

He opened his eyes and was smiling, but a tear slipped down his cheek.

"Hey, no, baby. Don't. I want that too. I feel the same. But

I also know Stellar has to take priority. You guys are riding a high and you need to stay on it. I would never want to get in the way of that."

"But what we've created together is incredible, Shane. You push me as a songwriter, as a musician, as a man. I think it's some of the best music I've ever made, and I wish that it could just all come together into one big kumbaya moment!"

I snorted. I know, not the kindest way to react to my boyfriend's existential crisis. "I draw the line at kumbaya. Taylor Swift revenge ballads are one thing."

Boone threw his arms around me and buried his face in my neck, and I wasn't sure how much of the sound coming from him was laughing and how much was crying, but I understood. I really did.

"How 'bout this," I said, smoothing his hair back and cradling his cheek in my hand so I could stare into those gorgeous eyes of his. "We go back to my room and I get all up inside of you until we're both wrecked and we put off making any decisions until the morning?" We hadn't fucked since that first week, though we'd talked about it. We'd definitely fooled around. We were both so tired by the time we dragged ourselves back to my room at the end of each day that we'd fall into bed and hold each other until we fell asleep. Making music had been all that mattered.

"I want that," he whispered. He lifted his head and stared into my eyes. "Love me, Shane."

He kissed me with his eyes open and it was so hot, so full of passion.

"I *do* love you."

My eyes were open. My heart was open, waiting for his response.

He blinked.

"God, I love you, too." He shivered as he bent to kiss me once more, only this time, he held my face and kissed me so deep, he fucked my mouth with his tongue until I was gasping. I yanked his stretchy, dark purple, crushed velvet pants down enough to get to his cock and stroked it with both of my hands, running my fingertip over his Prince Albert piercing, smearing his precum all over, and he shuddered, moaning my name.

"I want to watch you come," I rasped. I spit into my hand, and his eyes flared before taking on that heavy-lidded, lust-filled look I craved from him. The slickness of my hand over his shaft made us both moan and he gripped my shoulders for support. He pumped his hips forward and pressed his forehead against mine. The blissed-out expression on his face was the most beautiful thing I'd ever seen.

"You better still fuck me when we get back to the lodge," he said, his movements getting jerkier.

"I'd love to, babe, now come for me. I want it."

"It's yours," he cried, and then he was coming in my hand, his whole body spasming. He fell against me, barely able to stand up. "Fuck, Shane. Good, so good."

I held him against me while he caught his breath, and then he handed me a tissue, pulled his pants up and dragged me by the hand out of the studio.

"I can't believe we did that in here," he said as I punched in the code to lock and alarm the building.

"I can't believe we *hadn't* done it yet. I've caught Leland and Morrison getting it on in there, and I've heard Lydia and Unice have gotten a little freaky in there too. The studio has seen a lot of action."

Boone chuckled. "How do you make light of things when everything feels so heavy?"

I turned him to face me. "Because when I'm with you, I feel like I can handle anything. Like, it's all going to be okay somehow."

"Then *be* with me. Say we can figure this all out, because

right now? I don't want to be out of your sight. I know we'll have to be…eventually."

"Yeah, sure. When you guys go on tour."

"And you don't." He blinked up at me. "I want it all. I want Stellar, I want Butler Collins, and I don't know how to make it all work."

"We'll figure it out," I said, trying to reassure him, although I wasn't sure who needed it more. Could I sit back while he was in the spotlight and not fester? "I want you to talk to the twins tomorrow and see what they say, without me there. This should be your decision as a band. Don't make me the chick from *This Is Spinal Tap*."

Boone burst out laughing. "Yeah if you come in with their star charts done, they'll run you out of town."

"I'll try to keep that in mind. Now, get that ass up those stairs." I smacked his right cheek hard enough to make him squeal, and he took off running.

"Come get it," he called over his shoulder, which got me running after him. We were ridiculous. We were that sappy couple everyone makes fun of. We were in love, and damn it felt good.

We were out of breath when we got to my door. He reached around and unfastened my pants while I was trying to get the key in the lock.

"I want you to fuck me in that window seat," he said, and his words went straight to my dick.

"You don't care if we're seen?"

"Let them be entertained," he said as I got the door open and he pushed me inside. Within minutes, we were naked, and he knelt beside me on the window seat, in full view for anyone out front of the lodge at midnight. I worked him open with my fingers as I sucked on his neck.

"Those were almost healed," he said, but his sigh was less annoyed and more desperate.

"I know," I said, nibbling on the tendons that attached to his collarbones. "Time for new ones."

"Oh, God, Shane. Give me that dick."

He straddled me and lowered himself slowly until he was fully seated, his knees on either side of my hips on the window seat cushions.

"Take what you need, babe. You're so fucking gorgeous like this." I leaned back, supported his hips with my hands, and then watched as he got himself off, coating my stomach and chest. It was a damn beautiful sight. I slowed him down, sat up and wrapped my arms around him, thrust into him twice, three times, and when I came it was from the depths of my fucking soul.

He did that. He made me reach down inside myself and feel things I'd shut off a long time ago. Whether I wanted to feel them again or not, he brought it out of me.

When I stopped moving, he started to stand up.

"Please, wait." I looked up into his face and brushed his hair back. "I love you," I whispered. "I mean it, Boone, and it fucking scares me."

He smiled at me and ran his thumbs over my cheekbones before kissing me. "You won't be sorry. I'll earn it, I swear."

We showered together and then crawled into bed. We were quiet, though, and I couldn't help it when my thoughts began to spin out. If life wanted to teach me a lesson about letting go of my need to control, this was definitely the way.

The next morning I woke up feeling raw, like every nerve was exposed. I groaned and rolled over to find Boone gone. I figured he was talking with his band and that didn't help what was shaping up to be a foul mood.

It doesn't do any good to second-guess yourself. You laid it all out there, Butler.

I growled and rolled over, pulling Boone's pillow over my face. The minute I got a whiff of his...what did he call it...some fucking candy mixture that made my goddamned mouth water and my dick hard, I calmed down a little.

I'd have to trust Boone. It was as simple as that. He had my fucking heart in his hands. What else could I do?

At this very minute, I could get up and write about how my feelings were at war, how my fucking insecurities had me doubting myself, doubting him, doubting everything, and how I wanted to rage against the helplessness of it all.

The only paper I could find was in Boone's notebook. It was pretty banged up and I was sure he'd probably used most of it, but I flipped it open to get to the last few pages...and my curiosity got the best of me.

At the top of a page in the middle were the words "Feuds and Interludes."

It wasn't one of the songs we'd worked on together. Did I chance taking a look?

At that moment, I heard footsteps running up the hall. I threw the notebook onto a pile of Boone's clothes and lay back in the pillows. Yeah, like a coward.

The door flew open and Boone ran in, jumped onto the bed, and then very carefully removed his pillow from my face.

"Are you awake?" he whispered.

Twenty-Six

B oone

"Anyone ever tell you that you're a bit of a chaos demon in the morning?"

Shane had my pillow over his face, the sheet pulled down below his navel, and his hand dramatically draped over what would be his forehead if my pillow wasn't in the way.

I kicked my shoes off and crawled onto the bed next to him on my knees.

"I'm not sure anyone ever put it quite so adorably, but yes, I've been called lots of things in the morning. Annoying, obnoxious, gassy—"

He pulled the pillow away and I loved his sleepy scowl. It was somewhat laughable, him trying to look scary when he was all soft and warm with creases in his cheek from the pillow.

"Gassy? As in—"

"Oh, yeah. We're not there yet in our comfort level, so you're safe. It's honestly better since I quit drinking but Shane! I have news! Are you awake enough for me to tell you news?"

I pressed kisses down the middle of his chest, taking time to lick his navel and blow on it.

"While you're down there—"

"You're awake. If you're thinking about sex, you're awake."

He shoved the pillow back on his face and let out a long, loud exhale, and then he pulled it off. "Okay. I'm awake. Speak, but at a lower decibel, please."

"Sorry," I whispered with a chuckle. "The twins are gone, they got flights out this morning, but they said they're open to discussing recording with us after Rocktoberfest."

"So, not a resounding yes," Shane said, and he pushed himself up to sitting. "I get it. I should have talked to you about it before I brought it up."

"It's fine. It'll be fine. They'll get to know you better and we'll come up with a business plan for them to look at, not just 'hey, come play on our *looove* album.'" He gave me a half smile.

"As long as you don't say kumbaya again."

"Right. And I definitely won't sing it, but Shane! I had an idea!"

I knew I was coming off a little manic, but I'd woken up in the wee hours full of thoughts and it had taken every ounce of restraint I had—which wasn't much—to keep from pouncing on him then and unloading on him.

"What's your idea, babe?"

"God, you're so fucking gorgeous. You have no clue, do you?"

"The idea?" He crossed his arms over his chest and smiled for real this time, only it was that indulgent smile that let me know he was doing his best to be patient because he really did love me.

He loves me. And he'd said it last night. More than once.

"The idea! I woke up from a dream in which you and I were on TV, you know, like those interviews they do before a big movie comes out? And like the interviewers are asking probing questions."

"You dreamed about this?"

"Yes. I think you and I should do a mini press tour before Rocktoberfest! Get people excited about our performance. Of course they're going to ask questions about our so-called beef with each other—"

"I never had beef with you, Boone."

"You did, but it's okay. I was an asshole. I deserved it. But this way, if we pick the media and we control the narrative, we can hype up the performance, turn it into hype for the foundation, and then hint at a project together. We can gauge what the reception will be, maybe get our prospective labels excited about it…and if everything goes as well as I think it's going to, we'll have paved a nice little path for future Butler Collins collabs. It will also take a bit of the gossipy bullshit out of the story. We say yeah, we're dating, we're working together, but it's about the music. Our music and the legacy of our families. What do you think?"

I wasn't sure if it had come out as polished as I'd hoped, but the walk back from breakfast, where I'd said goodbye to the twins and gotten their blessing on all things Rocktoberfest, hadn't been a super long time to craft my pitch.

"So we get out ahead of all the speculation. We tell them upfront. It could work. Who did you have in mind to talk to?"

"I did an interview with Sammara Gunderson not too long ago. I'm sure she's going to be at Rocktoberfest, since Maggie's Bones is playing. Did you know they were reuniting for the festival?"

"I'd heard. I'm tight with Devon Boudreaux and his wife Jaylene. She's my tattoo artist. I used to work on his guitars way back when they were recording their last album in LA. That was fetus Wicked Soul days."

"Fetus," I said, laughing at Shane's Emo side that came out every once in a while. He might play music that had the classic metal feel of Metallica and Megadeth in terms of heaviness and vibe, but he was from the generation that made Emo a massive force in music, and Maggie's Bones had been one of the heaviest, alongside Bullet For My Valentine and pre-pop Bring Me The Horizon.

My vocal stylings with Stellar were on the other side of the rock spectrum. I spent my formative years not only trying to emulate my grandfather, but also being influenced by singers like Scott Weiland, Myles Kennedy, and of course, Freddy Mercury. Shane's vocals on Wicked Soul songs were frankly a little terrifying in the pure evilness he managed to pour into his performances, and I'd always found them sexy as fuck. Rather than scare people with my music, though, I wanted to get them hot and bothered so they'd go home with their partners and do what nature intended.

He rolled his eyes playfully. "I could also call up Krish Guruvayoor. I bet he'd do a piece. Now that he's taken Chaz Vella's position at *Alt-Scene* things have gotten a lot better. I've got contacts at *Kerrang!* and Pops's buddies at *Classic Rock* mag would probably dig it." He frowned a bit. "So Annie and Bran aren't keen on the Butler Collins project, huh?"

"It's not that they aren't keen on it. The thing is, you and I wrote the music. They're not used to being sessions musicians, you know? I don't think they're opposed to *me* doing it, per se, but I think they recognize it as *our* baby and they don't want to be, like, rock 'n' roll godparents."

Shane rubbed at his mustache. It was thin, just barely covering his upper lip in a line, but I fucking loved it. It made him resemble a villain or like an old-timey performer in a speakeasy. Watching him rub it? Did things to me. But we needed to have this serious conversation, which meant I needed to focus on something other than that, or his pleasure trail leading underneath the sheet.

"We'll get through Rocktoberfest and regroup, then. And if they don't feel comfortable recording with us—"

"*We* do it. Hell, between the two of us, we can play everything."

"You play the drums?" he asked me.

"Oh yeah. I'm not as fancy as Bran. I kinda look like a gremlin when I play, but it's fun."

Shane grinned at me. "This I gotta see."

I wiggled my eyebrows and walked my fingers to the edge of the sheet. "Speaking of seeing—"

He put his hand over mine. "Hey, I'm serious, Boone. I don't want to put any discord between you and your band. They're right. Let's talk about it after Rocktoberfest. Besides, you can't really make any plans until after you meet with your label. They're going to put you guys everywhere. We have time, babe. I'll be around."

That made shit real, quick. "What are you going to do?" I asked him.

"That's a really good question. I don't know. And right now, I'm okay with that. I'll go back to LA and regroup. That's all I can do. We've got Rocktoberfest and that's as far as I'm worrying about right now. I want to enjoy my time with you until you go on your way."

He smiled, but it was a little sad.

"I don't want it to be me going on my way. I want it to be me going on tour, talking to you every day over FaceTime, and if you're free, seeing you when we can meet up. People have relationships that continue when they're on tour, right?"

Shane tugged on my hand and pulled me to straddle his lap.

"Of course they do." He pushed my hair back and ran his thumb over my pulse in my throat. "You sayin' you want me around?"

"God, yes. I do, Shane." I bent over and kissed him. "I fucking do. I don't want this to be over when we go home."

Shane moaned and pulled away from the kiss. "Move in with me."

I froze. His eyes were a little wide, like maybe he hadn't planned on saying that.

"Are you... Seriously? Haven't you seen what I do to a domicile?"

He pulled my shirt up and over my head. "I can live with your mess. I have a cleaner come in every week anyway. As long as your shit's picked up before she comes." He ran his finger over my nipple. "How come these aren't pierced?"

"They were. I had to take them out when I had all my tests done and I never got around to putting them back in."

"But the Prince Albert you did." He grinned.

I ran my fingers over his muscular chest and shrugged. "I didn't want it to close up and have to go through the healing process again. Plus, it feels good."

"It sure does. I love it on my tongue."

"Fuck, Shane." I was about to rip the rest of my clothes off, but we were having a serious conversation. "How about a trial run? I won't move my shit in, but I'll stay with you."

"Stay with me," he said, wrapping his arms around me. "Sleep with me. Make a life with me. Love me, Boone. The rest is just details we can figure out later." He kissed me, and I fucking melted. He was offering me everything I ever wanted wrapped up in a gorgeous, kind, talented, thoughtful, loving package, and I was ready to jump in with both feet. And pray I didn't falter.

"Just remember," I said as he went to work pulling down my pants. I lifted up to slide them off my legs and pulled the sheet down, putting us skin to skin. "You asked for it."

He chuckled against my throat as he grasped my shaft, causing me to make sounds I couldn't even describe if I tried, and I kind of describe things with words for a living.

"Then gimme it. Give me what I want, Boone," he murmured. He slid his fingers between the globes of my ass and tapped on my hole. "I promise I'll make everything good for you. Always, babe. I want all of you."

Believe me, I said a whole lot of yes after that. Yes to his fingers inside me in the gentlest way, coaxing my body to open for him. Yes to his cock in me as he drove home his point that I belonged to him, and he took care of what was his. *Oh*, did he take care. I lost track of the number of positions he folded me into over the rest of the day as we fucked and fucked and fucked as only two fairly young men, in decent shape and ludicrously in love, could do.

We napped and went at it again. We soaked in the tub and went at it again. I could barely lift a finger by the time nightfall came, so Shane dressed and went to get us a feast from Felix before he shut the kitchen. Shane fed me from his fingers. He sang to me as he attempted to braid my hair and barely managed to not tangle it before he figured out what to do. He played guitar for me. If he were trying to convince me to do something ridiculous like sell all of my belongings and go live off the grid in the wilderness (I liked my creature comforts, thank you), I'd give him anything he wanted at that point.

Turned out, all he wanted was for me to hold him as he fell asleep.

We packed our shit the next morning, said ta ta for now to the crew at Bolder Breed, and departed for Shane's place in LA.

We'd debated renting a car and driving like our grandparents had, but I assured Shane that sitting for that long might be a little uncomfortable after our Gay Sex Olympic Games the day before. Instead, I booked time with the private jet company I was a member of and Rose drove us and our gear to the airport.

Neither of us was up for joining the mile high club. We were both a bit too tender for that, but he did give me another love bite, this one on my hip so only he could see it. I bargained with him to please keep them under my clothes until after Rocktoberfest. He begrudgingly agreed.

We opted to get settled into domesticity at his place before going to see our grandparents. It was nice to hold on to a little bit of that feeling we'd nurtured while up at Bolder Breed, like we were cocooned, and the world couldn't hurt us.

Shane's place was a sweet condo in Silver Lake that was part of a super-cute Spanish-style home with archways and tile that gave it a lovely touch. The downstairs contained a kitchen and the rest was a sprawling workspace full of recording equipment. Upstairs he had two bedrooms, laundry, and a gorgeous view of the reservoir. He had a private patio out back with a grill and what looked like an herb garden. It was, like everything else about Shane, not at all what I expected.

"The only thing metal about your place, darling, are the stainless-steel appliances in your kitchen," I remarked as we stepped inside. We dropped off our guitar cases in his great room and I looked around expecting...something else?

He sniffed. "Wait 'til you see my room."

I followed him up the stairs and he directed me to leave my duffel in the laundry room.

He stood in front of his bedroom door and raised an eyebrow at me so severely, it set me to giggling.

"I don't know if you're ready for this."

I clapped my hands together. "Oh please oh please. I can't wait!"

"All right, but what goes on in this room, what you see in this room, stays between us."

My eyes flared. "Do you have a sex dungeon in there, Shane? Restraints? Ooo! One of those swings?"

He rolled his eyes. "Is that all you think I am?" He absolutely was messing with me.

"Fine, I promise. Just open the door!"

He sighed. "Don't say I didn't warn you."

He opened the door—and he was right. I wasn't ready.

The room had high ceilings and arched doorways leading to the master bath and a large walk-in closet. There was a medieval-looking king-sized four-poster bed in the middle of the room, and on each of the four sides hung black and white flags from what I assumed were Shane's favorite bands —Led Zeppelin, Black Sabbath, Judas Priest, Metallica, Megadeth, Van Halen—and on the ceiling above the bed were posters of Dio, Spinal Tap, Tenacious D, Ozzy Osbourne and more.

But the walls...

"Oh my God, Shane..."

The far wall was covered with a detailed mural that was the artwork from California's debut album cover.

"That was my test run. I wanted to do it as a surprise for Pops in his new place, so I did it here first. His turned out better."

"And now someone else has it. Oh, Shane—"

"It's fine. I did it like six years ago, I think. Maybe seven."

I linked my arm with his. "We'll have to think of a house-warming-slash-engagement gift for the happy couple. Besides me moving out."

Shane put his arms around me and kissed my head. "I meant what I said, Boone—"

"I know. And if you still mean it after Rocktoberfest, I'll take you up on it. This place is amaz—is that a snake?"

Shane smiled bashfully. "Yeah, that's Duncan. Pops got him for me when I was fifteen. I thought it made me more metal, having a snake. Turns out he's on the small side for a ball python and he's kind of clueless. Every time I've let him out, he's tried to end his little slithery life. Poor guy. Inbreeding has not been kind. So now he's a pampered pet, not a badass prop."

"I take back what I said. This place is definitely metal." This man was so freaking adorable.

"And you haven't even seen the best part yet."

He gestured for me to go into the bathroom, where I found a shower that would absolutely fit seven people with several showerheads pointed strategically, and an intricately tiled bathtub tucked into a corner with a full-length stained-glass window surrounding it.

"Shane..."

"All this could be yours," he said in a cheesy gameshow host voice.

"And I want it." I placed my hand on his cheek. He seemed nervous showing me around his place. "I'm just a lot to take, Shane. I don't want you to regret any of this. Ask me again after the festival, okay?"

He dropped his head and nodded. "Gives me time to persuade you."

"Persuade me?"

He grinned. "We have the best Persian, Greek, Japanese, Brazilian, and Peruvian restaurants in SoCal in this neighborhood. What can I tempt you with tonight?"

I fluttered my eyelashes at him. "How 'bout pizza?"

He groaned. "You're not going to make it easy, huh."

"Just for tonight. Please? Doesn't pizza and a movie sound awesome?"

His frustrated expression softened and he smiled that soft smile I loved so much. "Totally awesome."

"Great. You order and I'll get the laundry started."

"You don't have to—"

"If I'm going to be here, I'm going to attempt to do my part. Besides. I'm great at laundry...making it messy *and* getting it clean. Do you have any requirements?"

"Not that I can think of? I've got three baskets for sorting and one for stuff that goes to the cleaners. Oh, yeah. No fabric softener."

"No?"

He shrugged. "I used to get rashes as a kid. Mom yelled at me for getting into shit with my good clothes on, she thought it must be pollen or grass or something I was allergic to. Turned out it was her fancy fabric softener. She didn't like having to stop using it."

I nodded. "Good to know." My Metal Menace had more than an emotionally sensitive side. I kinda loved it.

We sorted our clothes together like an established couple and he showed me how to use his machines. Then he ordered mushroom and olive on pesto for me and spinach and white sauce for him, along with salads. He gave me a pair of comfy lounge pants that I had to tighten up with my hair tie, and we crawled into his massive bed. He lowered a screen from the ceiling at the foot of the bed, turned on a sound system, and we talked about our favorite movies until the pizza came.

We ate standing up in the kitchen, crawled back into bed, and watched *The Big Lebowski*, which turned out to be both of our favorites. We curled up and recited lines together, laughing until my stomach hurt, and I thought, this...really is everything I ever wanted.

I just hoped I didn't fuck it up.

TWENTY-SEVEN

S hane

"We really are going on an orgy bus, aren't we?"

Boone and Bran cracked up at Annie's drama as we loaded up the kitted-out RV we rented to drive up to Rocktoberfest.

"We're happy to give up the room in back for you, Annie, and we'll bunk it if you prefer."

She rolled her eyes. "You're too tall for the bunks." She sighed. "I will take the over-the-cab bed though. I can change up there and I won't have to smell my brother."

"She smells worse than I do," Bran called out. "She denies it, but if she eats lentils or curry? Watch out. There's no hope for you."

"Fuck off," she said, throwing Bran's backpack at him.

I was looking forward to being on the road with Boone and the twins. We'd had a phenomenal week rehearsing for our set at Rocktoberfest. I felt like they trusted me a lot more than when we were up in Oregon. They gave me shit freely and the three of us even ganged up on Boone a few times, which had been so fun. I loved watching him squirm.

Our domestic life had been fucking perfect, too. In just a couple of weeks, we established a routine that worked for both of us, and when we weren't working on music together, I retreated to my bedroom to read or draw, and Boone took over my spare room. He put his clothes in the dresser in there and I encouraged him to use my Warhammer table for writing or handling Stellar business. He didn't need to know that under the surface was an elaborate, hidden countryside with battle-ready creatures I'd painted myself. I had to keep some secrets. He could be messy in there and we could share my room without any disputes.

The only hiccups had occurred the day after we'd returned from Oregon.

Boone and I were folding laundry when my phone buzzed.

"Mom? Everything okay?"

Boone's eyes had gone wide and he'd gestured as if he should leave, to which I shook my head. I wanted him in all parts of my life, including the sticky ones.

"I don't know, Shane, that's why I'm calling you. Your grandfather hasn't returned any of my calls, and when I went by his place, there were strangers moving in. Do you know anything about that?"

I pinched the bridge of my nose and sighed. "I take it he hasn't told you about his change in relationship status."

"Change in what? What's going on? Is he using?"

I sucked in a breath and it took all of my skills learned in Al-Anon and therapy to answer her in a neutral tone.

"He is sober and he's sold his place. He moved in with his fiancée."

"His *what*? At his age? *Jesus*, will that man ever—"

"Mom? I'm happy to tell him you'd like to speak to him

and then it's up to him whether he contacts you. I can tell you that he's safe and healthy. Is there anything else you need?"

Boone's eyebrows went up to his hairline as he clenched a pair of my boxers in his fists.

I could just imagine my mother standing a little taller and kicking her chin out. "I'm sorry, I was just worried. How are you? Anything exciting going on?"

I grinned at Boone. "Things are good. I'm doing really good. Thank you for asking."

She sighed. "Your stepfather's sixty-fifth birthday is coming up at the end of the month, and we'd like it if you'd attend."

My nostrils flared. I would go. Arman Grigoryan had mostly been good to me, and he respected my need to set boundaries with my mother.

"I'd love to. Text me the details?"

"I will, and perhaps you can pass them along to my father." He was my grandfather when she was pissed at him and her father when she was pissed at me.

"I will," I said, though her tone let me know in no uncertain terms that she was displeased. "I'll be on the road the week before, but I'll be back in time to come to Arman's birthday. Thanks for calling." Even if she was calling primarily to find out about *her* father.

"Thank you. And Shane?"

"Yeah?"

"I...I'll look forward to seeing you. Will you be bringing a guest?"

I gazed at Boone standing on the other side of the bed watching me, still clutching the underwear.

"I'll ask, yes. Thank you. Good bye." I disconnected and shoved my phone in my pocket with a sigh.

"That was... Wow."

"Yeah. Mom and I have very narrow parameters in which

we engage. I had to set limits when she tried to embroil me in her problems with Pops. I told them I refused to be in the middle of their issues, but in this case... Shit. I can't believe he didn't tell her he moved. That's major even for him."

Boone shrugged. "Maybe he and Gran are too wrapped up in each other to have sent change of address notes?" His lip twitched, and I laughed.

"Yeah, how would they write that up? 'It is after a brief courtship and fifty years of being in love that we have decided to join our lives together for the remainder of our time on this Earth. Please respect our privacy in this happy time while we act like teenagers and make out in restaurants all over town.'"

Yes, the tabloids had been so busy with the news of their engagement and impending nuptials, that our news had almost been overshadowed.

Until the pictures came out later that day.

It started out innocently enough when pics of the two of us at the restaurant in Portland, hamming it up, appeared on Stellar's fan site. But then TMZ got ahold of pictures of us boarding the plane together...of me smacking Boone's ass, him turning to me with mock shock, and then us kissing at the top of the steps before slipping inside.

Audra called me right away, at the same time Stellar's manager, Dickie Henderson, called Boone. They wanted to know if this was a publicity stunt because of the Rocktober-fest gig.

"Absolutely not," I'd told Audra. "Our grandparents started dating, we were united in our determination to protect them, and in the process, we kind of just happened."

"I want to say 'aw that's adorable,' but we need to get ahead of this."

"Already on it," I'd said. "We're talking to some trusted media folks."

Audra was pleased with our plans, and when Sammara's

and Krish's pieces went out, she was ready to handle all the phone calls so we could focus on the performance.

Bran and I took turns driving the RV from LA to Black Rock, Nevada, with one overnight along the way in a funky campground none of us were eager to visit again.

When we pulled up to the gates of the festival grounds, Boone took the seat next to me and the twins were standing behind us.

"Holy shit, we're actually here," Annie said. "On a scale of Lollapalooza to Download, how crazy is this going to get?"

"Good question," I said. "Soul played here twice before, the last time was before the pandemic, though. Food's good, nights get chilly, days are warm. We play tomorrow night, which is opening night, so crowds might be a tad smaller, and folks will be high energy and curious. They're not going to know what to expect, other than what we've put out in the media."

"I love the logo you designed, Shane," Bran said. "I didn't know you were into visual art, too."

Boone's gaze shot to me and he gave a shake of his head, which I interpreted to mean he hadn't said anything.

"Yeah, I found a font that was as close to the one California used as I could find. We just needed something for the media for this festival."

"Yeah, well, it's awesome," Annie said. "And I love the t-shirts too. I'm glad you guys picked out the soft cotton. I hate the scratchy ones."

Along with performing, Boone and I had scrambled to put together merch in a rush order. Thankfully I had good connections, and his assistant, Cat, was willing to ride in the van with our techs, Rowan and Martin, and staff our merch tent.

"It feels good to DIY this shit again," Boone said. "It's like the old days."

"OMG, remember when our mom was our merch girl for that first tour?" Bran said. "And Dad was our roadie?"

"And he nearly electrocuted himself," Annie said. "Those were the days, man."

"You guys met at Berklee right?"

"Yep," Boone said. "By the end we were all, like, ready to go do our thing. Gran wanted me on Broadway, and their parents wanted them doing symphonic shit, and we were like—"

"Hell, no," Bran said. "We're going to be those assholes who throw away our fancy education for rock 'n' roll!"

"I mean, symphony is boring."

It was my turn to check in at the gate and we were directed over to the artists' campground. There was a collection of fancy tour buses and rickety RVs. We were kind of in the middle. Loads of folks I recognized were milling around their areas, setting up overhangs and outdoor sitting areas. The weather was forecasted to be perfect. We were scheduled to headline the second stage on opening night, which was the perfect-size crowd to test out our little experiment. Boone and I had several conversations before we left about what we wanted out of this venture, and I felt like we had a vastly-appealing project.

It would all depend on what the twins wanted and what his label decided on.

Oh, yeah. Stellar's label loved the new music, but they wanted to keep a lid on it until they saw what happened at Rocktoberfest. If it was a success, they thought they could use the performance as a jumping-off point for a huge release. Boone wasn't too comfortable with their attempted money grab to snatch up rights to Butler Collins. He told them in no uncertain terms that Butler Collins was not on the table at this time, that whatever we decided to do with our music, we'd decide together.

God, it was hot knowing he had my back.

But there was a part of me that was panicking about the unknown.

Thank God for Rocktoberfest, because at least I had a couple of days to not freak out about the fact that my band was done and I had nothing else lined up.

"All right, my darlings," Boone said. "We're going to have eyes on us the whole time we're here. Be coy about the project, tell them we're working on some things, bat your eyelashes and walk away. Got it?"

"So we get to be big teases," Bran said. "I can do that."

"Our set is going to blow the lid off this place," Annie said. "That California shit is fire. The other bands are going to be like 'how the fuck do we follow that?'"

I loved hearing her cocky attitude. I just hoped by the time we finished here, I'd win her over. But I wouldn't be selfish. If it made more sense for Stellar to ride out their album cycle before we jumped in, I'd be fine with that too. Somehow.

An attendant directed us into our parking spot and it was on. I turned off the motor and turned to my companions.

"Okay, before we go outside, I just want to thank you all for taking this ride with me. This only works because the three of you are stellar musicians—"

"Nooo," Annie groaned.

"Ha! Butler with the dad jokes." Bran slapped my shoulder.

Boone grinned. "And we're thrilled you brought us along," he said. "This is going to kick ass."

"On three," Bran said, and we all put our hands in the middle.

Boone counted, "One...two...three..."

And the three of them shouted, "ASSLICKER!"

"What the..."

"Oh," Bran said. "It's from our first tour in Italy. One of

the journalists called us ah-Stellar, and the way he said it, it sounded like Ass Licker, so it kinda stuck."

"Forget I asked. You guys are something."

Boone leaned over and kissed me before climbing into the back. "Get with the program, Butler!"

"Right."

And with Boone's gorgeous ass barely covered by another pair of those corduroy pants I loved so much—these ones a dusty rose—I couldn't wait to get onstage with him tomorrow night and turn this place upside down.

The rock world wasn't ready for Butler Collins.

TWENTY-EIGHT

B^{oone}

"Are you ready for Butler Collins?"

Shannon Gunz from SiriusXM announced us and the crowd went wild, sounding much louder than the approximately twenty or thirty thousand people who'd gathered at the second stage for the opening day of Rocktoberfest. All afternoon, I'd been wandering around the grounds trying to get an idea of what the crowds would be like, but it was tough to tell. Shane said first day numbers might not be as big, but there were people as far as the eye could see, so that didn't tell me anything.

"You're going to be great, babe," he assured me that morning when I woke up covered in sweat from a nightmare that we'd been performing in front of five people who kept yelling "you suck" at us. "We gotta do something about these dreams. They can't be helping your fasting sugars."

"I know. I wake up in a panic at least a few times a week. I'm not even drinking alcohol or caffeine, so it's not that."

"Let's see if we can get you into a nice relaxed state," he'd whispered, and when he went down on me with his talented mouth, I nearly bit through my thumb trying to keep from screaming at the strength of the orgasm he brought on. At least I'd been quiet.

"You promised no orgy bus, Boone!" Annie shouted.

Shane snorted from under the covers and cracked up.

"You're getting me in trouble," I whispered. I climbed on top of him and tried to take care of him, but he was laughing too hard. Then Bran started rocking the RV, and someone banged on the door.

"Did someone say orgy bus?" Rowan and Martin, our techs for the festival, must have heard Annie, because then they were making porn-shoot noises outside the door while Annie howled with laughter.

Rowan and Martin had worked for Wicked Soul for years. Shane had already hired them to come on this trip, which was fine with me. Our roadies were off doing other gigs at the moment. I was glad he had someone from his team, and though they were being assholes at the moment, they were damn good at their job. Sound check had gone off without a hitch and now that we were standing backstage, ready to face the screaming desert hordes, I was grateful they'd had experience with this venue, since I was totally out of my element.

"On three," Shane shouted, putting his hand out. We all followed suit, he counted us down, and as I shouted "asslicker," the three of them shouted, "orgy bus!"

It was enough to get me out of my head.

Bran climbed up the back of his riser and started with a kick drum beat that Annie picked up as she sauntered out onstage to feral screams from the women in the audience.

Shane and I walked out together playing the opening riff of California's "Entertain You," which was their opening number for most of their career. Papa and Bruce harmonized on the guitar, then with their voices. It was one of my favorites that we added to the set. We came to the front of the stage together, and Shane waved to the crowd.

"Friends, Fans, and Nonbinary Stans," he said. "Thanks for giving us such a warm welcome. I'm Shane Butler, and this is the incomparable Boone Collins!"

He held his hand out for me, and I played a little variation on the riff.

"We are the grandsons of the legendary John Boone and Bruce Duncan of California—" He was cut off by loud shouts from the side of the stage, where we looked to see a whole contingent of our musical peers who, apparently, were just as excited to see what we'd come up with as we were to play.

"Thank you," Shane continued, shaking his head. "We're going to play the classics, a few songs from my band, Wicked Soul," there was another loud shout from the fans, "and a few songs from Stellar, which features Boone and our rhythm section, Annie and Bran Thompson."

There was applause, but it was a little less feral, a little more reserved.

"We thank you for being here. Now, get ready..."

He turned to me, and I approached him at the mic. His smile was almost lecherous as we both took a deep breath, put our mouths close to his mic, and we belted out, *"Weeeeee are here to entertain you."*

The noise from the crowd almost overwhelmed my in-ear monitor as I backed away from Shane. We played a complicated set of notes before I turned to the mic and sang the first part.

. . .

When you're down and life gets mean
  turn your back on the in between
  Join us in the California scene
  Grab a honey and smoke that green

Shane laughed every time I sang that line, and he was still smiling when he came in on the chorus.

We are here to entertain you
  Got nothing but love and joy
  to wrap around you
  We'll all get high as the sky
  and entertain you
  Everything's all right
  Everything's gonna be all right

Shane sang the next verse, and I couldn't help it. I moved to his side and watched him as he sang the wacky words our grandfathers wrote all those years ago.

Girl, come on along with me
  You're the prettiest girl I ever did see
  Say you want my company
  and say you wanna get down and be free

Weeeee are here to entertain you
  Got nothing but love and joy
  to wrap around you

We'll all get high as the sky
and entertain you
Everything's all right
everything's gonna be all right

The dueling solos were so much fun to play, but I had to concentrate. Shane was so much better than me, but I was proud I was able to keep up with him.

We repeated the chorus with just the drums backing us, and Annie got the whole crowd to clap along. Our lips were so close on the mic I could feel every word he sang. Our guitars knocked once and we laughed, but it was like we were created by some otherworldly deity to make this music together, like destiny reached down from the aether and brought us together to make this unique sound no one else could duplicate, not even our grandfathers, who were touted as being the best singing duo in rock for the longest time.

I was so wrapped up in his eyes, I almost missed the cue to start the next song, which we'd rehearsed to flow directly from the first one.

I headed back to my microphone and stayed there for the next couple of songs, as I was singing lead on them, then I went wandering along the edges of the stage during Annie's vocals on the song, "Do Right By Me," which was a favorite from Brothers and had featured a duet with folk singer Tess Miller. Annie's sexy-ass delivery had the crowd dancing and ripping off their clothes. There was more nudity in the audience than I'd ever seen at a show, and a few couples were making out up against the rail. Shane sang backup to her, but she was the fucking star. She sang a couple Stellar songs on her own, but man, I was starting to think we should rework some of the new songs and put her front and center.

Then it was time for us to play two of Stellar's biggest hits. Shane watched me the whole time for cues and they went off without a hitch. We'd practiced with my band, we'd practiced after hours together in his house, and I'd been pleased to see that he played them effortlessly.

I was not as great with the Wicked Soul songs we chose to play. Thankfully he played all the really tough parts, so I only had to play the chords and I only fucked up twice. Shane smiled at me after the second time and raised his eyebrows to make sure I was okay.

I mouthed "sorry" to him, and he winked at me. God, he was so hot. So fucking competent and in control of the set. I hated making mistakes, and he knew that. He made it a little easier to accept I wasn't perfect, because he thought I was. That was all that mattered to me.

It all went by so fast and then it was time for us to perform "Paisley," so we were back on the mic together.

"Thank you all for being here tonight for the inaugural performance of Butler Collins. This show all came together while we were sharing studio time, and I want to thank Stellar for accepting my invitation to play tonight."

More loud shouts from the sidelines as well as the stage. Jesus, even more of our peers had arrived. Plus, the entire journalist pit was jam-packed with photographers all climbing over each other to get shots of us.

"It was our pleasure," I said, as we'd rehearsed. "We've saved something special for last. If any of you happened to see the Rock Hall Ceremony, you may know that my grandfather was posthumously inducted this year. John Boone accomplished many great things in his career, but the one he was most proud of was the work he did with my grandmother, Vera Jean Collins, on the Collins Foundation, which provides assistance to our fellow artists in the industry experiencing catastrophic medical emergencies. Many of us have health issues that impact our ability to work, and no one should live in fear of losing everything if the worst happens. If this cause speaks to you, please scan the QR code at our merch booth and give what you can. The majority of the proceeds from our merch will also go to support the Collins Foundation. There's also an online auction in case you want to bid on gear donated by various members of our community, including Maggie's Bones, who will be playing the main stage in just a little while." I paused while the crowd lost their mind. "But before we say good night..."

I turned to Shane and smiled up at him, and my heart leaped in my chest. We'd made it. Almost. There was just one more song, and it was the most emotional of all.

"If you saw that performance, you'll also know that my grandfather, Bruce Duncan, got to perform the song 'Paisley' with Boone, and he dedicated it that night to the one who stole his heart, Ms. Vera Jean Collins. Tonight, I'd like to dedicate it to the person who stole mine—Mr. Boone Collins."

Well, shit. We hadn't rehearsed that. And the crowd's gasp when he turned and smiled at me let us know that they hadn't *all* heard the news yet, but now they knew, and they screamed like Elvis had just wiggled his pelvis.

He bent down and kissed my sweaty cheek, and I was so startled that I missed him playing the opening notes. Thankfully, I caught Annie's wide-eyed stare and picked up the riff.

The vocals were challenging on this song, so I mostly stayed at the mic while I stretched my voice and tried to commune with my grandfather's spirit, only cursing his decision to go up an octave in the middle of the song.

But Shane was there, and I felt grounded as we stood together playing the harmonized guitars, our grandfathers' signature sound, and when he sang with me, I could practically feel him holding me up.

By the end of the song, I was out of breath and a little

light-headed, but I was stunned. We'd pulled off a massive performance with only a month to prepare, my band slayed, and Shane was there to support me the entire time. My eyes filled with tears as we played the final notes and I sent up a little prayer to my papa.

I hope you're proud of us, old man.

The song ended and Shane pressed his forehead to mine as the crowd went absolutely apeshit and started chanting *But-ler Coll-ins But-ler Coll-ins But-ler Coll-ins.*

Shane gestured for Annie and Bran to come up and take our hands, and we bowed together, me going through the motions as my hearing fuzzed out and my vision was blurred with tears.

It was the greatest performance of my life—and it was all because of Shane.

He gave my hand a squeeze and waved as he dragged me offstage. Rowan took my guitar and Martin handed me water with electrolytes and a towel as I passed by. I was sure Shane had told him to do so.

I followed Shane backstage in a daze as we were surrounded by people I knew only by name and face, not personally, but they all knew Shane. There were so many hugs and congratulations that all I could do was smile until my face was about to break. Shane was pulled away, and I searched frantically for Annie and Bran, who were also deluged. The three of us grabbed onto each other and made our way away from the crowd.

"Are you fucking kidding me," Bran squealed. "That was fucking awesome!"

"Did you see all those people practically fucking in the audience? What kinda drugs are they handing out?" Annie looked shock, and I elbowed her.

"It was all you, sweetie. Damn, you were hot."

She rolled her eyes and threw her arms around my neck.

"And that fucking Shane Butler, trying to make me cry onstage. Can you believe he told the whole fucking world he loves you?"

"He does." And then the tears really hit. Annie and Bran held me as I sobbed. "I miss the old man," I said.

They totally got it. They'd been with me through Papa's illness and death. They'd held me as I mourned him while trying to be strong for Gran.

"Hey, hey, babe, what's—"

Shane's arms went around me then while the twins still held me, and I was able to let the emotions roll through me.

"He misses John," Annie said.

"Damn," Shane said, holding me tighter. "He was here tonight, singing with us. You were amazing, baby. So good."

"Dude, *you're* fucking amazing," Bran said, slapping hands with Shane. "I'll fucking play with you anytime, anyplace."

"Back atcha. You two are so fucking solid, man." He slapped hands with Annie too, who laughed.

"I was just trying to keep up. And why did you not tell us people be taking off their clothes and making out like that? A bitch needs to be prepared for that kinda shit."

"I've never seen that before either," Shane said with a shrug. "That was all you, Thompson."

Annie blinked at him and then rolled her eyes, trying to play it off. "Yeah, well, that was some distracting shit. I think Bran and I should go get a closer look at the crowd."

"Yeah," Bran said, clearing his throat. "For research purposes."

"What about Becca?" I asked him, and he shrugged.

"Who do you think told me to get pictures?" The two of them trotted off, and Shane pulled me close to him.

"You okay?" he whispered.

I nodded and smiled up at him as I wiped my eyes. "I'm great."

His expression was concerned. "You *are* great. How's your sugars? You okay for a bit?"

I pulled out my phone and sure enough, I was in the good zone.

"Can we go watch Maggie's Bones?"

"I'd love that."

Twenty-Nine

S hane

My teenage self was in heaven. Not only was I watching my favorite band perform live from the side stage at a ginormous metal festival, but I had my arms around the most wonderful guy I'd ever met. He'd also just managed to blow me away during our performance. He was so vulnerable and passionate, and then he unleashed that massive voice and I was carried away. So what if I just told tens of thousands people that I was in love with him? So what? I was riding a high unlike any I'd ever known, and I was going to enjoy the spoils for a bit.

We'd run over to the main stage and managed to arrive as Maggie's Bones was finishing their first song.

"They sound amazing," Boone said, his eyes wide. He spoke in my ear. "Is it bad that I had the biggest crush on Marcus when I was like fourteen?"

I shook my head. "As long as it's not bad that I had a

ridiculous crush on Devon. That was before I met him. It went away when we became friends. At least I never hit on him."

Boone's eyes went wide, and he took my arm and draped it over his shoulder. He stood with his back to my front and I held him close as my idols showed the world that after many trials and tribulations, they still had it.

Maggie's Bones formed in 2005 in Houma, Louisiana, when brothers Marcus and Jade Lambert joined with cousin Devon Boudreaux and best friends, Mage Dumas and Star Stevenson. The band rocketed to the top of the metal and hard rock charts, thanks to the keen management of Devon's older sister, Maggie Boudreaux-Stone. As they were riding a huge wave of success, Maggie was killed in a single-car accident with her intoxicated husband at the wheel. He got away with it, the band nearly fell apart, and thankfully they managed to survive the grieving process with the help of tattoo artist Jaylene Charles-now-Boudreaux.

But strife continued to plague the band, and eventually singer Marcus left for a while to pursue a solo album. Devon and Mage continued to make music under the name Houma. Jade went to university and Star ended up in rehab. That was eight years ago, and I worried they were done. When Devon hit me up to tell me the Bones were playing Rocktoberfest, I knew I'd move heaven and earth to be stage side for their set, and they did not disappoint.

"My God, it's like no time has passed," Boone murmured as I was tapped on the shoulder.

"Jaylene!" I greeted Devon's wife, and then Marcus's wife Sherry, at the same time Boone squealed in delight when he recognized Mage's wife, music journalist Sammara Gunderson. The women stood with us while the band played and man, my world felt complete. The only thing that would have made this perfect would have been to have Pops there. I pulled out my phone and texted him a pic of the crowd.

Missed you, old man. We did you guys proud.

"You guys were brilliant," Sherry said into my ear. "I heard what happened with your band." She shook her head. "I hope you know that you're better off without them. And Jeff was a dick for letting that happen."

"Thanks," I said, and then the crowd roared, making it impossible to talk anymore. Boone kept a hold of my hand while he danced to the music with the women, and once more I wondered *how*...how had I not known?

My phone buzzed and I pulled it out.

Caught the set on YouTube with Vera Jean. We're so proud of you both.

I held the phone out to show Boone, and he grinned at me.

Their set was over too soon. We all cheered for them and when they came offstage, Boone and I stepped back to let them hug their wives before we got sweaty hugs.

"You guys should come hang out with us," Devon said. "I want to hear about *this*." He wagged his finger between Boone and I. "Killer fucking set," he added, as he shook Boone's hand.

"Thank you," Boone said, grinning way up at Devon. The dude was nearly six foot seven. He made *me* feel short.

"Please come!" Jaylene said. "I barely know any of these people."

"We'll come for a bit," I said. "You okay with that?" I whispered to Boone.

He nodded, his eyes big as saucers. I forgot that this wasn't his scene and there were likely a lot of folks he didn't know. I needed to do better introducing him around. At least I'd kept him away from the drama. Some of the guys from Warrior Black got into it and security had to get in there and break it up. We passed by as things were still being sorted out, tempers were still flaring.

The Bones camp was much more our speed. They had four RVs parked in a square with a couple of couches in the middle with a canopy over them and a bar. They were serving smoothies, energy drinks, and a bunch of hot teas. They had been through it with the health issues, too. I knew Boone would feel comfortable with them.

"What can I get you to drink?" I asked him.

"I'd love a smoothie, but tea sounds great, thank you."

"Coming right up." I heard him asking Jaylene about doing my tattoo as I walked over to the bar, where Devon was talking to Sherry.

"Great set," I said to him, clapping him on the shoulder.

"Thanks man. Felt good to be back out there." He looked around at his bandmates, his gaze lingering on his cousin, and took a long drink of a smoothie. "Sure would be nice if we could keep it together long enough to go out on tour."

"He's doing great, Devon. He wants the same thing." Sherry squeezed his arm. "He's been sober this time for two years, he's following doctor's orders. There's no reason he can't work back up to touring again."

Devon nodded. Then he turned on me with those all-knowing eyes of his. "Boone Collins, huh? Never thought I'd see the day."

"What?" I crossed my arms over my chest.

"Relax, big guy," he said. "Never thought I'd see the day

you two would share a stage, much less get involved. He used to drive you crazy." Devon's lip quirked, and I rolled my eyes. Fine, I'd take it from him.

"A lot can change when you're working in close quarters. You begin to appreciate things you never let yourself want before." I tilted my head toward Jaylene. Devon had been very resistant to getting involved back in the day. All it took was a whip-smart, freakishly talented tattoo artist to change his mind. "Blame my pops. He started dating Vera Jean, and Boone and I were united in our determination to keep them apart, until we realized we were being assholes and they belonged together."

"Yeah. Lotta history there. John Boone was one of my idols, man. California was my dad's favorite band." He crossed himself and kissed his fingers.

"They were pretty great."

"So what are you doing next?" Sherry asked me. "I heard you're working with Audra now. I don't know her well, but she came up under Arthur Frye and he's amazing."

"Yeah, I don't know what's next. I've got an album's worth of songs I was ready to record with Wicked Soul, and now I've got no band."

Devon grunted and shook his head.

"Boone and I wrote some really great stuff while we were up at Bolder Breed, but Stellar also just recorded an album and will likely go out on tour. I don't know. I'm a man without a country for now."

Devon nodded. "You get yourself a band, I'd love for you guys to open for us." He frowned in Marcus's direction. "As long as certain people keep it together. That's what we want to do."

Sherry poked his shoulder, and he held up his hands.

"I'm just saying."

"That would be awesome. Thanks man." I had no idea if I

wanted to continue as Wicked Soul, but it would be a dream going on tour with my favorite band. Maybe a fresh start was what I needed.

But then I thought about Boone. Was there a chance he'd want to tour as Butler Collins? I felt like I might have won over the twins tonight, but I still needed to have Audra draw up an agreement. The more I thought about my future, I wanted Boone to be front and center, professionally and personally.

"Let me think about it."

Devon nodded at me and then he laughed. "Probably we should go remind Jaylene that she's on vacation before she starts tattooing your guy."

Sure enough, Jaylene had Boone's shirt pulled up in back and was looking over his skin. Was he ready to let me design something for him? A shiver ran through me, but then I remembered his concern about his health.

Devon and I joined them as Jaylene was saying, "I've had plenty of diabetic clients. We just need to go in small chunks, make sure you're handling it okay. Maybe even do a small one first and see how you do with it before we attack a big canvas."

"Thanks," Boone said, grinning at me. "She said it would be okay if my numbers are good."

I sat next to him on the couch and Devon sat beside Jaylene.

"I was telling him that diabetes definitely doesn't have to mean you can't get tattooed. I have a client who beat breast cancer, but the chemo made her diabetic. We still have skin to work with." She grinned at Devon.

"That woman is a goddamned warrior. I don't know, dude. I think women can handle that shit a lot better than us men."

"I think Boone can handle anything." I smiled down at him and he winked at me.

"We should go to Jaylene's shop in New Orleans. She said her friend Mackenzie could re-pierce my nipples."

I laughed, and Devon groaned. "Just keep her away from your drummer. She did Star's and he nearly ripped them out a time or two. We had to force him to wear a tank when he plays now."

Boone leaned back against me, and I caught him stifling a yawn.

"We should probably get you back to the RV."

Boone sighed. "Probably. We've got press to do tomorrow, right, Sammara?"

She turned around from where she was talking to the guys from Embrace the Fear. "Yes! I can't wait to talk to you guys!" She waved and went back to taking notes.

"It was great to meet you," Jaylene said, giving Boone a hug. "I'll definitely let you know when we're going to be in LA again."

Devon and I stood and shook hands.

"Still miss you working on my guitars," he said. "No one's as good as you."

I rolled my eyes, but Boone elbowed me. "You're right. You should see his rig for playing slide! He played on one of our songs and I was blown away by how he set that thing up."

Devon looked between us and smiled. "He customized that Gibson I played tonight. It's still my favorite after all these years."

We said good night and I put my arm around Boone to lead him out of their encampment.

"They are so awesome," he said. "You have nice friends, Shane."

And just then, we were faced with the last two guys I wanted to see here. So much for avoiding the drama.

"Dude," Dean said, looking between us. "I can't believe

you replaced us with *them* and fucking played cover tunes." He wrinkled his nose at Boone, and then elbowed Drew.

"Fuck off," I said, feeling my blood boil. How dare they insult Boone? "What are you even doing here?"

A third man turned around and joined them. "Oh, hey, if it isn't the nepo babies."

The lead singer of one of the nineties' pop punk/ska bands stood before us with spiky blond hair and a dyed goatee, looking like a Guy Fieri wannabe in a bowling shirt with flames on it and pink board shorts. Mike Broward had been a has-been since Boone and I were toddlers.

"Mike," I said, giving him a chin lift but not a handshake. He didn't deserve to breathe Boone's air, much less mine. "The fuck are you doing here? Shouldn't you be playing nostalgia cruise ship shows? Warped Tour's over, man."

"We're headlining second stage tomorrow night. I've got a new album coming out, and your band made themselves available for me. They decided to come on over to the side of commercial success rather than wasting away in the doldrums with you."

This scenario was so ridiculous, I was beginning to wonder if perhaps I was living in a nineties teen comedy.

"Yeah, well, good luck with all that. I'm glad to not be carrying around dead weight." I put my arm around Boone and led him away, but he stopped and turned around.

"We might have benefited from nepotism, but at least we're making music that's relevant to this century. By the way, *Now That's What I Call Music* is still making CDs. Maybe they'll be able to finally get you that hit on the pop charts. Buh-bye."

Mike laughed and called out, "Damn, Shane. Hey, if the twink doesn't put out or runs his prissy little mouth, just grab him by the hair. He's much more cooperative that way."

I froze, and Boone's eyes narrowed. I was about to get up in his face when Boone took my hand and dragged me away.

Dean and Drew turned on Mike, though, and I could hear their raised voices from a distance. *Good.* They were assholes, but at least they weren't worthless pieces of shit.

"That's not even an original burn. Nepo baby? Jesus. Who the hell dressed him? He's rather old to be shopping at Hot Topic."

"Hold up," I said, pulling Boone to a stop. "Why did he say that?"

Boone rolled his eyes. "Why do you think?"

"Did you...with Mike Broward?"

"Not after he pulled my hair, not willingly. But yeah, I did some stupid shit when I was young. You got a problem with that?"

"No," I said, putting my hands on his arms. "God, no. My first time was almost with a roadie for Motley Crüe."

Boone stared at me for a moment and then he sighed. "I'm sorry."

"It's fine. He couldn't get it up, so I left. But Boone...did he hurt you?"

Boone rolled his eyes. "Not really? It just...scared me. He didn't want to take no for an answer and when I tried to leave, he...yeah, he held me by my hair and tried..." He threw his shoulders back and blew out a breath as he shook his hands and bounced his knees. "It was close. He didn't hurt me nearly as much as I hurt him. Piece of shit thought he could treat me like trash. You know, he needed medical attention after I left. I heard he lost a testicle."

My hand went involuntarily to my groin. "Good," I said.

"I wish it would have been both of them, honestly. Just knowing there's even a chance he could procreate is a crime against humanity."

"I thought I was supposed to be the sarcastic one," I finally said.

"Yeah, well, those were the polite options of what I had to say." He huffed out a breath. "Kind of a shitty way to end our night. You okay?"

I put my arms around him and pulled him close. "If I've got you, I'm golden."

He tilted his head back and kissed my chin. "Same. Take me to bed?"

"Gladly."

THIRTY

B oone

Shane and I made it back to the RV before the twins, and I laughed when I realized it wasn't even midnight.

"Sorry I'm such a party animal," I said as I pulled off my sweaty clothes and pulled on one of Shane's t-shirts. "If you want to go back out there—"

"I want to curl up with you and go to sleep. We've got three more days of fun ahead."

"And press. I've got about thirty notifications from the label, my manager...everyone wants to talk. Right now, I just want to be with you."

Shane crawled into bed next to me and held out his arms.

"We did it." He kissed my head. "That was probably my favorite performance ever."

"Really? Not when you guys played that massive show in Brazil? Or that time you played with Brothers?"

"You remember that?" he asked with a laugh, covering his eyes. "Pretty sure my voice hadn't fully changed at that point. Brazil was intense, but no. Tonight was my favorite."

I shook my head at him and poked his chest. "You and your grandfather with your declarations."

He pushed up and smiled at me. "Couldn't help myself. I love you."

"God, I love you, too, Shane." I curled up against his chest and yawned. "Thank you for bringing me."

"I'll take you anywhere," he said.

That was the last thing I remembered until both of our phones went nuts on the shelf above our heads at five-thirty in the morning.

I sat up and fought off the dizziness I sometimes had first thing in the morning. Shane grunted so I handed him his phone.

"Shit. I've got two missed calls from my mom," Shane said, as I read my text.

Bruce was taken by ambulance to Cedars-Sinai. I'm waiting for a car so I can join him there. If you could please let Shane know?

"Shane, honey, we need to get dressed and find a way to the airport."

"What's wrong?"

"Bruce was taken to the hospital. I don't know anything else."

His face paled and he shot out of bed, scrambling for his pants.

"What's going on?" Bran called sleepily from his bunk.

"I need to get Shane back to LA. Bruce isn't well."

"No worries. Let me get dressed. We'll take you to the airport and then drive the RV back."

"Thanks, man," I said, and I placed my hand on Shane's back.

"What did the doctor say? Why did they call an ambulance? Well, call me when you know something. I'm headed to the airport now with Boone. We'll be there in a few hours. I know, Mom. I'm coming. I know. I'm sorry I'm not there. If you'll quit yelling at me...I *know*, Mom, shit. Can you just... I'll meet you there. I'm hanging up. Call me— Mom, come on. I'm coming, I'll be there as soon as I can. I'm hanging— I know. I— Fuck! She hung up on me."

Shane looked at me with the most terror I'd ever seen from him, and I wished I could sprout wings and fly him there myself, or spontaneously invent a fucking teleporter.

"GPS says it's just over two hours to Reno. I think that's the closest."

"Wait, let me call my rep. Maybe the jet can get closer."

Shane rubbed a hand over his head and nodded. He was pacing in the narrow walkway as I called the company.

"Great. Thank you. Shane? They can get a jet to Empire Farms Landing Strip in forty-five minutes. It's not far from here."

"Thank you," Shane rasped, and he excused himself to go into the bathroom.

I shared the location with Bran and he got the RV started. I texted Gran to let her know we'd be flying into Burbank and we'd meet her at the hospital.

Thank you, Boone. I'm quite frightened. My car just arrived. I'll see you soon. I'll text you if I hear anything. Love you.

. . .

Shane was on autopilot for the quick twenty-minute drive and the hour-and-a-half flight. I would be writing rave reviews for the flight company for taking care of us and being so speedy about getting us there. My rep even hired a car to take us from the airport to the hospital. I hadn't been able to get any updates on the flight and once we landed, all Gran would say is they were waiting for test results but that Bruce was awake and talking.

The car dropped us off in front of the hospital, and I practically had to run to keep up with Shane. I was groggy and hadn't been able to clean up beyond what I could find in the airplane bathroom, but thankfully I'd brought my medication and my blood sugar was only a little bit high.

We made our way to the emergency room waiting area and were told only one of us could go back, and that one of Mr. Duncan's guests would have to leave. Shane gave me a sad look, and I squeezed his hand.

"I'll be here," I said, giving him a small smile. I hoped he knew that I would be there for him no matter what.

He pushed the doors open a little harder than he should have and stalked back down the hallway, the harsh lighting glinting off his wallet chain.

I sat down with a huff and texted the twins that we'd made it. I'd told Bran and Annie when they dropped us off that they should go back and stay at the festival.

"Maybe you guys can do some of the press? If you want."

They shrugged. "Whatever we can do for you, Boone. And for Shane."

I loved having such supportive partners. My hackles rose just thinking of those jerks who shall not be named who'd abandoned Shane and then shown their full asses by joining up with a festering boil like Mike Broward.

I looked up as the doors opened again, and Gran floated toward me with her arms out.

"My dear boy," she said as I stood to embrace her.

"What happened?" I asked, but she took my arm and led me outside the ER and around to an alcove, where we were out of sight of folks coming and going.

"Oh, Boone, I'm so embarrassed. We were...intimate last night, and when he woke up this morning, he wasn't feeling well. I panicked. I thought, well, he's had issues with his heart in the past. The ambulance came and he told them he was fine, but they insisted. The poor man has been poked and prodded...and do you know the doctor said he might have just been light-headed and had indigestion from the curry we had last night? That was all and...and I overreacted."

I held my Gran and pressed my lips together, trying not to laugh out loud. "You did what you thought was best. At his age, it's better to be conservative, isn't it?"

She wiped at her eyes. "Then his daughter showed up here. The hospital called her when they couldn't reach Shane, because she was listed as his next-of-kin. Boone, darling, she wouldn't even speak to me, and she yelled at him for carrying on like a young man and further embarrassed him. She's quite an angry person."

"She wasn't kind to Shane on the phone either. Are you all right?"

"Yes, of course. A little tired, but I'll rest later when they let him come home."

I gave her another hug and sighed. "At least he's going to be all right."

Gran burst into tears, and it was as if a five-alarm fire had just broken out. My grandmother *never* sobbed like this.

"What's wrong, Gran?"

"I don't think I can do this," she whispered. "I was so terrified! I cannot bear the thought of losing him like I lost John. I don't think I could take it."

"Oh, Gran, but the doctors said he was all right. I know

this is scary, but you two are so happy." I couldn't believe I was encouraging her to stay with him when two months ago, I was determined she would not become involved with the man. "At your age, he may just need to take it a little easy, that's all. But he loves you, Gran. You deserve to be happy together."

She nodded and wiped at her eyes with a tissue she'd pulled from her coat pocket. "I'm afraid I'll be worried about him every second, that if he so much as sniffles, I'll have him carted off to the laboratory for blood tests. Why am I like this?"

"Because losing Papa was hard, and it took a long time until you were ready to get close to another person. But you are now—"

"I never thought I'd survive losing your mother. I don't know what I would have done without John by my side. I was so lost. I didn't know how I would take care of you. I was distraught. But he was so determined, so sure we could give you the life you deserved..."

"And you did." I smiled and brushed her hair back that had come loose from her bun. "Gran, you and Papa gave me a wonderful life. Everything I could ever dream of. You deserve to be happy, and I know *Bruce* makes you happy. You've been glowing ever since the Rock Hall show. Sure, there are going to be tough times, but I'll be here, and Shane, and we'll make sure you're both able to enjoy the time you have."

"Bless you, my dear boy. I am so blessed to have you in my life. Not many young people would have come running when a silly old woman panics."

"You are neither silly, nor are you panicking. You had every reason to be concerned. Bruce is up there, Gran, and you're a lot of woman for a man at any age to keep up with."

She shushed me, and I kissed her cheek.

"It's going to be all right, okay? Now, can I get you some water? Some tea while we wait?"

"I'm all right, dear. Just sit with me, please?"

So we did. I pulled up the video of our performance from the night before and we watched it together, sharing my earbuds I'd happened to shove in my pocket on the plane.

"It's like listening to the two of them as young men," Gran said when Shane and I sang together. "That Shane is a wonderful performer."

"He's pretty wonderful period," I said with a sigh.

She elbowed me. "I'm glad you two found each other."

"We didn't have much of a choice! Who was going to keep an eye on you two?"

She chuckled, wrapped her hands around my arm, and rested her head on my shoulder.

I'd gone from being a complete disaster who couldn't take care of my own damn self to this place, a few months later, where I was beginning to get a handle on my illness, I managed to prove myself worthy of man like Shane, and I was able to be there for my Gran when she needed me to be strong for her.

Maybe I had a little of that determination Papa had. Maybe he really was with me, channeling a bit of that gumption that kept him on top of the world for a long, long time. For the first time since my diagnosis, I felt like I could handle what was thrown at me, and that felt like a pretty big accomplishment.

I hoped Shane was faring all right. I wished I could be with him right then.

THIRTY-ONE

S hane

Man, I wished Boone was with me. He helped me keep my cool, and right now, with the hospital staff as witnesses, I really needed to do just that.

"Dad, this is ridiculous. You need someone looking out for you. Vera Jean Collins is a high-maintenance harlot who—"

"Mom, come on. Don't speak badly about her. You don't even know—"

"So you're going to take her side because you're shacking up with her grandson? Is anyone in this family in their right mind?"

"Mom—"

"Christina, I'm going to ask you one last time. If you cannot show some respect for my fiancée and for me, then I want you to leave. You're not helping this situation."

"I've already had my lawyer draw up medical power of

attorney paperwork and you need to sign it. This was a close call. I don't want your health left to her the next time—"

"Christina, I'm fine. It was indigestion, for the love of Christ—"

"Mom, I want to speak to you outside." I took her gently by the arm and led her out into the hallway, where I knew she'd be less likely to raise her voice.

"Shane, I know you and *my* father are close, but you have no idea—"

"Mom, I have power of attorney for Pops. We took care of it a few years ago before he had his last surgery."

I hadn't seen my mother in person since that day four years ago, when Pops had to go in for a procedure to give him some peace from a back injury. Mom had thrown a fit a year prior to that, when he'd had to have an emergency triple bypass surgery and he hadn't told her until the day before. She'd threatened to take over his medical decisions at that point, so Pops and I went to see his attorney and took care of the paperwork. We agreed we would tell her if any more health issues arose, but he'd been doing so well, I think we both forgot about it.

Mom meant well, but she hated not being a part of the decision-making process. She felt she knew best and thought Pops and I were too lackadaisical about his healthcare.

She had no idea what I'd done with my life, how much I'd accomplished, how robust my financial portfolio was, because I didn't feel like she'd earned the right to be invited into my inner circle, not with the way she'd treated me since I was a teenager and decided the life path she'd chosen for me was not the one I wanted for myself.

But having to tell her to her face that her father had chosen her son over her, well...it was not sitting well.

"So you two just took it upon yourselves."

"Mom, it's not like that."

"Then what's it like? I lost my mama because the two of them didn't have their shit together and were too busy partying to get her medical attention when she needed it. She had cancer, and they chose to let her die rather than take her in for treatment."

"Pops did what she wished, Mom. She didn't want to go through chemo and radiation. She wanted to go out on her own terms."

"How do you know? You were a child!"

"And I'm a man now, and I've been taking care of Pops for the past fifteen years. He trusts me to make his decisions for him if the need arises. I'm sorry if that's not how you want it. It's up to you to decide whether you can accept it."

Her lovely sepia face, that so resembled her mother's, turned red in the cheeks and storm clouds passed before her eyes. "What did I ever do to make you treat me like this?"

I sighed and shook my head. "You refused to accept that you are not the only person in this family who knows what's best. There is room for all opinions and experiences to coexist, and I hope someday you realize that."

And I hoped it was soon, so that she didn't lose her father before she made peace with him.

"I guess you got it all figured out, huh, rock star?"

"Mom."

"Tell *your* grandfather when he's ready to talk sense, I'm a phone call away."

She slung her bag over her shoulder and walked out of the hospital, her fists clenched at her sides.

I let out a long breath and tried to focus on keeping the tears at bay. When I felt like I had control of my faculties, I went back into Pops's room.

He took one look at my face and shook his head. "I'm sorry, son. Come here."

He gave me a hug and kept a hold of my hand as I took the seat next to the bed.

"She loves you in her own way, son. She's like her mum. Headstrong. She thinks if ye don't agree with her, yer disrespecting her. I just hope she realizes what a wonderful son she has before it's too late."

I squeezed his hand and nodded. My phone buzzed, and I pulled it out. "It's Boone. Would you like Vera Jean to come back?"

Pops's smile fell, and he patted my hand. "I'm not sure that's a good idea."

"What? Why? What's wrong?"

"I don't know if it's good for her, bein' with a broken old man like me. She really panicked, son. She said..." He bowed his head and took a deep breath. "She said she couldn't stand it if she lost me like she lost John."

"Pops, man." Vera Jean was a tough lady, true, but like Boone said, she'd experienced a lot of loss in her life. It had only been two years since John passed. I understood what Pops was saying, but *he* was my concern. "I think it's her decision whether or not she wants to be with you. You're not broken. Maybe scratched and dented, but you've got a lot of miles left in you."

"I appreciate you saying that, I just dunno what's the right thing to do."

"How about—"

"Hello, Mr. Duncan, I'm Dr. Abad, the cardiovascular specialist on call."

"I'm Shane Butler, his grandson," I said, shaking the doctor's hand.

"Wonderful, I saw you're his medical designee. I wanted to let you know, Mr. Duncan, that everything looks great. Your tests all came back normal, so whatever you've been doing to keep your heart healthy since your last surgery, keep it up. I would only caution you that if you use Viagra in the future, be careful that your blood pressure doesn't drop too low. It's likely that the light-headedness you experienced was due to a drop in blood pressure, especially if you'd—"

"Thank you, Doctor. I'll follow up with my cardiologist about the, eh, future use of the medication."

My fucking jaw was on the floor. On one hand, go Pops. On the other? I did not need to know what he and the very classy Vera Jean Collins had been up to that required certain pharmaceuticals.

"Wonderful. We'll get your release paperwork together in just a bit. I'm glad this was just a precautionary visit. Have a lovely day."

The woman had her lips pressed together as she walked out the door, and I was grateful for her professionalism. As soon as she shut the door, I turned on Pops with raised eyebrow.

"Now, Shane—"

"Let's get you dressed, old man. We can talk about how much I don't want to know when your ass isn't hanging out of a hospital gown."

"Very well," he said. "Do you think... D'ye mind not mentioning this to Boone?"

"There's no way in hell I'm talking to him about what you two were up to, and *he* sure as hell won't want to hear it from you either."

Pops nodded and shook his head. "It's good to know I haven't lost it," he said, and then he cracked up as he got a load of my look of disbelief. "I'm just takin' the piss."

"Keep it up, old man, and you'll be dealing with Mom."

He patted my shoulder. "She loves you, son. Just give her time."

It had been fifteen years, though. I'd given up hope that we'd ever see eye to eye.

Pops got dressed, I texted Boone we'd be out soon and to please order a Lyft, the nurse brought in his papers, and they pushed him out to the waiting room, where we found Boone and Vera Jean and our bags in a corner. She'd dozed off against his shoulder, and he gently nudged her awake. When she saw Pops, she stood shakily and walked over to him, uncertainty on her face.

Pops took her hand, brought it up to his lips and kissed it. "I'm fine, love. And you did the right thing."

She let out a very un-Vera-Jean-like sob, bent over and wrapped her arms around him in his wheelchair, which the nurse had insisted on.

Boone gave me a sad smile. "Our Lyft will be here in two minutes."

"Thank you," I whispered, so grateful to see him. So thankful I hadn't had to do this by myself. I couldn't wait to get him home—

Shit. Reality cascaded over me like an ice-cold shower, waking me up to my current situation. The festival performance was over. That meant my time playing house with Boone was as well. We'd agreed he'd stay with me until after the festival, but now, he was most likely going to be taking off with his band, and I'd be home stewing. I had to take care of my grandfather and deal with my mother. I had to figure out what I was going to do with the rest of my life.

My mom's criticisms throughout the years echoed in my mind. I'd thought I had it all figured out, and my band quit on me. I'd stepped up for Pops, but when he'd needed me, I hadn't been there. How the hell was I supposed to be there for Boone, for Pops, and deal with the fact that I was nursing some wounded pride of my own? Boone needed to focus on Stellar, on the next step of his career, and any talk of Butler Collins was only going to take his focus away from where it needed to be.

With a heavy heart, I followed our seventy-agers out the front doors of the ER with a tired Boone by my side but feeling miles away.

"We'll get them settled at their house, and then—"

"You can stay if you want," I said. "I can Lyft home from there."

I couldn't make eye-contact with Boone, and thankfully our Lyft pulled up because there was no way we could continue this conversation. I had Pops sit in front and that put me in back next to Boone with Vera Jean on the far side. Boone's phone was blowing up the whole ride back. His brow was furrowed as he punched responses in with his thumbs with a huff. I wanted to ask what it was all about, but it was none of my business. Not anymore.

We were quiet for the ride up to Laurel Canyon. When we arrived, Boone climbed out my side, gave me a funny look, and then rushed around to help Vera Jean while I tried to help Pops up the driveway. He kept swatting my hands away, proving that he really was fine, and so I followed the group with my chest so tight it was ready to burst.

Once inside the gorgeous mansion, Pops turned to me and told me they were fine, that he was okay, and we hugged.

"I'll call you tomorrow," I said. "But if anything happens, you better call me."

"I know the drill, son. Thank you, I'm sorry to take you away from your festival."

Boone was speaking quietly to his Gran, and then he kissed her on the cheek. He walked up to me with an expectant look on his face.

"My car should be charged or we can Lyft."

"It's fine, I'll just Lyft. You've probably got things to do here."

Boone frowned at me, turned and gave his Gran one last

smile, and then he took my hand and yanked me down the stairs to what I assumed was his room.

Or rooms, I should say. I'd sneered at the fact he lived with his grandmother once, that was true, but the bottom level of the house was no basement scenario.

A wall of windows offered a gorgeous view of the Los Angeles basin. There was twice as much music equipment as I had at my place strewn about. There was a room off to the side with a treadmill and gym equipment, a kitchenette, and off to the other side, there was a hall that I assumed led to his bedroom. It was a cavernous space. You couldn't tell from the front of the house how much square footage the house actually took up.

"Look," Boone said, dropping his bag on the floor and parking his hands on his hips. "I know we're both tired, you had to deal with the double whammy of your grandfather in the hospital and your mother, but did you just try to dismiss me?"

I used to think he was a prick when he'd talk all prissy like this. I mistook his assertiveness for attitude. Right now, he was about to hand me my ass, and I wasn't up to the challenge.

"Boone, I'm tired. You have things to take care of, so I'm going to get out of your hair."

He bounced his knee and scowled at me. "Since when have I ever wanted you out of my hair? Shane Butler, don't you dare push me away right now."

Before I'd kissed him, he'd irritated me with his drama. After I'd kissed him, I thought it was cute. It was endearing. He was everything I'd ever wanted. Now? I knew I was being an asshole and I just didn't have the spoons to take care with my words. I was a coward who couldn't take the chance that Boone would figure out that I was full of shit. I needed to cut ties and go.

"Don't think I don't know your phone has been blowing up all day. You have Stellar to think about now."

"But you said—"

"Let's not complicate things."

He snapped his feet together, his spine stiffened, and his gorgeous blue eyes went round like deep pools of despair.

"I don't... What did I do, Shane? I thought—"

"I'm just trying to divest you of dead weight. Get some rest. We'll talk later."

And for my next trick, I attempted to get the fuck out of there and ended up walking into a bathroom.

"Fuck," I said, and then found the stairs and took them two at a time as I heard something crash down below.

Thankfully no one was upstairs when I got to the foyer, and I was able to duck out the front door without any more theatrics. I took off at a jog with my bag slung over my shoulder, and then broke into a run. I was going downhill, which was a really fucking stupid thing to do, but it seemed that stupid was all I was capable of doing at the moment. I ran all the way down to Sunset Boulevard and puked when I got there.

And then I remembered telling Boone that running 'til I puked wasn't good for me.

A horn blared next to me, and I tripped over my feet and fell on my ass, narrowly avoiding the puddle I'd made.

"Get in the fucking car." Boone was there in Vera Jean's Cadillac, looking more pissed than I'd ever seen him.

"Boone—"

"Get in the fucking car, Shane, or I'm going to make such a scene—"

"All right," I said, trying to climb to my feet on rubbery legs. I tossed my bag into the back and then climbed into the passenger seat.

"Here," he said, handing me a box of tissues before he

pulled away from the curb, which pissed off several drivers, who all flipped us off as they drove by. "You're bleeding on your hand and your knee and you've got puke on your chin."

I took the tissue and did my best to clean up. Boone took off toward my place, driving like an elderly woman. He sat so close to the steering wheel, I didn't know how he'd managed to fit his legs under the dash. His seat was up perfectly straight and he hunched over, his gaze darting between his mirrors. He was even...

"You wear glasses?"

"Only for driving."

The rest of the twenty-minute drive was quiet, the only sound coming from the blinker, which Boone used obsessively. With his glasses on, he looked younger than he was, and he was driving as if he were taking his behind-the-wheel exam. Then I remembered him saying he didn't like to drive much. And yet he'd come after me.

I was such an idiot.

"Boone, I'm sorry."

He glanced at me, and then he shook his head and went back to steering. He pulled up to my place and parked in the driveway, setting the brake but not turning off the car.

"If you meant all that shit you said, then get out of this car."

"Boone—"

"If you were just talking out your ass because you're afraid of what the fuck is going to happen, well, join the goddamned club."

"Boone—"

"And if you *ever* say that bullshit about dead weight to me again—"

"Babe, I'm sorry. I'm fucking spiraling, okay? Pops, my mom, and you're leaving—"

He shut off the car, got out, grabbed my bag from the backseat, and then waited for me at the front door.

Which was just enough time for my fucking tears to start up. I grabbed a few more tissues, got out of the car, and trudged my way up to the porch, where Boone was trying to get the keypad to work. I'd shown him how to use it, but he'd never had to in the short time he'd been there.

"Here." I entered the code, opened the door, and waited for him to do something.

Without looking at me, he took a deep breath. "I suggest neither of us speak to each other until we've showered, eaten something, and slept for eight hours."

"That's fair," I croaked. I held out my hand for him to go inside first.

He glanced at me, nodded, and then walked inside. He went straight upstairs to the bathroom, took the quickest shower I'd ever seen, and then he shoved me into the bathroom and shut the door. When I got out, he was down in the kitchen fixing us eggs, toast, and the last of the fruit we'd left before going to Rocktoberfest.

He slid a plate toward me as his phone rang. He'd already eaten, and he rinsed his plate in the sink as he answered the phone.

"Hey, boo. Yeah, we're back at Shane's. He's fine, they're both fine. Yeah, I talked to them. I'm going to meet with them and Dickie tomorrow. No, it's okay. You guys enjoy the rest of the festival. I'll have everything set when you get back. I love you, too. Fuck off."

He hung up and slid his phone back in the pocket of his leggings.

"Annie?"

He nodded.

"You meeting with management tomorrow?"

He nodded again. "You were right. They want to build on

the momentum of the festival. They sent me a tentative plan, I read through it while you were in the shower, and they're pushing us to accept it."

"What do they want?" I asked him, my voice hoarse.

He blew out a breath and seemed to lose steam. "They want to release the first single from the album next week and they jumped at the chance to get us on TV. They got us booked to go to New York for *Saturday Night Live* a week later. Then they have a plan for us to go to Europe for six weeks, we'll be gone for the holidays, and that's all followed by Australia, Japan, and then dates in the U.S." He blinked his big blue eyes at me. "They've got us out until the end of February."

He sounded tired just telling me all that.

"You'll be back for the gala," I offered. "You need to do this. Don't worry about anything. I'll help Vera Jean and Pops with the gala. We'll handle it."

A tear ran down his face and he blew out a breath.

"Part of me hoped the label would hate the new material." He gave a humorless laugh. "I thought, if they hated it, we could just put it away and then you and I could... I don't want to leave." The last part was a whisper.

I went to his side and put my hand over his on the counter.

THIRTY-TWO

B^{oone}

I *did* have to leave, and Shane and I only managed to partially process what had happened. That meant spending the three nights I had left before I had to embark on a three-month-tour lying next to him in bed, where we only managed awkward conversation and chaste kisses good night. Gone was our easy way, our funny banter, our combustible chemistry. I could only imagine what was going on in his head. Had he just panicked and ran? Did he really not want me after everything we went through? Neither of us seemed brave enough to talk about what was really going on.

My assumption? It finally hit him that his band was over and he was left adrift, wondering what to do next. Me going out on tour was a reminder of what he didn't have, and he wasn't ready to put into words how he felt about that. And whatever his mother said to him in that hospital room really threw him for a loop. Shane seemed to be a stewer, and that's what he was doing. Stewing. And until he was ready to talk about his feelings, there was nothing I could do. Except yell at him, or beat him over the head with the reality that we'd found something incredibly special and that we could survive this setback.

That didn't seem to be the best option.

So instead, on day four, I packed up my shit, left him a note as he'd been gone when I woke up, and I drove over to Gran's.

"How long will you be gone?" she asked.

"The next three months. There are a few dates where I can come back if you need me, but our schedule is pretty tight."

She nodded and smiled sadly. "And what about Shane?"

"I don't know about Shane. I know he loves me, but I don't know if it's enough."

"I do believe in the saying 'absence makes the heart grow fonder.' Give him some space to figure out what he wants to do next. He's had the rug pulled out from under him, and men tend to need a bit more effort to bounce back."

"Tell me about it. I feel like I just got my numbers under control and now I'm going out on the road. I'm afraid. I don't want to be sick like I was before."

"What can you do to make a difference?" She was always good at making me think through things.

"Let the tour manager know about my dietary needs. Keep up with exercise. The twins won't let me go off the rails. Now that they know, we'll face it like a team."

"Then you're already in better shape than you were when you were out on the road last time."

"Yeah." My chest just hurt all the time. I missed Shane already and I hadn't even left yet.

"Come on, then. Chin up. Tits out. You can do this, dear boy."

. . .

So that's what I did. For three months solid. I sold Stellar to the world. I took the stage beside my two best friends and poured my heart out to audiences four to five nights a week. We traveled to more places than we had before, and conquered the hearts of fans around the globe.

But I took time for me. I ate the best I could. I worked out at every opportunity and when there was no hotel gym, I walked for miles with Annie and Bran.

And every stop of the tour, I bought postcards and wrote to Shane. Sometimes I sent three or four at a time. I didn't know if he'd care, but I had to get them out. Sometimes they were angry, sometimes they were about something I wished he was there to share with me. But I signed every one of them, "Yours. Still. Boone."

A month into the tour, I got a call while we were on a ferry heading from Helsinki to Stockholm.

"What do you mean, I twitch in my sleep?"

I barked out a laugh. One of the postcards I'd sent to Shane had been a diatribe about my adventures sleeping next to a puppy.

"You've heard of restless leg, right? You've got restless body, Shane. You twitch. Sometimes it was cute, sometimes you pulled my hair, and one night you even managed to knee me in the nads."

"Why didn't you ever say anything?"

Annie and Bran both had their headphones in, and I doubted anyone else understood my conversation. The talking around me had all been in different languages.

"Because it's one of my favorite things about you."

He made a disbelieving huff on the other end. "Why the postcards?"

My heart stuttered. "Why? Are they bothering you?"

"No, babe. I love them." He hadn't called me babe since everything happened. "But you have so much going on, why bother?"

I got up from my seat and took the opportunity to stretch my legs. I was winding up to let him have it, and I didn't want to take the chance that someone listening might recognize me and understand the conversation.

"Are you serious right now? Why *bother*? Oh, I don't know, Shane, because I'm halfway around the world and I miss you like crazy? Maybe because I'm trying to plant seeds in your stubborn, hard head that even after everything, I fucking love you? For all the reasons?"

"I love you too, Boone. I was an asshole. I'm sorry I lost my shit. It was a wake-up call that I still have some shit to deal with and you, unfortunately, were on the receiving end."

"God, I wish I was there with you right now."

"I don't know if I could be this honest if you were here, though."

"Then tell me everything."

He blew out a breath. "Okay."

Over that conversation, and the others we had during the next few weeks, he shared the things I wished he would have on that ugly day, but he hadn't been ready. He told me what his mom said to him. He told me he'd gone back to therapy and Al-Anon. He admitted that he'd hoped we would record our music together, and the fact that me being out on tour when he had nothing lined up was tough for him to swallow.

It went a long way toward healing the rift between us. I just wasn't sure it was enough.

"Come to London," I said during the last week we were in Europe. "Before I go to Australia and can't see you for another month."

"I wish I could, but I can't leave Pops right now. His cardiologist referred him to cardiac therapy as an extra precaution.

He admitted he hadn't been working out regularly like he did with me, so it's good for him. I'm taking him four days a week. We're also in crunch time for the gala. I'm sorry."

"It's okay. I know you have your hands full. How are the wedding arrangements going?"

"You know? They've been close-lipped. I think those two are going to elope after the gala. They haven't said as much, but I think they might do it."

"How do you feel about that?" I asked him. I knew he'd struggled with the fact that it wasn't Bruce and him alone against the world anymore.

"Glad I won't have to wear a damn monkey suit."

I burst out laughing, and Annie and Bran groaned. We were packed into a tiny hotel room because of some mix-up. Bran and me in a twin bed, and Annie in one alone with her gas. Not ideal.

"Sorry," I whispered.

"Bloody hell, Butler. Get your arse on a plane and do this in person." Bran's British accent was actually quite good. We'd been practicing all over town, which had Annie so done with us.

"I already tried. Go back to sleep." I climbed out of bed and went into the bathroom to give them a break. "I'd like to see you in a monkey suit. You were devastatingly handsome last year at the induction ceremony."

"I was an asshole at the induction ceremony."

"But look where we are now?" I joked about it, but we still hadn't made any firm commitments to each other. I was still concerned that I'd return to LA and he'd tell me he'd rather we just work on being friends, or whatever the fuck you were when your grandparents married each other.

Love's a fucking brutal bitch.

"Where are we?" he asked.

I whispered to him what he'd asked me all those weeks ago. "Where do you wish we could be?"

And he repeated my words to me. "Ask me when this is over."

Not a resounding, "I love you, I want us to be together, I want to wake up beside you whenever humanly possible, I want to grow old with you." Nope. Something was holding him back, and until I knew, I was the one adrift.

"Wake up, Boone."

I stretched in my first-class cubby on our flight back to the U.S. from Tokyo feeling like a defrosted and reheated twice airplane meal. Didn't look quite right, didn't taste right at all.

"Sir, we're making our final descent into PDX. Please put your seat up and stow your belongings."

The flight attendants had been wonderful, thank goodness. We'd been delayed two fucking days getting out of Japan because of weather and I felt like shit. My voice was gone, my blood sugar had been high the whole time we'd been stuck in the airport, and I'd broken my phone in the process. Bran and Annie had done their best to take care of me despite my shitty attitude.

We were likely going to miss the gala, and I felt like the worst grandson on the planet.

We deplaned and thankfully, there was a driver waiting for us.

"Your associates are collecting your bags," he said.

"Associates?"

"Greetings!" Rowan and Martin came trotting up. "We're going to get your belongings for you. Do you have your tags? We'll bring them in the van. You guys get out of here. You should make it in time for the gala if you leave now."

The driver hauled ass out of the airport and onto I-84 toward Bolder Breed.

"This sucks. I feel like I've been living in a dumpster for a week," Bran said.

"Or shaken up in a Honey Bucket shitter," Annie offered.

"God, you're gonna make me puke." I felt better being off the plane, but yeah. I was so gross. "I'd almost rather miss it than have anyone within a fifty-yard perimeter of me."

"Better make it a hundred," Annie said. "You reek."

"Thanks. You smell pretty sour yourself."

The driver piped up. "I'm supposed to let you know that there are clothes in your rooms in the lodge and you should have time to clean up. Ms. Collins says not to worry, they'll wait for you to begin the performance."

"Shit. I can't even sing, we didn't get a chance to practice. Fucking weather."

"It'll be *fiiine*," Annie said.

"Will you text Gran and tell her I don't have a phone?"

"Already done. She and Shane have been texting me the whole flight. Thank goodness the plane had good Wi-Fi."

The ride was bumpy and loud. I was just about to fall asleep when the car stopped abruptly.

"Go, go, go!"

Annie and Bran dragged me up the stairs to our rooms and we all split off to shower and change. I was in a daze, like that spacy feeling you get when you're woken up from a deep sleep, and I tripped over my pants trying to get out of them. I pulled myself up by the bedpost and got a look at what was laid out for me.

Gran had brought my blue velvet suit and my sparkly gold Converse shoes.

The outfit I'd worn to the induction ceremony.

It felt like a good omen.

That night had been the start to me getting my life together, and tonight I was going to at least look *put* together.

There was also a white box next to the suit with no markings on it. I opened it up and there was a beautifully crafted boutonniere made with dark flowers, nearly black. Not exactly Gran's taste...

I had no time to ponder. I took a shower, washed my hair three times to get all the funk out of it, and scrubbed my skin raw. I banged on the wall, knowing Annie was on the other side, since I didn't have my phone. A minute later she was banging on my door.

"What is it?"

She was dressed in a slip dress in a gorgeous blue to match my suit. Bran came trotting over too. "Come on, man. We gotta get out there."

They both had their hair braided in Australia before we left, and they were able to pull their braids back to look decent.

"Can you guys French braid my hair, please? It will take me forever to blow dry it."

They both went to work on either side of my head and then Annie joined the two braids together at the base of my neck.

"Damn this shit is long. It goes almost to your ass."

"I haven't had it cut in forever." It had thickened, too, since I'd gotten better with my food and medicines.

The three of us crowded around the bathroom mirror, applying makeup, and then they rushed me through getting dressed.

"Uh," I said, moving the pile of clothes around on the bed. "No one brought me underwear."

"Fuck it. Go commando, come on, we gotta go."

Fuck it was right. There were also no socks, so I was going to have to go barefoot in my Converse, which I hated. Hopefully I wouldn't have to be dressed like this for long. I wanted to crawl into bed so bad, but the show must go on.

"Let's do this," I croaked, and my besties patted my back as we made our way out to the covered amphitheater.

The grounds were packed. There were loads of people wandering around the path that led to where the studio and rehearsal rooms were, looking at all the displayed items available for silent auction. There were servers carrying drink trays and hors d'oeuvres, and I was tempted to snag a whole tray.

"You should drink some water," Bran said. He grabbed a server and asked them where there was bottled water. He pointed toward the bar, where I found Bruce.

"Hey, you made it."

He pulled me into a hug, which felt nice, but weird. We didn't hug. Hadn't. Was that about to change?"

"Barely. Is Gran okay?"

"Boone, darling."

I turned to find Gran coming toward me in a gorgeous royal blue sparkly gown...and a cane. With a boot on her foot.

"Gran! What happened?"

She grinned at Bruce, who winked at her.

"It happened weeks ago, I'm almost out of this dreadful shoe."

Bruce took her other hand and led her to me for a hug. "We went snowboarding after Christmas in Lake Tahoe. We had a fantastic time."

"Well, it was fantastic until I twisted my foot getting off the ski lift and managed to fracture it. I never even made it onto the slopes." Gran laughed.

"What the h-e-double hockey sticks were you doing snowboarding?"

Gran put her hand on my arm. "We've got a bucket list of things we want to do together. As soon as I'm out of this boot, we're going to try hydrofoiling."

"Hydro *what*?"

"Yes! Shane bought boards and we're going to take them to Hawaii."

"Hawaii?" My head had already been spinning, but now I was in full-blown shock. "Where is Shane?"

Just then, applause sounded from inside the amphitheater and everyone hurried to their seats.

"Come along, Bruce. Boone, we'll see you after. Kiss kiss."

Bruce led my gran away to the backstage area while I stood there in shock.

"Come on," Annie said, taking my arm. Bran took the other. "Rose has seats reserved for us down front."

"What about performing?" I needed to stretch, warm up, I—

"Just hurry up."

We took our seats as Shane took the stage, and my breath caught.

He was wearing a pair of form-fitting black slacks and a black dress shirt with the arms cut off.

Close enough to a monkey suit.

He was stunning. He was also wearing a matching boutonniere to mine.

God, I'd missed him.

I wanted to cry.

Instead, I chinned up and titted out and hoped I could make it through the gala without swooning.

THIRTY-THREE

S hane

"The package has arrived."

When word came through my in-ears that Boone and the twins had arrived, I sighed with relief, but then panicked.

"Copy," I answered.

"You good?"

Danny Black, lead singer for metal gods Blackened, patted me on the shoulder. He'd been so much fun to work with for this event. He and his wife, choreographer Jesse Martin-Black, had become a Hollywood power couple when it came to organizing fundraisers like this, and Danny, it turned out, was a massive fan of Brothers' music.

"I'm...wow, I don't know."

It had taken me a full month to realize just how badly I'd fucked up with Boone. Four therapy sessions, six Al-Anon meetings, and thirty-six postcards from all over Europe later,

I'd been ready to accept my licks and plan for how to get him back. I'd thought Boone would go off and forget about me, or he'd remember how much of a jackass I'd been. When I finally called him, ready to grovel, I'd realized that he deserved so much more than that. I didn't want to discuss our relationship over the phone. I wanted to make a grand gesture in person.

And how else would a bonehead musician do that but to write a song and sing it in front of their collective friends and family?

It sounded good in theory. It was the stuff of romance novels. It was also taking a big chance, and I think by now, I've established how not great I tend to be about taking chances.

Go me.

"You ready, big guy?"

Leland and Morrison were there with hugs, and so was Lydia. They'd all be playing with Blackened, as well as Aldous Archer, and even Pops and Mack from Brothers.

And then my dumb ass was going to get up and sing a fucking ballad to the man I loved with all of my heart and hope he'd forgive me, come home with me, and, if all went well, agree to marry me.

God, just thinking the words made my legs buckle. It helped to see that Pops was just as nervous about marrying Vera Jean, despite the fact he'd spent the majority of his life in love with her.

"Son, you're going to have times when you're apart, times when your career is in the toilet and his is in the stars, but that's when you'll be the closest. That's when you'll need him and he'll be there for you. He's already proved that he loves you. Ye can't spend yer whole life hiding from things you can't control."

For an old man who'd made many mistakes in his life, he sure had great advice.

It had been his idea for me to invite my mother to the gala, and shockingly, she'd agreed. She'd arrived the day before with my stepfather, and the three of us had gone into Portland for dinner. It had gone well, actually, and we agreed to keep the lines of communication open. She'd had a civil conversation with Vera Jean as well, and I think she was coming around to the idea that Pops was truly living a happy and healthy life.

The show went off without a hitch. Aldous acted as a lovable yet unhinged emcee, as well as performing one of the massive hits he'd recorded with Morrison and Leland a couple years ago, which resurrected his career. He kept everyone in stitches, and I was laughing my ass off when he started talking about me.

"Along with creating some of the biggest rock songs of the seventies, Bruce Duncan had himself a lovely little family. His daughter Christina is here—hello darling. Love to buy you a drink after the show. Oh, and her long-suffering husband Arman, so lovely to see you again. If you need a good financial advisor, they're the two to see."

I peeked out and saw Mom rolling her eyes but clapping begrudgingly. Aldous was one of those guys who was so wrong but you couldn't help but love him.

"Thankfully for Bruce's grandson, Shane, Bruce's stubborn Irish temper seems to have skipped—oh, that's right. It didn't skip him. Our firebrand, Shane Butler, has torched the airwaves with his band Wicked Soul, and rumor has it, there's been some sheet-scorching recently as well. Ahem, but this is a family show, so I won't go into the prevalence of love bites around this place. Perhaps there's a colony of vampire bats living here. Lydia, Morrison, you should have that checked out."

"Har har," I said to myself, as I pulled my acoustic guitar on over my head.

"Without further ado, let's welcome Shane Butler to the stage."

The guys from Blackened all passed me as I took the stage, clapping me on the shoulder. They'd come back in a few moments to accompany me on the last song of the show.

I approached Aldous and he held his arms out for a hug. He kissed me on the cheek, patted my other one and turned to the audience. "Look at this handsome lad. If only I were thirty years younger—oh, hello Boone! Ladies, gentlemen, and nonbinary brethren, say hello to the *other* grandson, Boone Collins."

Boone's cheeks flushed, and he stood and waved. He was stunning in that blue suit. I'd asked Vera Jean to bring it for him, as well as the shoes, which she bitched about. Turned out she wasn't a fan. Thankfully, she and I had reached a place in our relationship where we could work as a team, both in taking care of Pops and, I hoped, supporting Boone. I felt bad that I'd ever doubted her motives for getting involved with my beloved grandfather. They were good for each other. If they could put the past behind them, I could too.

I wasn't used to seeing Boone with his hair pulled back so tightly. Occasionally he threw his thick hair up in some sort of bun, but today it was expertly braided, and the look enhanced his widow's peak and cheekbones. And those giant blue eyes.

God, I was so in love with him. I'd missed him more than I thought possible. We'd gotten close so quickly, and when him going out on tour seemed like a maybe-someday thing, I thought it would be good for us to have some space. Turned out maybe someday happened really fucking fast, and I'd managed to screw it all up. My ego used the time to recover and my rational side reminded me of reality. I could love Boone and still be frustrated with my career. The two were separate, and if someday the two merged, if we continued to work on material together, then I would have to shove that ego back in the box where it belonged.

Boone was more important than my bruised pride.

But I could see that Boone was struggling. His face was pale and he had circles under his eyes. I knew he'd been dragging the past few weeks, and I wanted to curse out his manager for agreeing to Australia and Japan right after Europe. It was too much for him. Hopefully my elaborate gesture would go over well, and he'd let me take him home and nurse him back to health.

"Take it away, Shane. I'll just be over here keeping out of trouble." The whole audience laughed riotously while Aldous faked shock. "It could happen. I'm a redeemed man, didn't you know?" He winked and then gestured for me to take the mic.

"Thank you, Aldous, and thank all of you for being here. The Collins Foundation has done so much good for our rock 'n' roll family, and I'm pleased that Pops and I could join Vera Jean and Boone this year to help raise funds to support our fellow musicians who are struggling financially due to health-related expenses. We never know when we might get that diagnosis, have an accident, or struggle with our mental health, and as a community, we need to support each other, lift each other up."

There was strong applause, a few shouts, and everyone in the amphitheater seemed tuned into my words. Boone watched me intently, with Annie and Bran beside him looking just as wrecked. Part of me wanted to call an end to the show and let them go to bed, but I had one more thing to say first.

"I know most of you are used to seeing me with an electric guitar in front of a massive Marshall stack, but my purpose today is a bit more heartfelt." I strummed the guitar, taking a deep breath. "The past year has been special for many reasons. John Boone was inducted into the Rock Hall." I paused for applause. "Pops decided to let us in on the real meaning behind 'Paisley.' Thanks for that. And congratulations to Pops and Vera Jean on their impending nuptials." Laughter, applause, and whistles filled the air.

"For me, this year has been special because I finally discovered what an incredible person Boone Collins is. Yeah, I know I'm late to the party, and I'm going to ask you to bear with me for a minute while I do a little groveling."

Everyone laughed, and Boone put his hands over his mouth, which didn't hide his flushed cheeks. *Good.*

"For various no good, very bad reasons, I spent my formative years bitter and angry." Feigned shock from the audience got me a few laughs. "I know, right? Those of you who've known me my whole life, my apologies. It wasn't until I formed my band Wicked Soul that I learned how to channel that anger into an acceptable outlet. It worked, for the most part, but that temper Aldous mentioned? Yeah, I come by it genetically." I shrugged. "But whatever my reason or excuse, any time Boone's name came up, I found that little green monster peeking it's ugly head up, and over the years, I judged him erroneously.

"Then our grandparents started dating." I dramatically rolled my eyes, and everyone cracked up. "You can imagine the conversations Boone and I had when it became apparent we were going to be seeing a lot more of each other didn't go smoothly at first.

"Then both Stellar and Wicked Soul were booked simultaneously up here at Bolder Breed last summer. It appeared the universe was trying to tell me something. I finally got to witness the magic Boone makes when he's in the studio, and I was blown away. The man is truly a wonder."

A long, steady, thunderous applause rang out, until Boone was peeking up at me with narrowed eyes. I kinda liked watching him squirm.

"Then my band broke up with me."

A shocked gasp.

"But it's fine," I said quickly, holding up my hands. "The market has changed, people change, and I wish my former bandmates well. In the wake of that event, I found a new songwriting partner...and along the way, I fell in love with him."

There was a loud chorus of *awwwwww*, followed by more applause and laughter.

"And, in true Shane Butler fashion, I managed to mess that up. But today, in true *songwriter* fashion, I'm going to try to use my words to get my message across, so I hope you'll be patient with me as I try to make things right."

Boone pressed his hands to his heart and said my name. Then I saw Annie and Bran take his hands, and the sight of the three of them sitting together with concern in their expressions spurred me on.

I started to play the song I'd written for Boone, inspired by the words I'd read in his journal before realizing I was trespassing. The audience clapped and then sat riveted as I began to sing.

I am the darkness
   And you are the light
   And whenever we meet
   We fuss and we fight
   A collision of forces
   Both wrong and both right
   But not when I look at you tonight

Can't we take a moment
   to breathe each other in
   To fill in the spaces
   no one has to win

whatever the fear
whatever the sin
why can't we let love begin

You're so close I want more
     Please don't shut the door
     You're so close I can't breathe
     I never want you to leave
     Despite all the feuds
     I crave the interludes
     Let's do something rash
     With this emotional whiplash

The crowd swayed and swooned along with me. It was that moment all artists crave, when the audience just gets it and they're right there with you. I was nearly out of breath as I played the break. I took a chance and glanced at Boone.

He sat upright with tears running down his face, still holding hands with Annie and Bran, but staring at me. His brow crinkled in confusion, and for a moment I thought I'd gone too far, but then he blew out a breath and smiled through his tears.

So I sang the last chorus and...prayed.

I stand before you now
     I'm not sure I know how
     I'm all out of breath
     I should never have left
     Despite all our feuds
     I want more interludes
     I know this is rash

I blame emotional whiplash

I want all our feuds
  Let's have more interludes
  Who cares if we're rash
  Gimme all that emotional whiplash

It was done. It was all out there. Pops shouted, "That's my boy!" Vera Jean kissed his cheek. The crowd lost its mind. Even my mother and stepfather jumped to their feet and clapped for us.

But Boone didn't move.

And my heart stopped.

Maybe it was too much.

Had I fucked up again?

He shook himself as if he'd had a sudden realization. He flew out of his seat and I barely had time to take off my guitar before he dove into my arms, knocking me back a couple of steps.

"Goddammit, Butler," he cried, before he kissed me with a force that matched my colossal swell of emotion.

The shouts and applause nearly tore the roof off the place, but I didn't care if the sky was falling. I wanted the world to stop and let me hold this man who'd rocked my world, turned it upside down, and forced me to let go of my need to control everything in my life. I didn't know if I'd ever enjoy feeling out of control, but for Boone, I was willing to give it a shot.

"I love you," I said into his ear. "Please forgive me, Boone."

"For making me cry in front of everyone? Not a chance." But he barked out a laugh through his tears. "I can't believe you did this."

"So if I got down on my knee right now and—"

"Shane! Give me a minute to adjust! I thought I was coming home to live with the twins and somehow figure out how to get over you, which was not very likely by the way."

"Give me another chance, Boone. Come home with me."

"If you two lovebirds are done, we've got one more song to sing."

I pulled away from Boone to find the Blackened, Morrison, Leland, and Lydia all back onstage and in their places. Morrison handed me my guitar and Boone went to move, but I held his hand.

"Sing with me."

"I can't sing," he said in my ear. "My voice is toast."

I pressed my forehead against his. "Then stand up here so I don't have to let go of you yet. I don't want to let go."

"How do you plan to play guitar with me— Oh!"

I draped the guitar over both of us, trapping him against me as I strummed the guitar to the start of "Paisley."

Pops came out and sang John's part, and I harmonized while I attempted to play guitar with Boone laughing against my chest.

"Lean your head back," I said to him. "I gotta see for this next part."

"Let me."

So he fretted while I strummed, and we made a joyful if not awkward noise together while the audience laughed and cheered for us. When it was over and we got untangled, Boone hugged Pops and shook hands with the rest of the band. Aldous stepped up to the mic to end the show, and Boone took the opportunity to drag me offstage.

He kept running once we were outside, and I followed him down the aisle and up the steps to the studio. He punched in the code and once the door was open, he dragged me up the stairs.

"Boone—"

He threw his arms around me and I groaned at the taste of his kiss.

"I can't believe you," he said against my lips. "I thought you were through with me, and you write a beautiful fucking song like that?"

"I'm sorry. I swear, I didn't read your notebook, I just saw those words at the top of the page—"

"'Feuds and Interludes?' Yeah, I wrote that after we had that first interlude right here in this room. I was so mad at you that night."

"And now?" I was shaking so bad. Had I just bared my whole-ass soul for him to tell me it was over?

"Shane, I haven't been mad at you since we spoke that night I was on the ferry going to Stockholm. I wrote a song that night too, about being in love with someone who held your heart hostage. It's pretty heavy."

"Can we try again? Will you m—"

"We've *been* trying. We'll continue to try. We'll go home and—"

"Home?"

"Yes, Shane, if you want me to come home with you, we'll try this again. And we'll keep trying until we get it right. Because I don't know if you realized this or not, but you're not the only one who is stubborn in this relationship. I'm not giving up on you, even when you literally run away from me."

"Please forgive me, Boone. I'm sorry." I kissed his mouth, his jaw, and headed for my favorite spot on his throat.

"I'm almost there," he moaned. "I just need a little more of that...ahhh, fuck, Shane."

That wild abandon I felt when I first kissed Boone was back with a vengeance. I couldn't get enough of him, couldn't bear the thought of letting him go.

I started unbuttoning his vest, and then cursed when I found more buttons underneath.

"Fucking buttons. Need you."

Boone threw his head back and laughed as I yanked his shirt open, sending buttons pinging off every surface. I went to work on his pants as I sucked on those tendons, right where they met his collarbone, and had just reached into his pants when—

"Ugh, we went from orgy bus to sexy times in the studio, geez. I can't with you two."

I pulled away from Boone's neck, and he squealed as I shoved his exposed body behind me. "Do you mind? You had him for three whole months—"

"Your grandparents are cutting and serving cake, and they would like the two of you to—oh shit, Boone. Never mind. You better not come out looking like that."

"What?"

I turned to look and... "Damn. Those are even bigger than the first ones. I'm, wow, I'm sorry—"

"The only thing you should be apologizing for is stopping. Annie dear, I love you. Please tell our grandparents that I am very, very tired, and Shane is putting me to bed."

"Uh-huh. If y'all make it to a bed. I'm out of here. Go on with your horny selves." She slammed the bedroom door and shouted as she stomped down the stairs. "I'm locking the studio door, ya heathens."

"Oh, thank God. Shane, you haven't finished groveling—Ah, fuck."

I'd dropped to my knees and had Boone's gorgeous cock in my mouth before he could yell at me anymore. I planned to keep him unable to speak coherently until he forgave me.

As long as it took.

. . .

Alt-Scene Magazine
    August 2025
    Feuds, Interludes, and Gratitude
    by Krishnan Guruvayoor-Franklin

It's a steamy summer evening on Frenchman Street in New Orleans. The chainsaw guitars blaring from speakers in the four corners of the ceiling and the buzz from tattoo needles provide the backdrop for my second exclusive interview with Shane Butler and Boone Collins, two remarkable musicians who spent the past year going from rivals to lovers to broken hearts to fiancés while their entire worlds were thrown into a maelstrom of family drama and professional upheaval. All of that is history now, according to Butler. He sits on a stool beside his reclined fiancé Collins, getting his hand squeezed to a pulp.

"You're doing so well, babe," he coos to Collins over and over, as veteran artist Jaylene Boudreaux works on shading the elaborate design Butler created for Collins. It's a sweeping, colorful logo for their musical collaboration, Butler Collins and The Thompson Rhythm Section, and once Collins is done, Butler will be undergoing the process. It's Collins's first tattoo and he asked Butler to design it for him. Butler drew the design on Collins's skin and, after five hours, Boudreaux has nearly finished.

"The plan had been to do a small tattoo first and see how I handled it, but we're on a time crunch, so in order to not have a half-finished tattoo on tour, we went ahead with it now. And I'm totally fine."

. . .

He doesn't appear totally fine, but then, I recall getting my first tattoo at my husband's urging. It was awful, yet totally worth it in the end.

I asked the songwriting duo if I could tag along tonight to ask them about their upcoming tour.

"Stellar spent the spring on the road doing festivals and shows in the U.S. and once we'd completed our commitments, we headed back to Bolder Breed Studios outside Portland and recorded the songs Shane and I had written together the year before. My bandmates Annie and Brandon Thompson welcomed Shane into our family and collaborated with us to make our songs even tighter, along with Morrison Jones, Leland Elliot, and Lydia Pride, who all share producer credits on the album." Collins sucks in a breath and squeezes Butler's hand tighter, this time with both of his hands.

"I know, this spot is tender," Boudreaux says apologetically to Collins. "We're almost done."

Boudreaux is the wife of guitarist Devon Boudreaux, of the legendary metalcore band Maggie's Bones, who Butler Collins will be accompanying on tour this fall. Butler is a longtime friend and collaborator with Boudreaux, and when the two met up at Rocktoberfest last fall, Boudreaux floated the idea of a co-headlining tour. Maggie's Bones reunited for that festival and then went into the studio to record new material after their triumphant return to the stage. Devon Boudreaux stated that a lot of things had needed to line up before the band would be ready to play together again, and their success at the festival proved to the band that it was time.

But what does the future hold for Butler Collins?

"We'll be on tour with Maggie's Bones through the fall, and, if we survive and are still wild about each other, we'll get married." Collins smiles at Butler, who bends to kiss Collins's hand.

"We've made it through a lot already. I'm confident we can survive anything."

Over the previous year, in addition to Stellar's tour, the pair have dealt with Collins's health issues, Butler's split with his band members in Wicked Soul, and the men's grandparents, Vera Jean Collins and Bruce Duncan, eloped and set off on a world tour of their own with Duncan's bandmates from the late-seventies band Brothers.

"We FaceTime with them every week and so far all is going well." Collins winces one last time, and then Boudreaux announces she's finished. She cleans him up and he stands, with Butler's help, and takes a look at the finished product. I'm not at liberty to disclose where it's located.

"You're a goddess, Jaylene."

. . .

She rolls her eyes. "Yeah, yeah. I've heard that before. I'll be right back to start on you, Butler." She leaves to take a break with her guitarist husband while their shop assistant, who I believe is Maggie's Bones drummer Star Stevenson, cleans up her workstation.

When I ask Butler and Collins whether they see this musical collaboration taking the place of any future separate endeavors, and whether Stellar will continue, they merely look to one another.

"We're taking this next year as it comes," Butler remarks. "Too much worrying about the future and trying to control everything led to issues with us in the past, so we're going to see how it goes."

"Ask us after our wedding," Collins calls over his shoulder while the shop boy-slash-metalcore drummer finishes bandaging his tattoo. Collins guzzles a bottle of water and attempts to get dressed without disturbing the bandage. I ask Butler if he has anything to add, but he seems to be preoccupied with watching his fiancé. I've spent enough time around musicians in love to know that this interview is over.

*I'll be covering the Butler Collins/Maggie's Bones tour firsthand, as my husband's band, Hush, will be joining them, along with opener, Ryan Wells and The Travelers. The tour is shaping up to be one of the most anticipated of the decade, so **Stay Tuned for more...***

Afterword

If you enjoyed *Feuds and Interludes*, how about checking out the rest of the Road to Roctoberfest books!

TL Travis: His Final Chase
    Layla Dorine: Broken Chorus
    Jenna Galicki: Half Notes and Highlights
    BL Maxwell: Tangled Weeds
    Lynn Michaels: Midnight Rhythm
    Gabbi Grey: Grindstone's Edge
    Miski Harris: Living The Legend
    CJ Barlowe: Beyond the Stix
    Anne Barwell: Divided Road
    Kaje Harper: Missing Chord
    Denver Shaw: When Stars Align
    Ann Lister: Three Part Harmony
    Sam Kraemer: Smolder
    Brina Brady: Busted String
    Kota Quinn: Zayden's Temptation
    Ari McKay: High Strung
    R.L. Merrill: Feuds and Interludes

And if you want to know more about the characters mentioned in this story, here are Ro's related books:

I Want, More: Bolder Breed Studios Book One - Morrison and Leland

Love and Pride: Bolder Breed Studios Book Two - Lydia and Unice

Haunted - Introduces the band Maggie's Bones, Devon and Jaylene's Story

Bated - Marcus and Sherry

Fated - Mage and Sammara

Summer of Hush - Introduces the band Hush, Krish and Silas

Brains and Brawn - Brains and Paul

You Can Do Magic - Ryan and Kal (Paranormal)

You Can Save Me - Dane and Walter, Tess Miller (Paranormal)

Teacher: The Hollywood Rock 'n' Romance Trilogy, Danny Black and Jesse Martin-Black

Stay Tuned for more Rock 'n' Romance...

Whether she's writing contemporary romance featuring quirky and relatable characters or diving deep into the paranormal and supernatural to give readers a shiver, R.L. Merrill loves creating compelling, diverse, and inclusive stories that will stay with readers long after. Winner of the Kathryn Hayes "When Sparks Fly" Best Contemporary award for *Hurricane Reese*, Paranormal Romance Guild's Best Rockstar Romance for *You Can Do Magic*, and Daphne DuMaurier finalist for *Connection*, Ro spends every spare moment improving her writing craft and striving to find that perfect balance between real-life and happily ever after. You can find her connecting with readers on social media, advocating for America's youth, cruising around town with Great Dane Velma, cuddling with twin black cat familiars Frankenstein and Dracula, or head-banging at a rock show near her home in the San Francisco Bay Area! ***Stay Tuned for more...***

Newsletter: www.rlmerrillauthor.com/all-the-links

Also by R.L. Merrill

Haunted Series: (Contemporary Romance)

Haunted

Fated

Bated

Jaded – (Coming Soon)

Minded Series: (Paranormal Spinoff of Haunted Series)

Minded

Blossomed

Father F'in' Christmas

A Peculiar Prom Night

Magic and Mayhem Universe: (Funny Paranormal Romance in the universe created by Robyn Peterman)

Shifted

Ghoul Me Once

Gator Me Twice

Magic and Mayhem/Shifted Collection

Fang Me Three Times

Fangtastic Four

Five Fanger Witch Punch

Hollywood Rock 'n' Romance Trilogy: (Contemporary Romance)

Teacher

Teacher: Act Two

Teacher: The Final Act

Contemporary Romance Series:

The Rock Season

Road Trip

You Fell First

The Heart Knows (Re-Releasing Soon)

A Match Made in Spain

LGBTQ Romance

Pinups and Puppies (Originally in Love Is All Vol. 2)

I Want, More – Bolder Breed Studios #1 (Originally in Love Is All Vol. 3)

Love and Pride – Bolder Breed Studios #2 (Originally in Love Is All Vol. 4)

Everything's Better With You: An MM Sports Romance

All I Wanna Do — Bolder Breed Studios #3 (Email Ro for your copy)

Under His Sheets: Accidentally Undercover – Out April 9, 2024

Feuds and Interludes: Road To Rocktoberfest 2024 - November 2024

The Banes of Lake's Crossing (Historical Horror Romance)

The Fourth Man (The Banes of Lake's Crossing) (Historical Horror Romance)

The Redemption of Nathaniel Bane

The Absolution of Jonah Bane

The Gifted Series: (Supernatural Suspense/Paranormal Romance)

Healer

Connection

Protector

Sundowners (M/M Paranormal Romance

<u>Sundowners Book One</u>

Sundowners Book Two (February 13, 2025)

Forces of Nature Series: (Gay Contemporary Romance)

Hurricane Reese

Typhoon Toby

<u>Earthquake Ethan</u>

Summer of Hush Series: (Gay Contemporary Romance)

Summer of Hush

Brains and Brawn

<u>You Can Do Magic: Carnival Of Mysteries (A Summer of Hush Tie-In</u>)

You Can Save Me: Carnival of Mysteries (Season Two, Book Two)

Anthologies:

Thanksgiving Day Parade From Hell (Worst Holiday Ever) (Gay Contemporary Romance

Valentine's Day From Hell (Worst Valentine's Day Ever) (Gay Contemporary Romance)

Salty and Sweet (Summer Fair) (Lesbian Contemporary Romance)

The Fourth Man (The Banes of Lake's Crossing) (Historical Horror Romance)

A Piece of Him (Gone With The Dead) (Horror)

<u>Breaking Bread</u>—Dark Divinations from HorrorAddicts.net Press (Horror)

Exchange (Renewal) (Science Fiction)

Tap-Tap-Tap (Impact) (Horror)

Human Sacrifice (Innovation) (Horror)

The Sitter (Clarity) (Horror)

Joy Is A Phone Call Away – A More Perfect Union (Lesbian Contemporary Romance)

The House Must Fall – Haunts and Hellions from HorrorAddicts.net Press – May 2021 (Horror)

A Kept Woman – BAQWA Presents: Horror Show 2021(Lesbian Horror Romance)

Gods of Rock 'n' Roll (Free on Wattpad)

How Bittersweet is Karma? Free on Wattpad)

Let Me Stand Next To Your Fire (Queer Cheer)

Midnight in the Renaissance Elevator

Holiday Romance

A Peace Offering (Re-release)

Love and Pride – Bolder Breed Studios #2

Once Upon A Holiday Story 2024 (Coming Soon)

Audiobooks

The Rock Season (Kiss App)

Brains and Brawn (Kiss App)

Teacher (Kiss App)

Hurricane Reese (Kiss App)

A Match Made in Spain (Audible)

Healer: Gifted Book One (Audible)

Under His Sheets (Audible Coming Soon)

Non-Fiction

Horror Addicts Guide To Life Volume 2 - Edited by Emerian Rich

Death's Garden Revisited - Edited by Loren Rhoads (Out Fall 2022)